"You're a liar, McGee," Marcie said quietly

Tucker McGee wouldn't tolerate a taunt like that from a man. But Marcie Browder wasn't a man. She was very much a woman. Besides, she was right.

"For someone who's been at the ranch only a few days, you seem to know a lot of what's going on," he replied, neither confirming nor denying her statement.

She wasn't the shaken rancher's daughter of two days before, he realized, but a confident woman, self-possessed and feisty. It made him smile with admiration. "I didn't know you—" he went on.

"There's a lot about me you don't know," she informed him. "Why did you lie?"

She wasn't one to mince words. He liked that, though at the moment it was putting him on the spot.

"Look—" he cracked a smile, but she wasn't moved "—no harm was done, and as you pointed out, you still need a foreman."

Her cool, calculating stare was piercing enough to make him squirm.

"You ride a horse well enough," she acknowledged, "and you obviously know something about cattle and ranching, but you're not a cowboy, McGee. *Now, who the hell are you, and what are you doing here?*"

Dear Reader,

We've all heard the saying "You can't go home again." Returning to an old favorite place often brings a sensation of distortion. The house isn't as big as we remember. The coziness seems more worn than warm. We see flaws we never noticed before and often come away with a nagging sense of disillusion. Maybe we should never have gone back.

After an abusive marriage and bitter divorce, Marcie Browder goes home to try to recapture her sense of self and security. The vast West Texas ranch is a little more run-down than she remembers it, but the difference in the people is what alarms her. They're not quite the way she remembers them—and perhaps they never were. Which raises another question—who is she?

And then there's the new foreman she finds standing over her father's body. He's not who he says he is, either. Is he friend or foe? Killer or savior?

Life is full of unanswered questions, and Marcie Browder's world is no exception. I hope you enjoy this story about a woman trying to solve the mystery of her father's murder, while searching for her own identity and another chance at love and happiness.

I love to hear from readers. You can write me at: P.O. Box 4062, San Angelo, TX 76902.

K.N. Casper

THE TEXAN
K.N. Casper

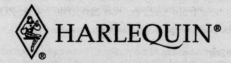

HARLEQUIN®

TORONTO • NEW YORK • LONDON
AMSTERDAM • PARIS • SYDNEY • HAMBURG
STOCKHOLM • ATHENS • TOKYO • MILAN • MADRID
PRAGUE • WARSAW • BUDAPEST • AUCKLAND

ISBN 0-373-70884-X

THE TEXAN

Copyright © 2000 by K. Casper.

This edition published by arrangement with Harlequin Books S.A.

® and TM are trademarks of the publisher. Trademarks indicated with
® are registered in the United States Patent and Trademark Office, the
Canadian Trade Marks Office and in other countries.

Visit us at www.romance.net

Printed in U.S.A.

To Barbara Jennison and Janet Branson, my partners
in murder and mischief

To Liz Flaherty, for coming through so quickly

To Gaye and Jim Walton, for their advice and encouragement

And, of course, to my inspiration, Mary.
May the stalls be with you!

PROLOGUE

MARCIE BROWDER WAS sitting on the patio, rubbing saddle soap into a brown leather bridle, when her father came charging up the driveway in his pickup, a white cloud of dust billowing violently behind him. It was obvious from the way he skidded to a stop and jumped out of the vehicle that he was both drunk and steaming mad.

He stomped over to where his wife knelt, loosening soil beneath a line of rosebushes. "You overdrew the damned checking account."

Wiping her hands on her worn canvas apron, Carlinda climbed slowly to her feet and brushed back an unruly hank of graying hair with her wrist. She didn't bother to make eye contact with her husband.

"No, Mason," she said as if talking to a querulous child. "I didn't overdraw the account. You did. I purchased groceries. You bought booze."

"You did it to embarrass me," he snarled.

"You don't need any assistance from me for that, Mason. You do it very well all by yourself."

She was studying the flower bed, so she didn't see it coming—the arm jerking up. He struck her across the jaw, sending her staggering into the rosebushes.

Marcie was instantly on her feet. She'd seen her parents fight in the past, listened to them bicker and snipe at each other for years. But physical violence went beyond the pale of tolerance. She'd felt the sting of the hand and the impact of the fist. More lasting was the pain of humiliation. She'd struck the word *victim* from her vocabulary.

"Stop!" Marcie shouted as she ran toward them.

The peremptory command stunned her father. He froze in midaction.

Marcie planted herself squarely between her parents. "Back off!"

Mason's florid features tightened into crimson rage. Jaw clenched, bloodshot eyes blazing with scorn, he balled his meaty hands into white-knuckled fists.

Marcie slipped to one side, her gaze fixed on his, drawing his attention away from her mother. "I'm warning you, Dad," she yelled at him. "Back off. Now!"

Her brother abandoned the girlfriend he'd been trying to help mount an old mare, and dashed over just as Mason made a move toward Marcie. But Dustin ignored his sister and the reeking, sweat-stained hulk of his father. He concentrated on his dazed mother, lifting her with gentle hands and soothing words from the needle-sharp tangle. Pulling a handkerchief out of his back pocket, he dabbed at the bright red droplets of blood dotting her arm where thorns had punctured.

Sudden awareness of how smoothly his daughter had distracted him from his real target infuriated Mason even further.

"Why, you little—"

Fist raised, he lunged at Marcie, an animal growl gurgling from his throat. Deftly, she sidestepped him. He staggered forward, tripped and landed on his hands and knees. Marcie stood over him, just beyond arm's reach.

"I'm warning you, Dad," she vowed. "If you ever lay a hand on Mom or try to take a swing at me again, I swear to God I'll kill you. Do you understand me? I'll kill you!"

Behind his father, Dustin wrapped his arms protectively around his mother. Over her shoulder, he said quietly but with convincing firmness, "Dad, I think you'd better get out of here."

Mason made no sign he heard his son. Breathing heavily, he clambered to his feet and took his time brushing off his pants. The thin line of his mouth held the unmistakable threat of renewed violence. He straightened, advanced one step, glared menacingly at Marcie, then looked away as if frightened by what he saw in her eyes. He wobbled stiff-backed to his truck, got in and drove off, leaving them all in a cloud of acrid dust.

When Marcie turned back toward her mother, she saw Tucker McGee on the other side of the split-rail fence. He sat astride his pinto mare, staring at her.

CHAPTER ONE

FOLLOWING THE DUNE BUGGY'S tracks, Marcie Browder had the eerie, nape-tingling sensation that someone, something, was watching her. She reined in her horse at the barbed-wire fence that used to separate the Lazy B from the Green Valley ranch, and scanned the area. In the long shadows of the afternoon, the craggy hills beyond the fence line looked secretive and forbidding. Her eye caught ground movement, but it was so fast, so distant, she wasn't even sure she'd seen it. Was it man or beast?

She sighed. Maybe she wasn't the only nervous rancher scouting around. Missing cattle had everyone alert, unsettled. A disappearing parent didn't help.

Marcie had known her father to rush off half-drunk before, and this certainly wasn't the first time Mason Browder had stayed out all night. His behavior, however, was becoming worse. He'd struck Carlinda and tried to hit Marcie, then he'd nearly started a fistfight with Dustin at the Beer Bucket Saloon a few hours later. Not that arguing with her brother was unusual, either. Father and son were too damn much alike to get along. But the old man's charging off in Dustin's stupid dune buggy worried her. He'd never done that before.

She had to find him and try to repair the damage she'd done yesterday. Maybe if she could get him to talk, she would understand why he'd allowed himself to degenerate into an abusive, alcoholic-bully, and why he'd built a chasm between them that had grown wider and deeper with time.

From hunting with him years ago, she knew better than to concentrate on the exact spot where she thought she'd seen the fleeting movement. Expanding her view to take in the whole hillside, she spied a break in the fence a hundred-and-fifty yards down the line.

She urged Sparkle to a slow walk. The breach, she realized upon getting to it, wasn't the result of ordinary deterioration. The shiny ends of freshly sheared barbed wire glistened in the bright sunlight. Someone had intentionally cut the fence and folded it back. Who? And were they still around?

Experience in tracking animals had taught her to examine the surrounding ground. There were hoofprints as well as the marks of a wheeled vehicle crossing the line. The dune buggy? What would her father be doing up here?

She ignored the quiver of apprehension that suddenly coiled down her spine. Keeping her mare in an easy jog, she advanced through a narrow ravine toward the sun-bathed hills across the vale. The cool springtime breeze that met her whispered something, but the message took a moment to register. Cattle. She could smell the mild pungency of cattle. She paused and listened.

For several months now, someone had been rustling small numbers of their livestock. If this was where they were being kept, she should be able to hear them. Yet the gentle wind brought no sound but its own as it wafted through stunted oaks and salt cedar. The tremor of danger grew stronger in her. Despite it, she moved on.

The ravine was a short one that acted like a gate to a depressed valley. Jagged, rocky peaks surrounded it like the rim of a chipped, cracked bowl. Pausing, she looked down. There, beside a muddy water hole, a man was inspecting a dune buggy, or rather, rifling through it. Even from this distance, she knew the man was Tucker McGee. Her father had hired him as their new foreman two weeks ago. Marcie had met him the previous Saturday when she'd come home to the ranch from Houston. Lean and hard, he exuded a raw strength that, even now, disquieted her, making her feel slightly self-conscious, not in control.

She nudged the horse into a careful walk down the sloping trail. From the way Tucker's body tightened and he squared his shoulders, she knew he'd heard her. She thought she saw him slip something into the hip pocket of his snug jeans as he straightened to face her. He put space between his scuff-booted feet as he watched her advance. The arrogant stance irritated her.

"I wish you hadn't come," he told her by way of greeting.

"I have every right to be here, Mr. McGee," she informed him. The slanting sun burnished the bronze features below the rim of his western hat. "This is Browder land, after all. But what are you doing here? I didn't think we were working this section."

"I'm not disputing your right to be here, Ms. Browder," McGee said, ignoring her question. "I'm just sorry you chose now to exercise it."

The words were spoken politely enough, but she saw wariness in his sea-green eyes. He was hiding something. "I see you've found the buggy. Where's my father?"

She dismounted and walked toward him, but when she started to approach the vehicle, he stepped in front of her and put out his arm. She looked down at the rolled-back sleeve, at the sinewy muscles of his forearm and its fine sheen of curly dark hair.

"Get out of my way," she ordered, placing a hand on his wrist to brush past him. His flesh was firm, his pulse thick and measured, and she could feel the heat emanating from the closeness of his brawny torso. For a moment, her heart raced.

"Wait." He shifted slightly, giving her a view of the off-road vehicle. Beside it lay Mason Browder.

Her face grew hot in spite of the chill that suddenly infused her bones. Whether it was at the sight of her father sprawled on the damp ground, or the warmth of this man's solid arm, or the unexpected tenderness of his voice so close to her ear, she wasn't sure.

"I didn't want you to see him like this," Tucker said.

She almost laughed. She'd seen her father spread-eagled on his back before—on his bed and occasionally on a floor. Dead drunk. It had taken years for her to suppress the disgust and revulsion, the shame and anger, his behavior provoked. But the emotions were still there, festering. The most powerful one was an overwhelming feeling that she was somehow responsible for what he had become. Her love had not been accepted—she'd been inadequate, a disappointment.

She stared at the still form on the ground.

"He's dead," McGee said softly.

At first the words made no sense, had no meaning. She glanced up at the tall man, aware of his sun-tanned complexion, the cleft in his chin, the hint of lines bracketing his full mouth. But they made little impression, until she looked once again at his eyes. The sadness in them jolted her.

"Dead?" she finally whispered, only vaguely aware when Tucker lowered his arm.

Later, no doubt, she'd experience all the normal reactions associated with death—sorrow, loss, regret. Right now she felt numb disbelief and a detached curiosity about why the man who had given her life had come here to die. She moved toward him.

"Don't," McGee said, not loudly, but with authority.

"Why the hell not?" she flared, her voice shaky. "He's my father."

She could see the breeze rippling the shiny shoots of new grass. Why couldn't she feel it?

"There's nothing you can do for him now," McGee said gently. "He's long gone. Best not to mess up the scene of the crime any more than it already is."

"Crime?" She looked again at the figure a few feet away. Only then did she see it—the dark brown stain in the middle of the burgundy-and-gray western shirt. "What happened?"

"He's been shot. I'm sure he died instantly, if that's any consolation."

She inhaled and exhaled deeply and slowly. She didn't like the man her father had become, hadn't had reason to for a long time. More recently she'd even come to fear him. But she'd never wished him ill. She wouldn't want him to have suffered. Physical pain could never compensate for or erase the mental anguish he'd caused. Nothing could. Yet, for no perceptible reason, she thought of how, long ago, he'd held her on his knee, read her bedtime stories and told her she was the prettiest little girl in all of Texas. No. She wouldn't have wanted him to suffer.

"Have you called anyone?" Marcie managed to inquire, her words thick.

"Not yet."

She wanted to ask him why not, but didn't trust her voice. McGee said he'd gotten here a few minutes ago. Was he the flitting shadow she'd observed? Why had he been going through the dune buggy?

She marched over to her horse, reached into the saddlebag and removed her cellular phone. There was no use calling 911. This wasn't a life-or-death situation. Not anymore. Death had already won. She punched in a longer set of digits. Her father'd had enough run-ins with the law that even after eight years of being away she remembered the number of the sheriff's office by heart.

She made her report concise and businesslike, answered a few questions, then broke the connection. Immediately, she hit an automatic dial button. Her mother answered on the second ring.

"Hello…hello?"

"Mom…I found Dad."

Carlinda heaved an audible, long-suffering sigh. "Where is he this time? In a bar or a ditch?" When Marcie didn't reply, Carlinda added anxiously, "He is all right, isn't he?"

Marcie's stomach knotted, and she hesitated.

"What's wrong, honey?" her mother asked more softly. "Did he finally land in jail this time?" Then another moment's pause. "You didn't…find him with someone?"

"No," Marcie answered, relieved she could at least spare her mother the indignity of learning her husband was shacked up with some bimbo again.

"Is he hurt? Did he have an accident? How bad is it?"

"Mom…I'll tell you when I get back."

"Don't play games with me, Marcie," her mother snapped. "Tell me what's happened."

"It's not good news, Mom. I'm afraid…Mom, Dad's dead."

There was total silence at the other end. Marcie tried to imagine what her mother was feeling at that moment. Was she numb, too? Marcie didn't doubt there would be pain and sorrow. But after nearly twenty-eight years of putting up with Mason Browder's moods, his abuse, his infidelity, irresponsibility and chronic alcoholism, maybe there was also an awareness of the inevitable and a sense of relief.

When Carlinda finally spoke, it was a simple quiet, "Oh." Then a moment later, a fragile, "What happened?"

"He was shot, Mom. Somebody killed him."

"My God!" Carlinda cried, her voice tremulous. Then a new anxiety. "Marcie, are you all right? Where are you?"

"Up at the bowl on the Green Valley place. Mr. McGee is here with me. I've called the sheriff."

"Green Valley? What was he doing there?"

"I don't know."

"Who did it, Marcie? Who killed him?"

"I don't know that, either, Mom."

"But…" Carlinda began, and let the word trail off.

"We'll be back as soon as we can."

"Be careful," her mother warned.

"I will. Mom, are you all right?"

"Just hurry home. I need to know you're safe."

Clicking the phone closed, Marcie placed it back in her saddlebag and, leading her bay mare, followed Tucker to a jumble of boulders where he'd left his horse. They could sit and wait for the sheriff there in the slanting evening shade. A justice of the peace would be coming with him to formally declare the rancher and one-time politician dead. Spring County, like most Texas counties, didn't have a medical examiner or a coroner. JPs proclaimed people officially deceased and decided if circumstances warranted further investigation.

Marcie sat on a coarse limestone shelf. The last of winter's chill was seeping out of its depths. She welcomed the bracing coolness. Tucker leaned against a boulder a few yards away, facing her, his long legs stretched out straight, his arms folded across his chest.

"You didn't answer my question," Marcie reminded him. "What are you doing here?"

"I got a call from Fletcher Doggitt, the foreman over on the Prudhomme ranch."

"I know who he is," she said impatiently.

"They lost fifty more head the night before last. I thought I might find a trail."

"You were looking for their cattle on our ranch? Are you accusing us of stealing Prudhomme livestock?"

"I'm not accusing anyone of anything," Tucker responded easily. "But someone has been corralling cattle here."

He was right, of course. She could see tracks and cow patties everywhere. The lingering odors indicated they had been here very recently, too.

"What are *you* doing up here?" he asked pointedly.

I don't have to answer him, she told herself. *He's not my father or my husband. He works for us.* But the nearness of her father's corpse somehow compelled her to keep talking.

"I was looking for Dad. He didn't come home last night."

"Word around the ranch is, that wasn't unusual. What made you come looking for him this time?"

Needle points of irritation stiffened her spine. Just because he'd witnessed her confrontation with her father, he'd concluded she wasn't concerned about him, that she didn't care. She resented his assumption. With all Mason's faults and failings, all the disappointments, she'd never completely lost affection for him. Of course, he'd never know that now. She took a deep breath.

"He had some sort of argument with my brother at the Beer Bucket Saloon yesterday afternoon—" *after I threatened to kill him,* she reminded herself "—and stormed off in Dustin's dune buggy. He generally has…had no trouble driving his pickup drunk, and he didn't always come straight home. But when he didn't show up at the house by this afternoon, I got worried he might have had an accident. As far as I know, he's never even ridden in Dusty's contraption before, much less driven it."

"Then why did he take it this time?"

Pure pigheadedness, she was tempted to say. "He told Dusty the truck was almost out of gas, and he didn't want to stop and fill up."

"But why come here? And what was so important that it couldn't wait?"

The questions had been gnawing at her, too. She shrugged. "Your guess is as good as mine. Dad didn't always make a whole lot of sense, especially when he was drinking."

"Which, from what I hear, was most of the time," Tucker added.

"I don't think you have any right to condemn," she erupted, surprising herself at the sudden urge to defend the man whose behavior she'd come to despise. "You didn't know him. Besides, he was your employer. That should be enough to warrant at least a semblance of respect." She expelled a chestful of air. "Anyway, he's dead. What he did doesn't make any difference now."

He gazed at her, his eyes never wavering. "Doesn't it?"

"What's done is done," she declared angrily. "It's over." *He's dead and the last thing I said to him wasn't that I love him but that I'd kill him.* "What's yet to be settled is his murder. I don't care what you or anyone else thought of my father, Mr. McGee. No one had the right to take his life. Someone murdered him. I'm going to find out who. Justice won't bring him back, but—"

Her words were interrupted by the fluttering drone of a Texas Ranger helicopter overhead. The sheriff had arrived.

Leaving the horses to nibble fresh green sprouts among the boulders, they moved back to the clearing. The chopper landed on a flat spot a hundred feet on the other side of the dune buggy. Tucker watched Marcie raise a slender arm to hold her western hat against the whirlwind of dust that rushed at them. The blast rippled her plum-colored shirt, outlining the generosity of perfectly shaped breasts. Discretion dictated that he be circumspect, but the male in him refused to look away. He'd experienced the same physical tug toward her on their first meeting and remembered all too clearly the tantalizing sensation of her hand slipping into his in greeting.

He tried to gauge her mental state. From what the ranch hands had told him about Mason Browder, the dead man had long since abdicated any right to his family's affection, but Tucker wondered about his daughter's tearless calm. Was she as cool as she seemed?

He replayed in his mind the scene she'd had with her father the day before. At the time, Tucker had had no doubt about the intensity or sincerity of her reaction, but he also hadn't taken the death threat literally. Should he have? Marcie Browder wouldn't have been the first woman to oppose violence with deadly force.

Maintaining his objectivity about this woman, with her light-brown hair and enchanting blue eyes, wasn't going to be easy. She was hanging tough now. No tears. No wringing of hands. No faltering speech. But she didn't fool him. He'd glimpsed, in the firm set of her mouth and unfocused stare, a deeply scarred sensitivity beneath her hard shell, detected the vulnerability she didn't want him to see. The emptiness she was feeling right now probably shocked her.

Death, he could have told her, always brought surprises, even when it was expected as a result of advanced age or long illness. But sudden, violent death robbed loved ones of even that preparation time.

Unbidden, he pictured Beth and little Ruth. His throat tightened. He didn't want to think of the family he'd lost. Not now. Not here. They filled his nights with an ache that could never be relieved. He couldn't let it torture his days as well. *Keep busy, active,* he scolded himself. *Think other thoughts.*

Two men emerged from the Jet Ranger's cabin and ran, hunched over, toward them. The older man, white haired, in loose-fitting jeans and khaki shirt with the six-pointed sheriff's star pinned on the left breast pocket, came to them. The younger man, middle-aged, balding and toting a camera and videocam, went directly to the body.

Tucker got through the introductions and preliminary report without any indication that Sheriff Kraus recognized him. That didn't mean he didn't, of course. Tucker had been warned that the soft-spoken gentleman was more savvy than he looked, and as up-to-date on technology as the county's budget allowed. Not that Coyote Springs had much call for sophisticated criminal investigative techniques. Drunken cowboys on Saturday night were still the town's biggest menace. There hadn't been a murder in the county in nearly six years. Until now.

"How'd you find him up here?"

"I was riding around, checking things out. I've been on the job only a couple of weeks and twenty-five sections is a lot of territory to cover. This was my first trip into an area I hadn't seen yet."

"Did you touch the body?" Kraus asked in a West Texas drawl.

Tucker shook his head. "His neck, to be sure he wasn't still alive, though it was pretty obvious he was dead."

"How about anything else?"

Tucker thought about when he first heard Marcie approaching. Had she seen him going through the buggy? After verifying there was no pulse, he'd put his leather gloves back on, so there wouldn't be any fingerprints, but it wouldn't do any good to have her contradicting him, or for him to give her doubts about himself.

"I checked the buggy," Tucker admitted. "I wondered if the gun might still be here."

"Why?" Kraus's gray eyes bore into him.

Tucker scratched the sandpaper stubble on his chin. "I know this might sound a little goofy, Sheriff, but I wondered if he might have killed himself, figured maybe the gun had flown out of his hand when he fired. Seems pretty dumb, I guess. Don't imagine too many people shoot themselves through the heart."

Tucker could tell the lawman was trying to decide if he was giving him a con job. "A few do," the old man commented as he regarded the body sprawled out by the side of the dune buggy. He looked back at Tucker. "Did you find a gun?"

"No, but I was here only a couple of minutes before Ms. Browder showed up."

Tucker used his peripheral vision to observe her. Had she seen him slip the piece of paper in his pocket? If so, she wasn't saying anything.

The sheriff ambled away to confer with the JP, who'd finished videotaping the scene. The police pilot had joined him, and they were stretching out a black plastic bag beside the corpse. While Marcie backed away, Tucker edged as close as he could to hear their conversation. He got only bits and pieces. "...dead some time...rigor dissipating...one shot...not self-inflicted..." Nothing Tucker hadn't already figured out for himself. "Make sure you take plenty of pictures of the buggy and all the footprints around here.

People and horses,'' Kraus concluded. ''Some of them have to belong to the killer, unless he was an angel of death who could hover above the ground.''

Tucker watched Browder's mortal remains being zipped into the body bag. He'd seen it all before, helped package friends, enemies and the scattered parts of both. It still brought a metallic taste to his mouth.

The sheriff came over to Marcie. ''I'm afraid we don't have room to take you with us. If you want to wait, I can send the chopper back for you.''

''Don't bother,'' she said. ''By the time it drops you off, returns here and takes me home, I can be there on Sparkle.''

''You're probably right. I just thought you might not feel like riding under the circumstances.''

''Under the circumstances,'' she repeated, ''I think I'd rather ride than wait.'' The sheriff nodded. ''What happens now?''

''We'll be taking your daddy to the hospital morgue. They'll probably do an autopsy tonight. I might be able to give you preliminary results in the morning.''

''Is there any doubt?''

''Not at the moment. But looks can be deceiving. I'll go out to your place and inform your ma as soon as I get back.''

''I've already called her,'' Marcie told him.

The sheriff nodded. ''I'll just stop by and offer my condolences, then.''

Tucker knew the lawman would have preferred breaking the news himself. First impressions at the announcement of misfortune could be revealing. Which raised a question. Did the sheriff suspect Carlinda Browder of involvement in her husband's death? There are two rules when investigating death by violence. Find out who profits. Then look to the people closest to the victim. Very often you're looking at the same person. So who would profit by Browder's death?

Tucker stood beside Marcie as the helicopter lifted off, again swathing them in a blast of blade wash. He glanced over at the young woman as she untied her mare. Beneath the black hat, her long chestnut hair was gathered loosely with a blue ribbon. Involuntarily, he wondered what that fine silk would feel like slipping through his fingers. An emptiness gnawed at his insides, a hunger he had no right to satisfy.

The sun had sunk low enough in the sky now that evening's gloaming was spreading across the basin. He untied the thick flannel shirt rolled up on the back of his saddle and handed it to her.

"I'm perfectly fine," she insisted.

"You're not dressed for a ten-degree drop in temperature. You've also had a shock that would be enough to give anyone the shivers. Rattling your bones with cold won't help."

She bit her lip, and he sensed she wanted to argue with him. Then suddenly there was a hint of a smile. "Thanks," she said as he held the shirt for her to slip into.

Tucker let Marcie ride ahead of him, content for her to set the pace. Her posture, erect, almost stiff, told him she was either unaware of or indifferent to his being there.

She was still in shock, maybe even denial. The full impact of her father's death probably hadn't hit her yet. A part of him wanted to soothe her, to hold her in his arms and tell her everything was going to be all right, that she had done her best, done what she had to do, that the time for recriminations was over. Tucker McGee understood too well the pain and anguish on the terrible sojourn in the shadow of death. The problem was that he didn't know how to relieve them.

How much did she know about what was going on? About him? What would her reaction be when she found out?

He'd have to stay close to Marcie and her family without giving himself away. His position as foreman should furnish him the cover he needed, provided the new widow didn't decide to terminate his services.

By the time they arrived at the ranch house, it would be nearly dark, even at the quick lope Marcie was setting. The prospect of riding under the stars had a certain romantic appeal, but it was also difficult and dangerous on a moonless night over unfamiliar ground. Riding against time as they were didn't give them an opportunity to talk, to exchange ideas and get to know each other.

When they reached the knoll overlooking the ranch house, she stopped, and he moved up beside her. He should say something, reassure her she wasn't alone. But he didn't know any adequate words. In the face of death, he ruminated, all of us are alone.

She glanced over at him as if expecting him to speak; then, before he had a chance, nudged her horse into an easy walk down the long slope toward the sprawling stone-and-stucco house. Her mother stood on the brick patio by the back door.

They reined in at the barnyard and dismounted. Carlinda Browder looked tiny in the glaring floodlights as she ran a hand nervously through unruly brown hair, streaked generously with gray. Tucker noted the grim set of her mouth and the blurred bruise along her jaw. Her posture was straight, almost stern, her dark-blue eyes clear and dry as she held her arms out to Marcie.

Tucker called to a new ranch hand who was coiling a hose by the barn, and told him to take the horses, unsaddle them, feed and water them, then clean the saddles before hanging them on their usual racks in the tack room.

"Heard Mr. Browder got shot," Jim Bob said in an undertone as he grabbed the split leather reins.

So word of how the big man died was already public knowledge.

"Just take care of the horses," Tucker instructed the young man, and marched to the house. Carlinda looked at him askance as he slipped, uninvited, into the kitchen. Did you kill him? her glance seemed to question.

"Where's Dusty?" Marcie asked her mother.

"He went into town this afternoon to see Calhoun. There was a billing problem on one of the feed deliveries this week. I expected him back by now. He probably stopped by the Beer Bucket as usual." Carlinda's expression was one of resignation.

"Or he went over to spend some time with Lula," Marcie suggested.

Tucker suppressed a smirk. Dustin and his girlfriend, Lula Crosby, were practically inseparable. No wonder. Her spandex pants and clinging sweaters didn't leave much to the imagination. The girl's blatant sexuality, however, had stirred no interest in Tucker. The feminine charm of the young woman across the room leaning against the counter in rumpled jeans and his oversized flannel shirt intrigued him in a way that was far more compelling.

Just then, they heard the low timbre of a sports car outside. The two women said nothing as they stood in the middle of the room.

Dustin Browder came through the doorway. His face was gray with shock.

CHAPTER TWO

"Is it true?" Dustin asked his mother, his eyes wide and glassy. "I heard on the radio..."

Carlinda bowed her head. Her son put his arms around her. Just under six foot, with good shoulders and strong arms, Dustin Browder looked very much like his father, or, Tucker supposed, what his father might have looked like thirty years earlier and fifty pounds lighter.

For a moment his mother hugged him desperately, the unbruised side of her face pressed against his knit shirt. A tear glistened, then escaped down her cheek.

Tucker glanced over at Marcie, who was standing by the teakettle on the stove. The purse of her lips suggested an attitude of forbearance; the older sister who did all the chores, while her kid brother took all the credit—and affection.

"Where was he found?" Dustin asked the room at large after his mother pulled away and resumed her make-busy work of putting out cups for tea.

"In the bowl on the Green Valley place," Marcie told him.

"Green Valley?" Dustin's brows went up. "Lennie's old place? What the hell was he doing up there?"

"Getting himself killed," Marcie snapped as she

placed tea bags in the two flowered cups her mother had set on the kitchen table.

"That damned dune buggy. He should never have taken it. I tried to stop him from driving it, you know."

"That wasn't it," Carlinda told him more gently. "Somebody shot him."

"Shot him?" The words came out as a whisper. "Somebody killed Dad?"

"He took a bullet in the chest," Tucker said. Apparently, the news report hadn't identified the cause of death.

Dustin spun around and faced the new foreman, as if seeing him for the first time. "What are you doing here? Aren't you supposed to be out making sure we don't lose any more cattle?"

"Mr. McGee discovered Dad just before I got there," Marcie explained.

Eyes narrowed, Dustin honed in on to the other man. "*You* found him? What the hell were you doing there? We don't keep cattle on the Green Valley place."

Tucker repeated the explanation he'd given Marcie and the sheriff; that he was trying to track some calves taken from the neighboring ranch the night before.

"What business is it of yours what happens on their place? You work for us, not Prudhomme."

"You've both got the same problem," Tucker reminded him. "Losing livestock. Green Valley is Browder property, but it's also smack in between the two ranches' major grazing lands. It seemed reasonable to see if any cattle were being kept there. It's got easy access—"

"Your job, McGee, is to prevent rustling, not investigate it. Leave that to the sheriff's department."

"I'm in a better position to find out things around here than the sheriff," Tucker countered, trying hard to keep from sounding argumentative. He couldn't accomplish his mission if he got fired.

"Well, you're obviously more interested in playing detective than doing your job," Dustin said angrily. "I just came back from Hawk Ridge. Seems we had another twenty head rustled last night."

"Damn!" Carlinda growled, then looked at Tucker.

"McGee's right," Marcie told her brother. "They must have taken them to the bowl. There were fresh hoofprints and droppings all over the place. Dad probably figured it out, went up there to confront whoever did it, and they killed him."

"We wouldn't have had this rustling problem if Dad had let me handle things," Dustin declared. "Well, I'm taking over now." He faced Tucker. "We don't need your services anymore, McGee. Pack up. You've got two weeks' wages coming. I'll give you three if you leave tonight."

"Wait a minute, Dusty," Marcie interceded. "I don't think it's your decision."

Her brother glared at her. "Dad's gone. I'm in charge now."

Marcie didn't flinch. "Dusty, I know you want to help, but this is Mom's ranch. Not yours. Not mine."

Dustin's face turned red—with rage and, Tucker suspected, with fear. "Who the hell do you think you are?" His words came out as a snarl. "You figure you can come back here and give orders—"

Her gaze steady, her voice firm, Marcie replied,

"I'm not giving orders. I'm..." She let out a long breath. "Dusty, why don't you just back off—"

"Or what?" he asked between clenched teeth. "Or you'll threaten to kill me, too?"

"Stop," Carlinda exploded. She'd watched her two children with wringing hands and pain in her eyes. "That's enough." She glowered at her son. "Dustin Clive Browder, I want you to apologize to your sister immediately."

Tucker almost chuckled. Besides being talked to like a little boy, Dustin seemed to recoil from the use of his middle name.

"Yeah, sure," Dustin mumbled. "Sorry." But he didn't sound very contrite.

The siblings stared at each other in tense silence.

"Things aren't always what they seem, Dusty," Tucker said, hoping he might be able to defuse the situation. "Those cattle weren't rustled from Hawk Ridge. I moved them yesterday after Fletcher Doggitt called."

"In any event," Marcie said, giving Tucker a sideways glance, "this isn't the time to be firing people. We're going to be busy enough for the next few weeks trying to straighten out Dad's affairs, much less running a cattle ranch and chasing rustlers at the same time."

Her brother walked over to the island separating the kitchen from the dining area and opened the lower cabinet. He removed a bottle of bourbon, got out a crystal old-fashioned glass and filled it halfway with the amber liquor.

"Dusty, please," Carlinda implored.

Scowling defiantly at his sister, as if daring her to plead with him, too, he swallowed most of the drink, put the glass down and turned to Tucker. "Maybe Marcie's right. I suppose you might as well stay."

Tucker breathed an internal sigh of relief. The bluff had worked. Phonies, he'd discovered a long time ago, usually backed off at the first sign of opposition.

"But I want a full accounting daily of what's going on," Dustin said forcefully. "Is that clear, McGee?"

Tucker groaned to himself at the twenty-three-year-old's belligerent tone. He'd seen the type before—the spoiled sons of doting parents. Kids who had intelligence, as Tucker suspected Dustin did, and occasionally even talent. The problem was commitment. They had all sorts of grandiose schemes and more than a little bravado to start things, but they lacked the focus and discipline to follow through on them.

Dustin Browder was no exception. He lived here at the ranch, supposedly to help his folks run the place, but he seemed to spend most of his time sniffing around his girlfriend like a hotshot cowboy. That didn't stop him, of course, from playing the boss from time to time.

But why was he so eager to get rid of McGee? He'd just found out his father was dead, murdered, and before he'd even asked who killed him, he was trying to fire the new foreman. Didn't make much sense. Or did he already know who'd killed his old man? Was he involved in some way? Obviously, he and his father hadn't agreed on who should run the ranch, but was that reason to kill him? Had Dustin found out who Tucker really was and that was why he was afraid of him?

Too early to be jumping to conclusions, Tucker reminded himself. People often act irrationally in a crisis.

He fixed his attention on Marcie. If he was reading the expression on her face correctly, some of the same thoughts were going through her head. Did she actually suspect her own brother of killing their father?

A knock on the door saved Tucker from acknowledging Dustin's demand.

"Come on in," Carlinda called out without even asking who it was.

Rudy Kraus, still wearing his badge, stepped inside. He tipped his hat to Marcie, shook hands with her brother, nodded to Tucker, then went to Carlinda. He held her hand in one of his and stroked it with the other.

"I'm real sorry, Carli. I wish things could have been different."

She nodded stoically. "Any idea who did it?"

"Not yet. But you can rest assured, we won't stop till we find him."

"I suppose you want to ask a bunch of questions," Dustin said as he polished off the rest of his whiskey and reached for the bottle on the counter.

"I have a few, yeah, but I reckon they can wait till morning. In the meantime, young man, I suggest you lay off that stuff. Seems to me whiskey's caused enough pain in this house already. Your mother and sister need your support right now—your sober support."

Dustin's eyes flashed with resentment. He glanced at his mother, then put the bottle back without pouring a second drink.

Carlinda said nothing, but as she gazed at Rudy Kraus, her back to her son, Tucker noticed a tiny curling of her lips that looked as though it might be gratitude.

Kraus, refusing the offer of tea or coffee, said he'd be back in the morning to report on what the autopsy found.

After the sheriff drove away, Tucker excused himself and went back to the foreman's cottage. It was Spartan, but adequate as far as he was concerned. Besides, he'd lived in much closer quarters under a lot worse conditions with men he didn't even know. At least here he had privacy.

On the wall between the makeshift cooking area and the straight-legged pine table was a telephone, an extension of one of the two lines available up at the main house. Since he didn't want to take a chance on someone overhearing him, he unfolded the cellular phone he carried with him when he was out riding fence line or checking stock.

The number was answered on the second ring.

"He's dead," Tucker reported. "Got him straight through the heart."

"Where the heart should have been, you mean. There's still the matter of missing cattle."

"Leave it to me."

"Are you sure you can take care of it?" the voice on the other end inquired.

"That's what I was hired for, remember?"

"I want this thing ended quickly."

Tucker thought about Marcie, about the look he'd seen in her eyes, the way the sight of her made him respond. He wondered how he would feel when he could no longer see her. It wouldn't do him any good to get involved. "That makes two of us," he said, and clicked off.

IN THE MORNING, WHEN HE heard a car crunch up the long, gravel driveway, Tucker strolled out of the horse barn into the open courtyard between the barn and the ranch house. It was a few minutes shy of eight o'clock, but ranchers and farmers rarely got to sleep late. Already several neighbors had stopped by to offer a few words of consolation to the new widow. This latest visitor, however, was different. The black-and-white Cherokee had the sheriff's emblem emblazoned on its door.

The heavyset man hauled himself out from the driver's seat, then reached back into the vehicle and removed a cellophane-wrapped fruit basket. After handing it to Tucker, he closed the door with a resolute slam and cast an accusatory eye on the foreman.

"'Morning, Sheriff," Tucker said.

"Did some checking on you, McGee. We need to talk, you and me."

Tucker didn't like the ominous ring of those words. But he shouldn't be surprised. After all, his status was a matter of public record.

"Can we do it later? I don't think this is a good time."

"For who? You or me?"

"For them," Tucker said, nodding toward the house.

The sheriff looked as if he were about to argue the point when Carlinda called out a greeting from the kitchen door.

"Later, McGee," he said in a truculent undertone, then faced the middle-aged woman standing in the doorway. "Do I smell fresh coffee?" he said more loudly. "You always did know how to brew it."

"Who do you think you're kidding, Rudy? I never

made a good pot of coffee in my life. I can burn water and you know it.''

The old man smiled. ''Yeah. Well, it smells pretty good anyway.''

''Thanks to Marcie,'' she said, ''and the wonders of modern technology.''

He winked. ''I will if you let me have a cup.''

Her tense features softened, and she chuckled. ''Come on, then.'' She swung the screen door open.

Tucker followed them inside and deposited the basket on the counter. Carlinda motioned them to the round oak table at the end of the oblong room, went over to the island and retrieved three mugs and the glass pot from the automatic coffeemaker. Tucker noticed when she joined them that her eyes were still clear and dry. If she was shedding any tears over the death of her husband, it was very much in private. The realization that a man could die without leaving sorrow behind saddened him.

''You have some news?'' Carlinda asked.

The sheriff nodded. He was putting his third spoonful of sugar in the steaming hot brew when Marcie came into the kitchen.

Tucker appreciated the way her jeans outlined her graceful hips and long legs. The casual T-shirt wasn't quite baggy enough to disguise the fullness of her breasts. The elusive fragrance he whiffed probably wasn't perfume, he decided. More likely the rinse used on the long, shiny brown hair that fanned across her shoulders. For an uncontrollable moment, lust twitched, until her brother came through the doorway behind her.

Dustin Browder looked as though he'd spent the night in hell. His hazel eyes were sunken and bloodshot, maybe from drink, too little sleep or both. The scruff of a brown beard reinforced the dissolute, almost sinister impression. So the new man of the house hadn't bothered to shave this morning. Tucker resisted a temptation to shake his head. If the death of Dusty's father was going to be the catalyst that would make the young man grow up, so far there was no indication of it.

After the new round of greetings and the pouring of additional mugs of coffee, Marcie took the seat across from the sheriff. "What can you tell us about Dad's murder? Do you have any idea who killed him?"

Rudy Kraus shook his head. "They did the autopsy last night," he said, addressing himself principally to Carlinda. "No surprises about the cause of death—a single gunshot to the chest. He probably died instantly, or pretty nearly so."

Nothing Tucker didn't know the night before.

"What kind of weapon was used?" Marcie asked.

The sheriff punched his nose. "The doc thinks it might have been a nine-millimeter."

Dustin aimed a suspicious glance at Tucker, then dropped his gaze when Tucker stared back.

"Was the bullet recovered?" Tucker asked.

"No," Kraus admitted.

"Then you really can't be sure of the caliber, can you? It might have been a .38 or .357."

The lawman's face turned sour, his bushy brows descending over his gray eyes. "Could be," he replied tersely.

"But that still means a handgun, doesn't it?" Marcie inquired. "Rather than a rifle? Was it at close range?"

"About six feet, the medical examiner estimates."

"What you mean, Sheriff," Tucker elaborated, "is that there were no powder burns, therefore the gun was fired from at least three feet away. Isn't that correct?"

Kraus's piercing gaze narrowed. "You seem to know an awful lot about this, McGee."

"Just trying to get facts straight. I don't think you'd want to repeat the statements you just made in a court of law. A good defense lawyer would tear them apart."

Marcie looked from one man to the other, confusion written in her glance. "So it was a face-to-face confrontation," she observed, toying with the handle of her mug. "Was there any sign of a struggle?"

"No. If there was a fight, it must've been verbal."

Dustin raised his cup to take a sip. "When did it happen?"

"The pathologist couldn't be absolutely sure," the sheriff told him. "You never can be, unless there's a witness. But he figures sometime between six and eight the night before last."

Dustin practically dropped the cup to the table, spilling a little of his coffee. No one made a move to clean it up. "That means Dad must have gone up there right after he left the Beer Bucket."

"How do you know that?" Marcie asked.

"Because I remember that when he stormed out of the place, the six o'clock news was just coming on the TV over the bar."

"Why'd he go up there anyway?" Kraus inquired. "Was he supposed to meet someone?"

"Damned if I know," Dustin replied with a shake of his head.

"What was he upset about?" Marcie asked.

Her brother turned down the corners of his mouth and shrugged.

"There's one other thing." Kraus looked at Carlinda, his voice mellowing. "Was Mason complaining of any aches or pains lately?"

"What do you mean?" Her expression was perplexed. "He was always complaining about something."

"But anything specific? Backaches? Things like that?"

She frowned. "Not that I recall. Why?"

Rudy Kraus paused. "He had cirrhosis as well as cancer of the liver."

Silence followed. Carlinda finally broke the spell. "I guess we shouldn't be surprised. Considering the way he drank, it was inevitable."

Marcie tightened her grip on the mug between her hands to keep them from trembling. "Did the doctor say how long he would have lived?"

"Apparently, both diseases were in the early stages. He might have been experiencing mild pain, but at this point, he could have dismissed it as a nagging backache, maybe even indigestion or heartburn. But it wouldn't have been too much longer before he would have realized it was something more serious. Without a liver transplant, he probably would have been dead in a year, two at the most."

"And it would have been painful?" Marcie pressed.

Kraus cleared him throat. "I'm afraid so."

She bit her lip and closed her eyes. "Well," she observed, "if there's any good in this, it's that he didn't suffer."

Her mother reached over, took Marcie's hand and squeezed it.

"When will you release the body?" Dustin asked.

"Might not be for four or five days, until all the tests are completed and they get back the lab results. Then they have to write up a formal report." He looked at Carlinda. "Smithson's when they do release it?"

She nodded. Smithson's was the biggest funeral home in town.

"The mayor got a call from the governor's office last evening wanting to know when the memorial service is going to be. Politics," Rudy huffed. "Seems he might send a representative to honor the former state senator."

Carlinda snorted. "'Honor.'"

"I'll let you know as soon as we work it all out," Marcie informed him.

Her mother was back at the sink rinsing out coffee cups when the sheriff got up from the table a few minutes later and said goodbye. She inclined her head lethargically. "Thanks for coming, Rudy."

He tipped his hat and sauntered to the door. Dustin seemed too busy pondering the mysteries of his coffee mug to notice the beckoning nod their visitor gave his sister. Rudy waited until they were outside and the kitchen door was closed behind them.

"Not much to come home to, Marcie." His frown deepened as he stroked his chin. "I'm glad you're back, though. I know it's a comfort to your ma. This is pretty rough on her. Probably gonna be for a while. Having you here will help."

Marcie had yet to see her mother break down and

really cry. "She's tough. Had to be to put up with him all these years."

The sheriff bobbed his head in agreement. "That bruise on the side of her face—looks like their relationship went into a new phase. I heard you got into it with him, too. That right?"

Her head came up.

"Heard he took a swing at you."

She held his steadfast gaze. "And missed."

"And you threatened to kill him."

"Sheriff, are you suggesting I murdered my father?"

"I'm not suggesting anything. Just checking things out."

"You don't really think I—"

"It doesn't matter what I think. I have a duty to investigate. I like to be thorough." He moved toward his car, then stopped and turned. "By the way, what were you doing up at the bowl yesterday?"

Her breathing stopped. "I told you. I was out looking for my father."

"Why there?"

She shrugged, feeling the answer was inadequate even before she gave it. "I'd already checked half a dozen other places he might have gone. The bowl was just another one of them."

She watched the old man lower himself into his car, start the engine and roll down the electric window. "Now, you take good care of your ma, hear? She's going to need you more than ever."

He drove slowly down the driveway, leaving her feeling hollow inside and just a little frightened.

TUCKER HADN'T MISSED the signal between the sheriff and Marcie. As they were going outside and Dustin was retreating to his bedroom, he took the opportunity to slip into the half bath by the kitchen door. He had to find out what the sheriff wanted, what he might have up his sleeve. Spying on people was the quintessence of Tucker's new profession, and listening to private conversations was a time-honored method of gaining valuable information, even if it did sometimes leave him feeling dirty.

At this time of year, when temperatures were moderate and neither the air-conditioning nor heating was in use, the lavatory's small window was wide-open. Kraus's car was parked below it.

Tucker wasn't able to make out all the words, but he heard enough of the exchange to understand its tenor. Did the lawman really suspect Marcie of killing her father?

It was true that she'd been back only two days before having a violent argument with him, and she had threatened his life. Could they have had another confrontation in which she followed through on her threat? From his sources, Tucker knew her marriage had been an abusive one. When she'd worked up the courage to walk out on a fist-wielding husband a year ago, wouldn't she have vowed not to submit to violence by anyone else, either?

If the sheriff was trying to frighten Marcie into revealing information she might not otherwise divulge, what did he expect to hear? That Carlinda had also sworn vengeance? Tucker couldn't imagine Marcie pointing the finger at her mother to save herself. Why not use the intimidation technique on Dustin? He was the one who'd seen his father last and who seemed most apt to cave in to pressure.

Had Kraus caught the look Dustin gave Tucker when the murder gun's caliber was identified? How many people in Spring County owned 9 mm handguns? Undoubtedly a few, but chances were not very many.

He waited until the sound of the sheriff's car had faded down the driveway before he stepped out of the bathroom and left the ranch house. Marcie wasn't in the yard. Probably in the barn. At twenty, Sparkle was getting long in the tooth, and Marcie impressed Tucker as the kind of woman who would diligently make sure the aging mare had recovered from the previous day's long ride. Or maybe the grieving daughter just needed the company of an old friend. He was tempted to check out the barn, but he had something he had to do first.

He closed the door of his cottage behind him, went directly to the desk in the bedroom, took out his key ring and unlocked the lower right-hand drawer. What he found didn't surprise him, but it sent a cold trickle of fear down his neck nevertheless.

He sat on the edge of the iron-frame bed and thought back to the day a little over two weeks earlier when he was unloading things from his pickup after being officially hired as the new foreman. He hadn't asked for help—there wasn't much to carry—but Jim Bob, the kid they had working around the house and barn and who seemed perpetually eager to please, had given it anyway. Then the teenager, trying to juggle too much, had dropped a box of books, and the pistol had tumbled out. Carlinda had been sweeping the brick patio and her son and his girlfriend happened to be passing by on their way to the barn for her riding lesson. Dustin had stopped and showed considerable curiosity about the weapon. How many rounds did the magazine hold? Did it have much of a recoil? How accurate was it? He'd asked to hold it, and to Tucker's relief had handled the side arm safely and professionally, checking the chamber, being careful to not point it at anyone.

"You interested in handguns?" Tucker had asked, thinking this might be an opportunity to get to know the young man better.

"I was on the rifle team in school," Dustin replied as he examined the bolt mechanism. "Took first in rapid-fire, long-range and small-target categories. Always wanted to try my hand at pistols." He stroked the barrel for a moment, then dismissively returned the weapon to Tucker. The fleeting moment of male bonding was gone.

And now, so was the 9 mm.

CHAPTER THREE

By noon on Wednesday the house was beginning to look like a church picnic and smell even better. The tantalizing aromas of Mexican spices, smoked meats and baked goods filled the kitchen and were beginning to waft through the rest of the house. Friends and neighbors stopped to drop off food or flowers and to linger a few minutes to offer their condolences. Shelby Turner, among the first to arrive, stayed.

She and Carlinda had been friends since high school. Six-foot-two and heavyset, Shelby had never married. Twenty or more years ago she'd transformed her father's small gas station on the north end of town into a big, modern truck stop. Her appetite for food matched her clientele's, and when the occasion demanded, she could keep up with their colorful language, syllable for syllable.

She greeted Marcie with a bear hug that threatened to smother her, but the affection was genuine and inevitably lifted Marcie's spirits.

Marcie chuckled as she fixed another pot of coffee, the fourth one so far. "We certainly will have a varied diet over the next few days. There's smoked sausage, roast chicken..."

"Fried chicken, too," Shelby added, almost smacking her lips.

"Rice salad, cheese and beef enchiladas, tamales, beans, four different kinds of homemade bread, three pies—two of them pecan—and a whole barbecued beef brisket," Carlinda recited.

"I hope someone likes pickled okra," Shelby boomed from the pantry. "I think you've got four quarts of it here."

Carlinda snickered. "Thanks, but no, thanks."

Marcie glanced over at her mother, confirming her suspicion that the levity didn't quite reach her eyes. Still, any attempt to maintain a sense of humor was a positive sign.

"Mom, where do you want to put these cold plates?" she asked. "We're running out of space in the—"

Shelby touched her arm gently. "Leave them. I'm an old pro at this. Why don't you and your ma sit down and relax for a few minutes—or until the next horde arrives. Pretend I'm not here."

Marcie cast an appraising glance at her mother. Dressed in a dark sweatshirt and her customary baggy jeans, Carlinda's slouched posture betrayed her exhaustion. Marcie had hoped the night before that the two of them could have a good cry together, but Carlinda had retired to her bedroom early and declined all invitations to come out.

"Coffee, Mom?"

"If I can have some that's hot. Every cup I've poured has gotten cold."

"How about a piece of Mrs. Kleinschmidt's strudel to go with it?" Shelby suggested, and served them two generous portions.

They ate in silence for several minutes, while the big woman fluttered in the background.

Marcie was worried about her mother. On her occasional visits to the Lazy B in the past few years, she'd noticed Carlinda becoming increasingly withdrawn emotionally, not in the hostile way her father had but with a sort of reserved fatalism. She'd been a positive and supportive parent when Marcie was growing up, but even her brother, who wasn't exactly known for his sensitivity, had remarked on their mother's bouts of near depression.

"Did Dad leave a will?" Marcie finally asked.

"Yes. Tad Radic, our lawyer, has it. There's not much. A few personal things, his guns, his share of the Green Valley place, some penny stocks—they're worthless—he left them all to Dusty."

To Marcie, it felt as if an old wound had been torn open. He'd left nothing for her. Not even a memento of the good times they'd shared. "What about the ranch? It's still in your name, isn't it?"

"It's mine. Gramps made sure of that. Mason couldn't touch it—though God knows he would have liked to."

"The place is pretty run-down, Mom." Marcie had been distressed to see the continuing deterioration of the homestead that had been in the family for five generations. The past couldn't be undone, but the future was still to be made.

"I tried," Carlinda said softly, "but..."

Marcie put her hand on her mother's and felt the tiny quiver beneath the cold skin. "I know you did. Nobody's blaming you."

She remembered fondly the sense of family and well-being when she was little and her grandparents were alive, though her specific recollections of them were few. Her father was around more after they died, and for several years he'd made her feel safe and cherished. They'd shared fun-filled times together. What had happened to break the bond between them she'd never understood.

Her mother had been different then, too. There had been more laughter in the house. The world had seemed greener and bluer and brighter, the ranch a happy place.

For no apparent reason, Marcie pictured Tucker McGee. He looked so proud and determined sitting on his horse.

Her father had ridden well enough years before when he'd been in shape, and her brother was a competent horseman. But Tucker McGee was more than just a good rider. She'd observed the proprietary interest he seemed to take in the things around him, not as possessions but as if they were somehow sacred, a trust. She liked the way he gazed off at the distant horizon from time to time, like a man seeing a vision, a dream. For this cowboy, the Lazy B ranch wasn't merely a place where he worked, and being foreman wasn't just a job he had to do. Marcie smiled to herself, knowing exactly why she was drawn to him. He looked the way she felt, like someone who belonged to the land.

She also felt an affinity with the melancholy she saw in his eyes, an intimation that the world, with all its beauty, had disappointed him, as well. Could he be a part of making the Lazy B better, more productive…more alive?

"Mom, will you let me help you rebuild the ranch—the way it used to be when Gramps ran it? I've got some ideas I'd like to talk to you about."

When Carlinda looked up, Marcie saw so much

desolation in her mother's watery eyes that it threatened to bring tears to her own.

"I'd like that," her mother said.

SHELBY LEFT A FEW MINUTES before two o'clock,
promising to come back in the morning with extra
coolers and bags of ice to store the cold food people
were delivering. The soft golden light of spring
melted like warm honey through the old sash windows as Carlinda, Dustin, McGee and Marcie gathered around the kitchen table. Each toyed with a mug
of coffee from the fresh pot she'd prepared a few
minutes earlier.

"What's this all about?" Dustin asked. He was still
unshaven, but at least he'd brushed his sand-colored
hair and put on a clean polo shirt.

"I think we need to talk about how we're going to
run this ranch, now that Dad isn't here to interfere."

"*You* think!" His hangover and appearance may
have improved, but his disposition, especially toward
his sister, hadn't.

"Dusty, please," Carlinda implored. "Your sister's
right. There are so many things we should have done
long ago…"

He slouched against the ladder-back chair, his chin
on his chest, arms outstretched so that the tips of his
fingers touched the sides of his steaming mug.

Marcie glanced at Tucker to gauge his reaction to
their family dynamics, but he merely took another sip
of coffee.

"Mom and I have talked about this," she continued, "but we all need to discuss it so there won't be
any misunderstanding about who's going to be doing
what."

She looked again at her brother, but he continued to stare morosely at his mug.

"Mom is going to set up our ranch budget."

"Nothing new about that," Dustin muttered. "She always does."

Frustration mounted, but Marcie refused to give it vent. "Except this time we're going to follow it," she said evenly. "All the accounts are going to be in her name. That means she's in charge of paying all the bills, including our wages."

"Wages?" Dustin sat up straight, his hands flat on the table.

Marcie suppressed a smile. She knew her brother would balk. Their father had given him an allowance when he was a full-time college student but had demanded little or nothing for it. After five years of lackluster grades, Dustin had finally graduated last semester with a degree in general studies. As far as Marcie could tell, he'd made no serious effort since then to get a regular job, but the allowance had continued.

"There's a lot to be done around here, and just because this is a family business doesn't mean we shouldn't be paid for our work," she reasoned, reversing the tables on him.

"I'm not some hired hand," Dustin sputtered.

"If you would rather work somewhere else, Dusty," she replied calmly, "that's your prerogative, of course. Naturally, should you choose to do so and continue to live here, you'll be expected to pay room and board. Or you can move out and get a place of your own. It's up to you."

She glanced again at Tucker. This time he winked at her before taking another sip of coffee. She nearly winked back but managed to catch herself in time. The impulse shook her. Flirting wasn't on the agenda—and wasn't going to be. She'd had enough of men, especially good-looking, sexy men.

The steam was practically rising from her brother's ears. He turned to his mother. "Mom, are you going to let her get away with this?"

Carlinda bit her lower lip, clearly uncomfortable with the situation, and for a moment Marcie was afraid she might crumble under the weight of her son's hostility. But then she stiffened her back. "I hope you don't leave, Dusty," she said. "We can use your help. This is supposed to be a family ranch."

Dustin's eyes widened. He was stunned by her response. To Marcie's relief, her mother didn't waiver.

"Just listen to what your sister has to say," Carlinda urged. "She's got a good plan."

He fell back against the chair once more, his mouth thinned into a taut line.

Marcie saw a subtle smile on Tucker's lips. His approval shouldn't matter to her, but his slow blink and encouraging grin were having an odd, stimulating effect on her.

"And what's she going to do for her wages?" her brother demanded, his still slightly bloodshot eyes blazing at her.

"To start with, I'm going to computerize us. I can't believe everything is still written down in ledgers and on scraps of paper."

"I thought about getting a computer," Carlinda said defensively, "but I don't know anything about them, and every time I saved up enough to invest in one, your father spent the money on something else."

You could have opened your own account, Marcie

wanted to say, but held her tongue. She understood all too well that in the past few years her mother's sole aim had been to avoid confrontations with her husband. As if it would keep peace. Marcie knew from personal experience that it didn't work. Bullies always found excuses for blaming other people for their own failings.

"That's okay," she told her. "I know what we need. If the computer place in town has everything in stock, I'll have us set up and running in a day or two. Then I'll start putting all our records on disk. Don't worry, Mom. You'll pick it up in no time."

Carlinda appeared doubtful, but Marcie also saw a spark of interest. She was looking forward to teaching her mother, imparting new technology and sharing a sense of achievement with her.

"And what, pray tell, is my assignment, oh, great leader?" Dustin inquired.

"I'll get to your job in a minute," she replied, unfazed by his sarcasm. She turned to Tucker. Unlike her brother, he was sitting up, his broad shoulders straight and imposing. The sleeves of his shirt were rolled up, exposing strong wrists and curly black hair. He had large hands, but as he rotated the half-empty mug between his palms, she noticed the nails of his long, blunt-tipped fingers were neatly trimmed, and she didn't see the hard, rough calluses she normally associated with men who made their living working outside in all kinds of weather.

"I realize you've been here only a short time," she told him. "But I imagine it's been long enough for you to have reached some conclusions about the state of this ranch. What do you see as our biggest concerns?"

"You have several miles of fencing that need to be replaced and some windmills that could do with major repair. There's a serious fire-ant infestation up on the north range, too, and you're definitely behind in your mesquite control along Cedar Wash."

How strange that the jade of his eyes was more pronounced here in the artificial light of the kitchen than in the bright sunshine at the bowl. It made her wonder how they would look when he laughed. She shook off her silly musings and took a quick sip of coffee.

"What about the cattle? How are—" she began, but he broke in.

"I was getting to that. Up until now your losses have been relatively small, but if the rustling isn't stopped, it's going to get worse. You're branding all your stock and using ear tags on prime heifers and bulls. That's fine for counting noses and tracking your breeding. Unfortunately, it doesn't do you any good when someone steals them. The other thing you might consider is chipping."

Chipping, the newest technological innovation, was to inject a computer microchip into an animal's neck muscle. The chip could then be scanned the way merchandise is at a supermarket. This was by far the most effective method of control and inventory because it allowed individual animals to be traced. It was also the most costly.

"Chipping's too expensive," Carlinda objected.

"I agree. I'd recommend it only for prize bulls or particularly valuable breeding heifers."

"Can you do it?" Marcie asked, "and how long will it take?"

Tucker shook his head. "I've seen it done, but I've

never done it myself, and I don't know if any of our hands have had any experience with it, either.''

Marcie gave him her executive ''that's not good enough'' look.

''Let me check with your vet,'' he added, shifting slightly in his chair. ''I'll get back to you in a few days.''

Careful not to smile, she nodded her agreement. ''If it's a matter of training, we'll get it. Okay. Here's what else I want from you.''

''Should I be taking notes?''

She eyed him over the rim of the mug she'd lifted to her mouth. He sucked in his cheeks, and she realized he was mocking her. After taking a long sip of cooling coffee, she slowly lowered the mug to the table, and stared straight at him. ''Depends on how good your memory is.''

He smiled, and for an instant, there was just the two of them.

Suddenly, she had to clear her throat before going on. ''I want you to make a complete list of all the fencing, gates, wells, windmills, outbuildings and other structures on the ranch and report back on their condition. Identify repairs you're comfortable having your men handle, and let me know which projects you would prefer to have outsourced.''

''Outsourced?'' her brother huffed. ''You make it sound like we're some multimillion-dollar corporation.'' He threw up his hands and let them drop to the table with a thump. ''Outsourced!''

''Wake up and smell the coffee, Dusty,'' Marcie replied. ''The Lazy B is twenty-five sections of land. That's twenty-five square miles. Sixteen thousand acres. Enough to be a very profitable multimillion-dollar corporation, if we'd stop running it like it was forty acres and a mule.''

Carlinda reached a hand across the table toward her son. ''She's right, you know. We've got plenty of good pasture land for cattle, but we ought to be diversifying—sheep and goats, for example. Your father wanted to keep pumping oil so he could have a steady income, but we ought to be conserving what's left until prices go up.''

Dustin's mouth fell open, and this time when he straightened, it was to listen.

''There are a couple of places where I advise drilling new water wells,'' Tucker went on. ''Several of your existing wells are close enough to power lines where I think you can put in electric pumps that will furnish you a more reliable water supply than you get now with the windmills.''

''Good.'' Marcie smiled approvingly. ''That's exactly what I'm after. Anything that will improve our efficiency. How soon do you think you can turn in your report?''

''It'll take a little time. There's a lot to check out on a spread this size. Too much for six men to handle. How soon do you want it?''

''Can you get it done in two weeks?''

He cocked a brow. ''If that's what you want, that's what you'll get. I may have to delay some other work—''

''I'll leave that up to you, Mr. McGee. All I'm interested in is the information.''

He raised his cup in salute. ''Yes, ma'am.''

Dustin smirked. ''Multimillion-dollar corporation with six people on the payroll. Yeah, right.''

She turned to him. ''Nine when you count Mr.

McGee, you and me, and in time, there'll be more. Now, here's what I'd like you to do, Dusty. When Mr. McGee gives us his report, I'd like you to consolidate and prioritize the requirements. Develop a plan to get the work done, then solicit estimates from the various contractors in town. After you've done that, we can get together again, discuss what you've come up with, and compare it with the budget Mom works out. Does that sound reasonable?"

"Yes, Your Highness. Anything you say, Your Highness. Will that be all, Your Highness?"

She tossed him a vicious smile. "It might just be the beginning, little brother. Do you think you could act as our general contractor? It'll mean coordinating schedules, supervising the work, performing quality control to make sure it gets done right—"

Dusty made a dismissive gesture with his hand. "I know what it means."

She hunkered down, stretched her arm across the table and pointed her finger at him. "Don't underestimate the amount of work you'll have to do," she warned, locking eyes with him. "If you take this on, you're going to earn every penny you make."

He bristled. "I'll take care of it, all right?"

Marcie studied him for a moment, then looked at her mother and finally Tucker. "Good. Now let's get to work."

THURSDAY MORNING, MARCIE saddled Sparkle, mounted her, then nudged the horse into a light, rhythmic jog. The sun was already high in the cloudless sky. The warm, gentle breeze still harbored a hint of winter's chill and brought with it the spicy sweetness of wildflowers and trees in bloom. Spring.

Sparkle shied when a jackrabbit popped up from the undergrowth and skittered across the open field of dry, gray broomweed and silvery green horehound until it found its haven hole.

Flight or fight, those were the choices, Marcie thought as they trotted on. The jack fled. Marcie wouldn't. Not this time. She'd fled Kevin. Fled her father before that. It was reasonable, even sensible, to flee such men, but not their ghosts. The sheriff might find the killer, yet a gnawing knot inside her said there was more she was seeking, more she had to discover—answers to riddles about herself as well as her father. It frightened her, but she wouldn't retreat. She couldn't. If her daddy had taught her anything, it was to never back off.

She spurred Sparkle into a gallop, as if together they could leave behind the undefined fears that haunted her. The momentary exhilaration didn't last, however, and she slowed the mare to a more conservative gait.

Following the route she and Tucker had used the evening before last, but at a more relaxed pace, she reached the bowl in under an hour.

What did she hope to find there? No answer came to mind. She reviewed the scene of two days before. The fleeting glimpse of someone or something before she'd crossed through the broken fence line, the scent of fresh cattle manure, the sight of Tucker McGee by the dune buggy.

She thought about the tall, strapping cowboy, the grace of his movements, the set of his square jaw as she'd approached him. But mostly she remembered his eyes. Even under the dim curl of his cowboy hat, they were transfixing.

She'd gone deep-sea fishing a few times and been fascinated when she peered into the water. The point of her vision was always a light, translucent green encircled in olive drab. When she tried to focus on another spot, it became the new center. Tucker's eyes were like that: a fathomless ocean of glowing jade, framed in sadness—and inescapable.

She retraced her steps to the barbed-wire fence. The same wind ruffled her hair, the same scent, milder now, of cattle, mixed with the slight minty fragrance of newly emerging mesquite. But there was no darting shadow this time. No creepy sensation of being watched.

What caused her father to come up here? Something to do with the rustling? Had he found out this was where the stolen cattle were being kept? How? And who was doing it?

She rode into the bowl. It was empty now. The sheriff had already removed the dune buggy. The ground where it had stood was a little drier than it had been. But she could still see the distinctive marks of horseshoes, cattle hoofs and balloon tires etched in the soft, fertile soil.

The sun was warm on her shoulders as she stared at the spot where her father had lain. Yet a chill settled in her stomach.

"Why were you so unhappy all these years, Dad?" she asked out loud. "I wish I understood. The ranch could have been so beautiful and productive if you'd been willing to give it some attention, instead of always taking from it."

Bitterness began to well up within her. She wanted to resist it, but there were too many unanswered questions.

"We could have been a happy family, Dad, if only you'd let us."

Throwing her head back, she gazed into the velvety depths of the azure sky and pressed her eyes shut. When she opened them, her vision was blurred, her nose clogged. "Why did you hate me, Daddy? Why couldn't you love me?"

She tried to wipe the tears that began rolling like raindrops down her cheeks, but it did no good. More came.

"Why wouldn't you ever tell me what I'd done wrong? I would have done better. I tried so hard to make you proud of me."

A single crow cawed overhead, a lonely cry in the stillness around her.

"Did you know you were dying, Daddy? Were you in pain? Is that why you hit Mom? Why you lashed out at me?"

Her throat burned. Her lips formed words, but no sound came out. "Maybe if you had lived...maybe if there had been more time...you would have explained. I would have made it up to you...and you could have loved me again."

Marcie took a thick shuddering breath through her mouth and let it out raggedly. "But somebody killed you," she muttered despondently, "and now I'll never know." Suddenly, her voice hardened. "I'll find him, Daddy. Whoever did this to you...to us...whoever took away our time together, I'll find him, Dad. I'll make him pay."

She stiffened her back and looked around, not sure what she was searching for. The trail of animal prints brought her to a rift in the rim on the other side of the bowl. The breach formed a hidden chute between craggy rocks and boulders.

Cautiously, she followed the churned floor of the narrow passage, not sure where it would lead her, or what she would find at the other end. The path opened into a kind of natural semicircular corral. Directly ahead was a broad, round-topped hill, at the base of which she glimpsed a roughly paved road. She settled back in the saddle, letting herself relax a little, and patted her face dry. This had to be the marshaling area where someone trucked rustled cattle to sales and auctions. She urged the bay mare forward to get a better view of the place.

Her heart nearly stopped. Just beyond a small out-cropping she saw a man on a horse, smiling at her. Tucker McGee.

She rode directly to him, unable to determine if the anticipation she felt was from suspicion or fascination. She knew only that the sight of him caused jitters inside her, a kind of tingling that thrilled and tormented at the same time.

"What are you doing here?" she called out, even before she had brought Sparkle to a complete halt.

He slipped the hat off the back of his head and repositioned it. "Good morning to you, too, Ms. Browder."

Her pulse was racing. "I asked you a question."

He could have been offended by her tone. Instead, he found her all the more intriguing. Maybe it was because underneath the brash facade he sensed a woman who was wounded, even frightened, but one who was also strong enough to fight her fears.

"The same thing you're doing here, I imagine. Checking to see where all the cattle are disappearing to. Would you agree this is where they're trucked out?''

Her red-rimmed eyes flickered a split second, as if she were trying to decide if he was serious or just playing with her. He could have told her it was a little of both.

"Obviously." She rested her right hand on her thigh, the long reins draped on the outside of her knees. "I expected you to be over on Hawk Ridge tracking down the cattle that were stolen yesterday.''

"I told you—'' he began.

"I know what you said to my brother.'' She smiled, giving him pause.

He placed one hand over the other atop the horn of the saddle. "Go on.''

"You're a liar, McGee,'' she said quietly, as though the words contained no challenge.

Involuntarily, he drew up his chest. He wouldn't tolerate a taunt like that from a man. But Marcie Browder wasn't a man. She was very much a woman. Besides, she was right. He forced a lazy grin. "Why do you say that?''

"Because there were no cattle on Hawk Ridge yesterday or the day before or the day before that.''

Damn, he told himself, and almost laughed. *I thought I was bluffing Dustin and he was bluffing me—except he didn't know it.*

"For someone who's been back for such a short time, you seem to know a lot about what's going on,'' he replied, neither confirming nor denying her facts.

"I also know how to read the logs my mother keeps in the office. It didn't take more than a minute to check your story.''

She wasn't the shaken rancher's daughter of two

days before, he realized, but a confident woman, self-possessed and feisty. It made him smile with admiration. He was glad her brother wasn't nearly as thorough. Had she talked to her mother about what she'd found? "I didn't know you—"

"There's a lot about me you don't know," she informed him. "Why did you lie?"

She wasn't one to mince words. He liked that, though at the moment it was putting him on the spot.

"I need the work." He hated having to make excuses. "Your brother caught me off guard. I had to say something to justify your defense of me." He cracked a smile, but she wasn't moved. "Look," he added contritely. "No harm was done, and as you pointed out last evening, you still need a foreman."

Her cool, calculating stare was piercing enough to make him squirm.

"You ride a horse well enough," she acknowledged, "and you obviously know something about cattle and ranching, but you're not a cowboy, McGee. Now, who the hell are you, and what are you doing here?"

CHAPTER FOUR

HE SHOULD HAVE REALIZED he couldn't fool her for long. No use making up another story. She wouldn't buy it. Besides, for all he knew, she already had the answer.

He breathed in deeply through his nose and let the breath out. "I'm a professional security investigator from San Angelo." He watched carefully for a reaction, but she only stared back, forcing him to continue. "Your mother and Vince Prudhomme hired me to look into the rustling that's been going on."

She sat motionless and said nothing. He couldn't tell if she believed him or was about to laugh in his face. He realized then he didn't ever want to play poker with Marcie Browder.

"Your mother and Vince thought that by working on your ranch I might have a better chance of figuring out who's been rustling your cattle."

"Have you?"

He held her gaze. "So far, no."

"Well, you've been here only a couple weeks," she excused him, while making it sound like an indictment. "My mother told me Dad hired you."

"In the formal sense, he did, I suppose." He lifted one shoulder and let it drop. "But only because your mother manipulated him into it."

He watched Marcie's brow furrow slightly, perhaps

in confusion, perhaps in dismay. Her mother had obviously not confided in her.

"Are you telling me my father wasn't aware of who you are?"

"Only your mother, Vince Prudhomme and his foreman know."

She flicked at an insect buzzing around her, but it was a mechanical response. He could see her mind was busy processing the information he'd given her.

"How about the sheriff?" she asked.

"No."

"Why not?"

Fair enough question, and he had an answer. "Kraus has been in a position to deal with these rustlers all along, but he doesn't seem to have accomplished much—"

"Surely you don't think he's in on it."

"He has a clean record and a good reputation for keeping an orderly town. But in this case he's either in over his head or he's got a leak in his office—or both. In any case, sharing information with him at this point doesn't seem like a prudent thing to do, not until I have a clear picture of the situation."

"So Dustin doesn't know, either?"

"I don't think his knowing would be a good idea."

The hint of a curl tugged at the corners of her mouth. She compressed her lips, trying to look cross, but he was convinced it was as much an attempt to suppress any show of amusement. One up on little brother.

"You may be right," she conceded. "But let me give you fair warning, McGee. Don't hold out on me. If I ever catch you lying to me again, I'll see to it that you're sent packing, and there won't be any generous extra week's pay. Is that understood?''

''Yes, ma'am.'' He touched his fingers to his hat in salute. ''But can I ask a favor from you?''

She cocked her head to one side. ''What is it?''

''Call me 'Tucker' or 'Tux'? 'McGee' makes me sound like I should be wearing a kilt.''

There was a moment's pause before she grinned. ''You'd rather be referred to as a penguin suit?'' She broke into a chuckle, the first genuine amusement he'd heard from her. It was a warm sound. Too warm. Its heat rippled through his body, settled and made him shift in the saddle.

''Okay, *Tux,*'' she emphasized. ''I guess you might as well call me 'Marcie.' 'Ms. Browder' is my mother.''

He had already noted that she'd reverted to her maiden name. Apparently, her experience with marriage had been so onerous she wanted to wipe out every vestige of it.

She nudged Sparkle into a walk toward the private road. It clearly hadn't been maintained in years. But it had been used. Tucker turned his pinto and rode up beside her.

''You said you're from San Angelo,'' she remarked, her mind toying with the image of him in kilts. ''Is that your hometown?''

''More or less. My father was an assistant foreman on the Leaning Cross ranch. My mother worked as a combination cook and housekeeper.''

So that was where he learned to ride. ''Do they still live there?''

''Dad died when I was ten, and we moved into town.''

"I'm sorry. Got any brothers or sisters?"

"An older brother and a younger sister."

"Do they live in San Angelo?" She glanced over at him, at his erect carriage and dark, chiseled features. His private life was none of her business, but she liked the sound of his voice. It was mellow and confident. There was a edge in it, too. Maybe it was the mysterious undertone, the subtle intimation of something hidden, the vulnerability, that prompted her to pry.

"Julia's a schoolteacher. Second grade."

"Married?"

"Not yet."

They reached the end of the dirt road where it intersected with the paved farm-to-market road, which in turn connected three miles farther on with the highway to San Angelo.

He waved an arm, taking in the whole scene. "An occasional cattle truck here, or even a small convoy of them, wouldn't draw attention."

"If it was even seen," she added. There wasn't a house or vehicle in sight. Only short telephone poles carrying a few skimpy power lines.

"What about your brother?" she prompted, as they turned back the way they'd come. "Is he married?"

"Very. He and Carmen have seven kids."

"Seven!" She'd always wanted children. Maybe not that many. But seven was better than none. Impulsively, she said, "They've found out what causes that, you know."

She watched a grin twitch the corners of his mouth. Just as quickly he erased it. The thought of sex seemed to bring joy and sorrow. She knew why it did for her, but why did it for him?

"So I've heard," he said blandly.

Mentally, she kicked herself. Whatever the reason, she wasn't about to discuss sex with him, though the thought of that kilt and the memory of his muscular arm under her fingertips were having a disturbing effect. "What does your brother do for a living?"

"Sean worked in law enforcement for a number of years, until he got shot by a crazy in a drug bust. Ended up taking an early medical retirement and starting a security investigative service." Tucker shifted in his saddle. "He's my boss."

She detected discomfort in his response. Was there some rivalry between them, resentment that he had to work for his older brother. He said he'd lied to keep the foreman's job because he needed the money. Could his brother be so disabled that Tucker was doing all the work, supporting his brother's family?

"What did you do before that?"

He paused this time before answering. "I was in the Marine Corps."

She could see him in uniform very clearly. Tall, straight, proud. "Why did you leave?"

He tugged at his ear, as if considering his reply. "It was time to move on."

She wanted to ask him where he had been, what he had done, but she sensed reticence. His military experience had apparently left a scar. It would be better to go on to a safer subject.

"Are you married? Got any kids?"

He didn't answer immediately. She looked over at him.

"No," he said simply but with finality.

They started back to the ranch house, this time skirting the bowl rather than going through it. She should be grateful he didn't want to discuss love and marriage. She certainly hadn't been successful at either.

After they'd ridden a short distance, she changed the subject. "When I got here yesterday, you were searching the dune buggy. You stuffed something in your pocket. What was it?"

So she had seen him. She'd already warned him about lying, and he had no doubt she meant it.

"What I told the sheriff was on the level. The possibility that your father had committed suicide seemed remote, but I had to consider it. I also wanted to see if there was anything that might give me a hint about the murderer."

"So what did you find?"

They stopped at a dingy gray knuckle of rock. He swiveled, one-handedly opened his leather saddlebag and extracted a transparent document protector containing a single piece of paper.

"Does this mean anything to you?" He leaned toward her and handed it over. She grasped the small plastic container. It contained an ordinary piece of white five-by-eight tablet paper with the Lazy B logo imprinted in the upper left-hand corner.

She recognized her father's sloppy scrawl. "Can you not read it, or do you just not understand it?"

"Your mother confirmed that it's your dad's writing, but she has no idea what it means."

Marcie looked at the paper again. There were four columns of numbers. She read them off horizontally:

8	10	2	10
9	14	5	15
10	28	6	18

11	17	3	26
12	4	8	22
1	6	10	30
2	15	7	36
3	27	5	18
4	14	6	49
5	3	4	27
6	17	9	34
7	23	12	43

The first column was in numerical sequence. Time? Was 8 a.m. or p.m.? What about the other numbers? They didn't seem to show any pattern at all. Adding, subtracting, multiplying or dividing one column by another didn't seem to relate to the remaining sets of digits.

"Does it mean anything to you?"

"I don't know." She read the numbers again, this time vertically, but they still didn't make any sense. Backward and sideways brought no enlightenment, either. They didn't even work as lottery selections, since they weren't in groupings of six.

"Let's forget about it for now," he said a few minutes later. "Maybe if we leave them alone, they'll come home."

He extended his hand, and she passed back the plastic-protected paper. He returned it to his saddle-bag.

"On Tuesday, just before I rode into the bowl, I thought I saw a fleeing shape among the rocks," Marcie commented, as they urged their horses forward. "Was it you?"

He looked at her warily and slowly shook his head. "I didn't dismount until I got to the buggy, and that probably wasn't more than five minutes before you arrived.''

''Hmm.''

''Can you describe whoever you saw?''

''I can't even be sure I saw anyone,'' she admitted. ''It was more like a shadow, a feeling.''

''Probably just a varmint,'' he offered.

They rode through a narrow ravine, the floor of which was loose and sandy, its borders scraggy with boulders, dark-green salt cedar and gnarled mesquite. The clear blue sky overhead was as smooth and depthless as brushed velvet.

''Pretty country,'' Tucker remarked.

''Picturesque enough,'' Marcie agreed, ''when it isn't flooded or ablaze from a range fire. But it's of only marginal use. It's too rocky and broken up by shallow ravines and dry creek beds to be useful for large-scale cattle ranching. Lennie Gruen raised hair goats on it for several years when all else failed, but ranching in any form doesn't seem to be in his blood.''

Lennie's place—that was what Dustin had called it.

''Lennie Gruen? Your father's friend? I've heard of him, but I haven't met him. Was he leasing the place?''

Marcie shook her head. ''This whole section used to be the Green Valley ranch—''

''Green?'' Tucker raised an eyebrow and looked around at the inhospitable terrain. ''A play on words, I presume.''

She nodded. ''Lennie pronounces his name Green but has never gotten around to changing the German spelling. Anyway, Dad bought it from him about two years ago.''

''Why,'' Tucker asked, ''if it's so worthless?''

She brooded. ''Let's see. From Mom's point of view I guess you'd call it blackmail. From Dad's, it was more like bribery. Everyone else called it charity.'' The note of irritation was only thinly veiled in her words. ''My father insisted it was simply repayment for Lennie's loyalty and past services.''

''Past services? What kind of services?''

The soft breeze brought with it the grape-soda scent of mountain laurel in bloom.

''Dad and Lennie had been friends since high school, played football in college together, drank together. Some years back, when Dad decided to try for the state senate, he hired Lennie as his campaign manager. To be fair, Lennie did a pretty good job. He ran a well-organized, if less than completely clean, campaign.''

She raised a hand to steady her hat against a sudden gust of wind. ''When Dad got elected, Lennie stayed on as chief of staff. I guess he did all right at that job, too, because when it came time for reelection, Dad was a shoo-in.''

Marcie unhooked the canteen from her saddle pack. Tucker gazed at her lips puckered against the plastic mouthpiece. She squinted out the bright sun as she tilted her head back and drank. The action wasn't intended to be erotic, but it was. The sudden impulse to press his lips to hers, the ache to hold her in his arms, was like a deep, searing pain. A pain whose intensity frightened him. He clenched his jaw and looked away.

She recapped the canvas-covered container and

hung it from her saddle horn, as Sparkle continued on at a comfortable walk. "About halfway through his second term," she continued, "one of the U.S. Senate seats came open, and Dad decided to take a shot at it. Mom was less than enthusiastic. She had no personal interest in politics, didn't care for all the protocol and socializing, and she positively hated campaigning. But she did what she had to do—be a faithful wife supporting her ambitious husband."

Marcie neck-reined her mare around a giant boulder that bisected the natural trail. Tucker followed her into a narrow gorge. Chalky white marks were visible on the stone above her head, where floodwaters had repeatedly coursed through.

"Dad's being away all the time had its advantages, though," she said when Tucker caught up and resumed his place beside her. "His love for the ranch was real enough, but it was the kind of devotion a book collector has for books he'll never read."

She looked to her right and left, alert for danger in the form of rattlesnakes or bobcats. "Mom got to run the ranch the way she wanted. The biggest problem was that all the money she earned he spent on his campaign."

Marcie was quiet for a minute, as if fortifying herself to go on.

"Then Mom caught him with a woman. Not even a woman, a girl really, a 'volunteer' who was barely past the age of consent, a kid younger than I was. Mom was furious. She demanded a divorce. Said she wouldn't stand by and let him humiliate her in public. Dad begged her to forgive him, swore he would never do it again, pleaded with her not to throw him out.

The upshot was that Mom gave him an ultimatum—give up politics or it was over.''

"Why didn't he divorce her?'' Tucker asked. "From everything you've told me and from what I've seen, they didn't exactly have a happily-ever-after marriage.''

"I wish he had,'' Marcie exclaimed. "But there was one little sticking point. The Lazy B came to Mom in a family trust. He had no legal claim to the place.''

With a flutter of wings, a covey of quail popped up from the ocotillo brush on their left. The horses skittered for a moment, then continued placidly forward.

"Even if Dad had managed somehow to break the trust and get a share of the ranch, it wouldn't have been enough to support him in the fashion to which he'd become accustomed. Like a lot of ranchers and farmers, we're land-poor. We own property with a big cash value, but it's all on paper. You can't spend it unless you sell it.''

"And if you sell it,'' Tucker added, "you don't have it.''

Marcie shrugged in frustration. "Anyway, there was no way Mom was ever going to let the place get away from her.''

"So how does the Green Valley place come into this?''

"A couple of years ago, Gruen was at the point of bankruptcy. His ranching attempts probably would have been marginal under any circumstances, but he wasn't exactly working himself to the bone trying to succeed, either. So he used the time he'd spent helping Dad as a lever to persuade him to buy the place from him.''

"How'd your mother feel about that?''

"She wasn't happy. Buying worthless land from a worthless crony, she called it, and added that between the two of them, the money would be wasted on booze in no time.''

They'd reached a narrow stream. Marcie went first across a sandy bar to the other side, her horse's hooves plopping in the shallow water. Tucker followed.

"I was visiting here for a few days when they were finalizing the deal.'' During one of her cooling-off periods from Kevin, but she didn't mention that. "I must say Dad was remarkably calm in the face of her rage. All he said when she finished was that Lennie liked to share with his friends. Surely she could understand sharing with friends. I don't think I've ever seem Mom so miserable.''

"But she gave in to him?''

Marcie shook her head, as if she still couldn't believe it herself. "Yeah, she gave in. They had to take out a loan to pay Gruen in cash for his thousand acres. Even at depressed market prices, the land didn't come cheap. She signed the papers without another word of protest. Maybe they could quarry some of the stone was all she said.''

They arrived at a gate. Tucker dismounted and opened it, let Marcie pass through, then secured it behind them.

They rode through a pasture blanketed in flowers of vibrant spring colors: electric-blue bluebonnets, radiant amber-and-maroon Indian blankets and delicate pink wild primroses.

"Has your mother filled you in on what's been happening around here lately?"

"About the rustling? Only in general terms. I know it started less than a year ago and that every month we lose a few more head."

"Is it having a big financial impact?"

To her left, she heard a red-tailed hawk squeal and automatically tracked the sound, catching Tucker's strong profile against the background of cloudless sky. The brown-and-white bodied bird climbed and circled gracefully overhead, eyes alert, no doubt, for prey.

"It's a concern, of course, but cattle aren't our sole source of income," she said. "Even with oil prices depressed, we're still pumping."

"Vince Prudhomme's lost nearly two hundred head," Tucker noted. "It's more than a concern to him. Cattle are all he has."

"We're down maybe a quarter of that number," she commented, then speculated, "perhaps it's a matter of access. It's less than a mile to the bowl from Prudhomme's prime grazing pastures, but closer to three miles from ours."

Their horses' feet made sucking noises as they crossed another muddy rivulet. It would soon be dry—until the next rain.

Tucker glanced over at the woman riding beside him. She intrigued him. Word among the ranch hands was that she'd been through a messy divorce. He knew for some people divorce was an acceptable way to end a relationship that hadn't worked out. For others it was a defeat, a mark of failure. Catching the slight upturn of her chin, her concentration on the path ahead, the moments of almost wistful loneliness

in her blue eyes, he suspected that Marcie Browder
was one of the latter.

"I understand you lived in Houston. Are you home
to stay now?" he asked, hoping to draw her out as
she had him. But Houston and coming home proved
to be the wrong approach.

"My only plans right now are to bury my father,
find his killer, then run this ranch better than it's ever
been run before."

She kicked her horse into a gallop, bounding ahead
of him.

She didn't like being reminded of the nightmare
she'd left behind. She'd dreamed of having her own
home and family when she'd wedded Kevin Hayes.
Dreamed of warm smiles and cuddly children. But the
smiles had turned to tears, and the children had never
come.

Now she was alone. Alone and lonely. But she
wasn't interested in getting involved with a man
again, certainly not with one who was a walking, talking advertisement for the male mystique. Her father
had been a handsome man, and look how insensitive
he'd been. Her ex-husband had been exactly the same.
Physically impressive. Shallow and vain underneath.
Good looks and character shouldn't be mutually exclusive, but in her experience they seemed to be. She
still wanted a family and children. But first she
wanted someone who would touch her in a way that
made her feel desired, not used. If she ever found
such a man, he'd probably be short, fat and bald—
not tall and bronze, with a head of thick black hair
that seemed to beg for her fingers to dance their way
through it. Certainly, not Tucker McGee.

Tucker watched her race ahead of him, annoyed

with himself for being such a jerk. For a few minutes he'd felt a bond forming between them, a bond he may not have a right to but one he couldn't help wanting.

He'd been thinking a lot about Marcie and the notion that she might be involved in her father's death. The sheriff's technique was tried-and-true: plant a seed of suspicion, foster a sense of paranoia and see what develops. It seemed grotesque to suspect Marcie of murdering her father, but the lawman was right to explore every possibility, every threat, every means, motive and opportunity. Given the incident with her father, Kraus had to consider both Marcie and her mother as suspects. What the sheriff couldn't know because he hadn't been there was that the anguish in Marcie's eyes completely belied the anger in her words.

She slowed her pace so he could catch up with her. They rode on, side by side, in silence.

This time when they got to the hill overlooking the ranch house it was still daylight. There was a single car in the gravel parking area near the kitchen door. She recognized the big, ten-year-old black Mercedes.

"Damn," she groaned.

After riding briskly down to the barnyard and dismounting, they put the horses in their stalls, removed bridles and saddles and hung them in their appointed places to be cleaned later.

She should have objected when McGee trailed along behind her to the house. He was here to catch rustlers. Family affairs were none of his business, but for some reason, which she didn't have time to analyze, she felt reassured by his company.

Lennie Gruen sat at the kitchen table, his beefy

right hand wrapped around a sweaty glass of iced tea. Even from half a room away she could smell the liquor on his breath. He rose heavily when Marcie entered, a crocodile smile creasing his pasty face. He'd been a linebacker when he and Mason were in college together. That had been thirty years ago. Since then the muscle beneath the mass had melted, leaving only blubber. He moved toward her in an attitude that suggested he wanted to give her a hug.

"Hello, Mr. Gruen," she said, gliding around the other side of the table.

He let his arms dangle apelike at his sides. "I'm real sorry about your daddy."

"Thank you." She glanced at her mother, who looked anything but pleased. "Any more tea?"

"He was a real fine man, Mason was," Lennie ruminated, still standing at the table. "My best friend. I wish I had known he was feeling poorly."

Marcie appraised Tucker's expression as she handed him a glass. He seemed as repelled by their visitor as she felt.

"This is Tucker McGee, our new foreman," Carlinda said.

"Yeah, Mason told me he hired someone new to take care of things." Marcie saw Lennie grimace as he shook Tucker's outstretched hand. Apparently, Tucker used a little more pressure than was customary.

"Why do you say Dad was feeling poorly, Mr. Gruen?"

"Your ma just told me he had cancer." He settled heavily onto the narrow cane-bottom chair. "I had no idea."

"He didn't mention anything about not feeling

well?'' Marcie persisted. If he'd told anyone, it would have been his old drinking buddy.

Gruen paused nervously, his attention darting uncomfortably to McGee before he answered. "Can't remember him telling me he was hurting. But he must have been in some sort of pain."

"How's that?" Carlinda asked.

Gruen took a big mouthful of the iced tea and clucked distastefully as he placed the glass gingerly back on the table. He avoided Carlinda's scrutiny, looking instead at Marcie.

"Your daddy must have been in terrible pain to hit your ma and then take a swing at you! No, he would never've done that unless he was really hurting. I'm sure if you had known, you wouldn't've threatened him the way you did."

Involuntarily, Marcie's mouth fell open. She felt as if she'd just been kidney-punched.

"You miserable bastard," Carlinda growled. "I've put up with your bad manners and boozing for damn near thirty years. But I'm not putting up with it anymore." She turned to Tucker. "Mr. McGee, please escort Mr. Gruen off this ranch. And if he ever returns, I want you to shoot him for trespassing. Lennie—" her seething scowl shot daggers at him "—I suggest you get out of here before I get a shotgun and pepper your fat ass."

"Carli—"

"Thank you for coming," Tucker said coldly.

"Yeah, sure," Gruen replied. He pushed himself up from the seat and lumbered to the door. He seemed completely baffled by the depth of Carlinda's rage. "If you need anything, you let me know. Anything at all. Mason would want it that way."

A minute later they heard Gruen's battered Mercedes rumble down the driveway.

Marcie went to her mother, who wrapped her arms around her daughter in a desperate hug.

Carlinda snuffled, the first real sign of emotional stress Marcie had seen since her return home. Ironic, Marcie thought, that it would take the insensitivity of an old lush to finally break through the steel armor her mother had shielded herself with for so long.

Marcie glanced over her mother's shoulder to where Tucker, looking none too comfortable, was standing against the wall. She shifted her eyes from him to the door, a signal for him to leave, which he picked up with apparent gratitude.

"If y'all will excuse me, I have some chores to attend to," he mumbled, turned quickly and left the house.

"Let's sit down, Mom." Marcie led her over to the table and sat her in a chair. Taking the one beside her, Marcie held her mother's hands. The bony fingers felt cold against her palms. "Are you all right? Would you like a cup of tea?"

Carlinda gave a wan smile and shook her head. "I don't know why I let that drunken old sot get to me."

Marcie's thumbs outlined small circles atop her mother's veined hands. "You're entitled."

Another smile, stronger this time, and Marcie saw her mother's brittle strength and determination returning. Maybe with time, widowhood would bring peace.

Carlinda brushed back a straggling wisp of hair from her forehead, a futile gesture filled with exhaustion.

"A little while longer, Mom, and things will settle down."

Carlinda jumped up and started removing the dirty tea glasses to the sink.

"Mom, why didn't you tell me you'd hired McGee to investigate the rustling that's been going on?"

Marcie hoped the distraction of another subject would help calm her mother. It seemed to have just the opposite effect. Carlinda spun around, her eyes glittering.

"When?" She returned to the table with a dishcloth and started wiping away the wet rings left by the sweaty glasses. "When have we had any time alone together? I wasn't about to discuss it in front of your father or brother, and you haven't exactly hung around the house."

It was true that one of the first things Marcie had done when she came home was to saddle Sparkle and go riding by herself. Sitting astride her old mare, letting the spring breeze ruffle her hair, had seemed the perfect therapy after all the turmoil of the past weeks and months. Taking decisive action to reorganize the Lazy B had been natural for her, too, and something she thought her mother appreciated.

"Mom, I didn't mean..." God, she was tired of being defensive. Kevin had blamed the failure of their marriage on her working full-time, not always being at home whenever he chose to show up. He'd even blamed her for his drinking and infidelity, claiming it was her fault he was lonely and had to find other companionship. "I thought we'd have plenty of time to talk."

Carlinda's features softened. "I know, honey. So did I."

A minute passed. "Are you saying you think Dad or Dusty had anything to do with the rustling?"

"Of course not." The response came too quickly. In a fumbling manner, Carlinda rinsed out the dish-cloth. "I just thought the fewer people who knew about McGee, the better. I certainly couldn't trust your father to keep his mouth shut. For one thing he would have told Lennie. After that, the Lord only knows how long it would have taken for the word to get out."

"And Dusty?"

Mechanically, Carlinda filled the sink with hot wa-ter. "I asked your father to make him foreman when Dixson left. I thought responsibility for running the place would give him a sense of direction. But Mason dismissed the idea, saying Dusty didn't have ranching in his blood."

"Like Dad didn't. He's a chip off the old block, all right, drinking and—"

Carlinda slammed off the water faucet and spun to face her daughter. "Your brother hasn't found him-self yet, that's all. There's a lot of good in him. He just needs some time—"

"He's twenty-three years old, Mom," Marcie in-terrupted, then softened her tone. "How long is he going to take to get over being fourteen?"

Her mother sighed. "With your father gone, he'll be able to settle down now and work this ranch the way he should. You'll see."

Did her mother really believe what she said, or was it wishful thinking? Was her mother setting herself up for more disappointment?

CHAPTER FIVE

BEING AWAKENED AT THE CRACK of dawn by the crowing of a cock instead of the buzz of an alarm brought a contented smile to Marcie's lips. She was tempted to turn over and luxuriate in the seductive warmth of her old bed, but conscience and a naturally restless spirit had her up and dressed in a matter of minutes.

Her goal today was to examine the ranch's books and ledgers, learn in more detail the condition of the family's assets and financial status and rough out a program for computerizing the management process. That was the plan, but she was soon reminded why some people leave farms and ranches to live in towns and cities, never to return. Chores among other things. Even with hired help in the barn to feed the horses, muck out stalls and maintain order, there were enough other routine and unexpected tasks to keep a team of workaholics exhausted. And just when you thought you might be getting close to catching up, a horse colicked or a dog tangled with a porcupine and had to have quills pulled from its muzzle.

Marcie was several hours into her research in the office when she heard Carlinda let out a bloodcurdling shriek. Her heart pounding, Marcie ran to the laundry room. Her mother was backed into a corner, arms raised stiffly against her chest, hands wrapped in a tight ball.

"What is it?"

"A s-snake," Carlinda stuttered. "In the drier."

Marcie looked at the white appliance. The door was closed.

"Are you sure? It's not a piece of clothing that looks—"

"Nobody in this house wears snakeskin, dammit. It's a snake."

"What kind?"

Carlinda shook her head violently. "A big one."

Marcie was tempted to smile, but didn't. Even though her mother had grown up on the ranch and could handle everything from birthing foals to castrating calves, she'd never gotten past her morbid fear of slithering serpents.

"I'll take care of it, Mom—"

"Be careful. It might—"

Marcie ushered her mother out of the room into the yard, then returned to the drier. Very slowly, she cracked the door open enough to look inside. Sure enough, there was a snake. A small harmless bull snake. Springtime temperatures were bringing the creatures out of hibernation and the warm clothes drier had no doubt seemed a great place to camp out. It had happened before. The screen on the hot-air exhaust hose must have come loose again. Another chore to be attended to.

She shut the door, looked around, found an old pair of work gloves, put them on and carefully removed the lethargic creature. It didn't even hiss. Carlinda took a clumsy step backward when she saw her daughter walk calmly by with the two-foot snake at arm's length.

"Where are you going? Kill it!"

"Mom, it's harmless. And it eats mice and rats. Better this than them."

Carlinda kept her distance, yet trailed like a frightened schoolgirl, as Marcie walked to the barn and released the mottled-brown creature along the side of the building.

She threw her arm around her mother's still-arched shoulders and walked her back to the house. "Where's Dusty?"

"I asked him to deliver your father's burial clothes to Smithson's so they'd have them when your father's body is released." She looked up at the copper skillet-shaped clock over the sink. "But that was hours ago. I expected him back by now. He promised he'd rototill the vegetable garden for me."

Marcie doubted her mother was really worried about her garden at the moment, but she understood her concern for her son and the need to have him close.

"Probably got held up talking with people. You know Coyote Springs. You can't go into a place, transact business and walk out. You've got to visit. Have you checked his girlfriend's house? Maybe he went over there."

Carlinda shook her head.

"Got her number? I'll give her a call."

"I...no, I don't have it."

Marcie removed the area telephone book from the drawer under the telephone. "Lula Crosby, right?"

She flipped through the pages. Several Crosbys were listed, but only one Lula. She dialed the number.

"No answer. I bet he got waylaid. Probably stopped to talk to someone and couldn't break loose."

Marcie copied down Lula's address and walked to the door. "Let me see if I can rescue him."

THE WEST SIDE OF THE LAZY B abutted the Prudhomme ranch's eastern boundary for about three miles, at which point the Green Valley place had formed a wedge between them. But Lennie's old place was Browder land now, so the two ranches had a common border all the way to the farm-to-market road that had once been Gruen's sole access to the world. Tucker had called Fletcher Doggitt on his cell phone and arranged to meet him at the point where the old fences originally split the three properties. The spot was several miles from the Browder ranch house, but less than a mile from their neighbor's. Tucker took one of the jeeps to their rendezvous. Doggitt rode there on horseback.

The Prudhomme foreman was wiry and ruddy faced, a man clearly used to spending his life in the elements. He rode a buckskin quarter horse up to the fence line, dismounted, let the reins hang slack and walked over to the wire mesh stretched tight between cedar posts.

Tucker slid out of the open vehicle and leaned against its rusty brown fender, facing the older man.

"Kraus says he's dug up some information on me he wants to talk about," Tucker told him.

Fletcher spit out an expletive. "I was afraid of that. Do you think he suspects you?"

An old familiar sourness formed in Tucker's stomach. "Probably," he said evenly. "Wouldn't you in his place?"

Fletcher paused to consider. "I reckon so." He rubbed his callused hands together. "You need to get out of here."

"Run?" Tucker shook his head. "That would only make matters worse. Besides, I can keep a better handle on things if I hang around as planned."

"I don't like it." Fletcher stared stone faced at a clump of prickly pear cactus. His features hardened as he looked back at Tucker. "You went to prison once. They send you up for murder again—"

"Relax. He hasn't got a thing on me." *Unless my gun turns up as the murder weapon,* Tucker thought. Circumstantial evidence had been enough the first time. He could feel sweat break out on the back of his neck, feel his gut begin to go watery. If they locked him in a cage again, he'd die there.

Fletcher fixed him with a cold stare. "You're underestimating Kraus. He's not some country yokel—"

"Maybe you didn't hear me when I said it the first time. I'm not running." He returned the old man's glare. "I was hired to do a job. I'm not finished yet."

"Okay, okay." Fletcher threw up his hands in disgusted defeat. "Stay longer if you insist. But I'm not letting you take the rap for this one."

"You won't have to. I told you Kraus hasn't got a thing on me, and he's not going to. Trust me."

"Famous last words." The two men measured each other, until Fletcher finally asked, "How's the family handling things?"

Tucker adjusted his hat and thought of Marcie. "His daughter's trying to tough it out, but she's taking it hard. Her last meeting with her father was a shouting match. She never got to say she was sorry." *The way I never got to say goodbye to Beth, never got to tell her how much I loved her. Never got to say I was sorry for failing to protect her and the beautiful daughter we made together.*

"She's wasting regret. Mason never deserved that girl."

"Her mother's another matter. I can't figure out if she's tough or cold. I haven't seen any tears. She must have really hated the son of a bitch."

"Or loved him. She'll do her crying in private." There was unexpected admiration in the statement. "What about the kid?"

"Dustin? No tears there, either. But he's drinking. I get the impression he's scared."

Fletcher's wrinkled face sank into a scowl. "Probably smart of him. He was arrested once, so he knows what it's like. If he's done anything else stupid, he won't have a powerful daddy to take care of things this time."

"Arrested? For what?"

"Robbery. Held up a liquor store."

Tucker blew out a chestful of air. If the young Mr. Browder had been involved in a face-to-face act of violence like robbery, what else was he capable of? Stealing cattle from his father as well as his neighbor? Could the old man have found out and confronted him? "Tell me what happened."

The old-timer rested an elbow on a cedar fence post in a familiar storytelling posture. "The way I heard it, Dustin and a friend of his, Gaverty, got blitzed one Saturday night at the Prairie Dog Saloon and started making a ruckus, so the bartender threw them out. Gaverty suggested they drive over to Tiny's Liquor Emporium in Spring Mesa and get a bottle of tequila.

Dustin drove but waited outside with the motor running while Gaverty went into the store.''

Tucker had a good idea of what was coming. Not a very original plea: *I was just there for the ride, Your Honor.*

"A few hours later," Fletcher continued, "Dustin was arrested at home and charged with armed robbery. He insisted he had no idea what the cops were talking about. At first, he even denied he'd gone to Spring Mesa. Trouble was, the store owner recognized him as the guy driving the getaway car. Apparently young Browder was as well-known there as his old man."

"How come Dustin didn't see the robbery taking place?"

Fletcher smiled. "I guess you've never been to Tiny's. The way the store's designed, the cashier can see out, but nobody can see the person doing the purchasing. Comes from the old days when Texas was dry, I guess, when one's clientele were considered strictly confidential."

Tucker smiled and nodded. "Go on."

"Well, the boy finally admitted they'd gone over to Spring Mesa but said all they did was buy booze."

"Did the cops believe him?"

"Seems like. His daddy got a high-priced lawyer to talk to the district attorney. I heard later Gaverty exonerated him, said Dustin had nothing to do with the robbery. Some people think the old man paid Gaverty off to take the rap alone."

"Did he?"

Fletcher shrugged noncommittally.

"When did this happen?"

"Toward the end of last summer, just before school

started, as I recall. Maybe six months ago. Gaverty pleaded guilty and got three years.''

Long before Marcie came home. Tucker wondered how much she knew about it.

''I did find one thing.'' Tucker pulled the plastic-encased paper with the numbers on it from under the seat. ''This mean anything to you?''

The old man pondered it, squinted his watery eyes as if trying to make sense out of it, then shook his head and handed it back. ''Can't say it does.''

''Probably isn't important,'' Tucker said, as he put it away.

They talked a few more minutes, then Fletcher remounted his horse. ''Keep in touch,'' he called out as he rode toward the Prudhomme ranch house.

MARCIE DROVE HER FOUR-YEAR-OLD Cougar directly to the funeral home. Dustin, she was told, had dropped off the burial clothes nearly two hours ago.

Lula's address turned out to be a small rock house at the end of a cul-de-sac on the edge of a mesquite woods. Dustin said she was a student at the Coyote Springs campus of the University of Texas. If she was serious about her studies, this place was ideal. Quiet, out of the way and probably cheap.

No answer to the bell. Marcie walked around the rear. The straggly back lawn, more weeds than grass, hadn't been cut recently. There was no response to her determined knock on the peeling back door.

She drove to the most likely other place she could think of where her brother might be—the Beer Bucket. She'd been there a few times over the years searching for her father. The saloon fitted its name, or vice versa—a gloomy, smoke-filled den that reeked of stale beer and body odor. There was a U-shaped bar at the far end, a small dance floor in the middle with bare tables and straight-backed chairs along the sides. The outdated posters and photographs pinned haphazardly to the walls were faded and dirty, the flickering neon signs garish. Everything looked tacky. Just being in the place made her feel sticky and sweaty.

It was still noontime, too early for the working crowd, even on a Friday, so the place had only a few customers, older men in shabby clothes with nicotine-stained fingers and rheumy eyes. The bartender, a man of about fifty, was shaped like one of his beer barrels. He was also the only one in the place who appeared completely alert. Marcie knew he never touched the products he sold. He greeted her familiarly.

"Marcie. I'm real sorry to hear about your daddy."

She heard a few other comments down the line: "Damned shame"; "Never would have expected it"; "We'll miss him."

I bet you will, went through her mind. Mason had always been generous with his drinking money. "Have you seen my brother?"

"Not today," the barman replied.

"It's Friday, ain't it?" one of the patrons asked. "He'll be at the orphanage."

"Orphanage?"

"Yep," another man answered. "Goes there every Friday. Seen him over there one time when I was visiting with a friend. Made me swear to secrecy." He chuckled. "Rightly so. Your pa wouldn't've liked it."

"I don't understand," Marcie said. "What's Dusty doing at the orphanage?"

"Out on Ranch Rock Road," the man said mysteriously. "You can't miss it."

Drumming her fingers on the steering wheel, Marcie drove the county road. What was Dustin doing at an orphanage? Or was it obvious? *God, don't tell me…* She wouldn't let herself even think the words.

The building was only a few years old, white brick, star shaped, clean but institutional. Marcie stopped at the information counter in the hub of the star.

"I'm looking for Dustin Browder," she told the silver-haired woman whose dark-rimmed half glasses dangled at the end of a gold chain.

The woman's preoccupied expression brightened. "Dusty? Take corridor C to the double doors about halfway down. You can't miss him."

Marcie walked along the hall. At least the inside of the building wasn't as cold as its exterior. Toys were stored on shelves. Posters and pictures adorned the walls. The rooms she passed might have been typical kids' rooms, bright and colorful, except they were a bit too neat.

She heard the squealing laughter and happy sounds of children even before she reached the double doors. Swinging one open, she entered a common area occupied by a group of young people ranging in age from toddlers to teenagers. They were sitting on couches, in chairs and on the floor, laughing at a figure dressed in black, his face stylized with stark-white face paint and red-dot cheeks. He moved in a stiff, puppetlike manner that nevertheless betrayed a remarkable grace and fluidity.

The mime's comic antics made it impossible not to

smile. It took her a minute to remember why she was there. Marcie glanced around the room for her brother, but he wasn't among the audience. She searched for an attendant to ask for assistance. Two were standing by a far doorway, talking to another actor. With a jolt, she recognized Dustin's girlfriend, Lula. She was wearing an old-fashioned pink-and-white hoop skirt and a coarse pigtailed wig of bright orange. Her face, all peaches and cream, was made up to resemble a young milk maiden's.

Marcie edged over to her. "Hi, Lula. I'm looking for Dusty."

"You found him." She nodded proudly toward the figure in the middle of the room.

Marcie stared blankly at the young woman for a moment before refocusing her attention on the mime. "That's Dusty?"

"Yep. Isn't he wonderful? The kids can't get enough of him. He's really good."

Marcie watched the man in black, whom she only vaguely recognized as her brother, then surveyed the expressions on the faces of the youngsters surrounding him. Lula was right. He was good, and the children did love him.

"How long has he been doing this?" Marcie whispered.

"A couple of months. He says he wants to be an actor. Did you see him when he starred in *Citizen Kane* on campus last year?"

"No." Marcie vaguely remembered her mother saying he was in a play. The foggy recollection reinforced a feeling of isolation, of no longer being a part of the family. She obviously didn't know her brother. "Is that where he learned to mime—in college?"

"No, I've been teaching him in exchange for him giving me horseback-riding lessons." Lula laughed. In the caricature of sweet innocence, it came across as a childish giggle. "I must admit, he's learned miming a lot faster than I have riding."

Marcie watched, entranced by her brother's unexpected skill. Using only two or three simple props, he managed to convey a remarkably convincing picture of a naive young man strolling through the countryside, awestruck by its natural wonders. The character—Sam, according to a name tag pinned to his baggy blazer—stopped to gape at a "wildflower," one of those black-eyed Susan pinwheels that were supposed to discourage gophers from taking up residence in the front lawn. He was enraptured by its imaginary scent, when Lula struck a gong in the back of the room.

Sam poked his long fingers into a watch pocket and extracted a piece of cardboard that resembled an oversized timepiece. But instead of showing the time, it said in big, bold letters: April 1. He turned it over. On the back it said: April Fool's Day. The hapless youth doubled over in soundless laughter just as Lula stepped forward in the same stiff-jointed manner, carrying a cardboard bucket.

For the next twenty minutes, Marcie was caught up in the misadventures of Silly Sam as he fumbled and tripped at the sight of the lovely milk maiden. He slipped on an imaginary banana peel, wobbled on unsteady legs and fell to the floor. "Pretty Polly" stood by in shock, then helped him to his feet. With his hand inside his jacket lapel, Dustin mimicked a throb-

bing heart as he gawked longingly at Polly's batting
eyelashes, then dropped the wildflower he was about
to present to her. He bumped his head against hers
when they both bent over to pick it up, making the
two of them stagger back woodenly and fall on their
butts. Sam gallantly covered his eyes—and peeked
between his fingers—when Polly's hoop skirt flared
to expose her ruffled pantaloons.

When they finally stood up again, Sam continued
to make a perfect fool of himself trying to impress
the pretty maiden, gaining the laughter-filled sympathy of his young audience. It was a remarkable act,
one that earned Marcie's unqualified admiration.

If Dusty had noticed his sister standing among the
adults against the wall, he didn't show it. As soon as
the pantomime was over, Marcie followed the two
players and squeezed with them into the room at the
end of the hallway.

"Dusty, I'm impressed. You were wonderful," she
told him with genuine admiration. "I didn't know I
had such a talented brother."

He looked at her over his shoulder. There was no
mistaking his pleasure at receiving the compliment.
But when he turned to face her, she saw a flicker of
unease, as well, as if he weren't sure the comment
wasn't a put-down. "There's a lot about me you don't
know."

It was the same thing she'd told Tucker. Excusable
in her case, but why did it sound like an accusation
coming from her brother? It had been over eight years
since they'd lived under the same roof. He'd turned
a very adolescent fourteen and was going into high
school, she eighteen and on her way to North Texas
University. Right after graduation she'd married

Kevin Hayes and they'd moved to Houston. The marriage had lasted less than four years. Eight years was a long interval to be separated from one's family.

"How did you get started doing this...and why at an orphanage?"

He began to answer but stopped, raised his eyebrows and shot her an ironic smile. "You think—" his grin broadened "—you think one of those kids might be mine, don't you?" He laughed. "Relax, big sister. You're not an aunt yet."

She lowered her head, embarrassed. "Well, the thought did cross my mind."

"I practice safe sex," he boasted, and smeared cold cream on his face to remove the grease paint. "What are you doing here, anyway?"

"Mom's worried about you."

His eyes flashed. "Look, I just told you. I'm a big boy now. I know how to take care of myself. You don't have to baby-sit."

Marcie considered the variety of personalities she'd seen in her brother in the past few days. The loving son to their mother at the announcement of their father's death. The whiskey-drinking bully set on firing the new ranch foreman—who happened to be a private investigator. And now, the accomplished actor whose skills might be good enough to portray all of them, including the angry young man he appeared to be at the moment.

"You're right," she said placatingly. "It's just that Mom...I'll let her know you're on your way."

"Thank you," Dusty singsonged, echoing the patronizing tone their father had used when he was feeling put-upon. He turned his back on her and applied a new layer of cold cream to his face.

Marcie straightened her back at the curt dismissal, observed the two thespians scrubbing away thick makeup and left the room.

She drove slowly on the trip home. Something more than her brother's attitude was bothering her, but whatever it was eluded her. Something he'd said or done was setting off little bells, but she couldn't figure out what it was or what it meant. The last half hour had furnished her a clue. A connection. But of what to what? She didn't even know that. Maybe Tucker would be able to decipher it, she thought, and wondered why the anticipation of seeing him lifted her spirits.

THE KITCHEN AND DINING AREAS resembled the bake sale at a county fair and Carlinda looked like a little girl lost in a sweet shop, when Marcie came in the back door. It made her pause, then chuckle. "Where's Shelby?"

"Left a few minutes ago. She'll be back later. She had some things to do at the truck stop. I really don't know what I would have done without her." Carlinda ran a hand through her lank hair. "Did you find Dustin?"

"He's on his way back now." Marcie was on the verge of telling her about his miming until she recognized the weariness in her mother's gesture. "Why don't you sit down, Mom, and I'll fix us a cup of tea."

"I've been trying to make one for two hours." Carlinda looped a tendril of hair behind her ear. "First, you'd better lock the door, though, and put a sign on it saying we've moved to Australia." She shook her head. "So many people stopped by today. I haven't seen some of them in ages. Your father had a lot of friends.''

Marcie set the kettle to boil. ''They didn't come for him, Mom. They came for you. You're the one they care about. With the exception of Lennie, I doubt Dad had any real friends.''

''Don't hate him, Marcie. In the end it will only destroy you. Deep down inside your father loved you very much.''

Don't speak ill of the dead. Carlinda had stood by her husband in life, too. Marcie respected her mother's loyalty, but over the years, she'd begun to seriously question its wisdom.

Mason had praised and encouraged his daughter's triumphs and achievements when she was young, but about the time she entered high school something had changed. The drinking he'd always indulged in began to increase until it was out of control. Marcie had done her best to please him; earned straight As in all her classes, was the head cheerleader, consistently took blue ribbons in 4-H; and she rode a horse as well as any boy or man in the county. She'd graduated from Coyote High with a full scholarship and still felt like a failure in his eyes. She couldn't seem to please him, and she had no idea why. Going away to college had come as a blessed relief.

''He had a funny way of showing it,'' Marcie muttered. ''He didn't even care enough about me to tell me what I was doing wrong. Except for Kevin,'' she added. ''He didn't make any secret of the fact that he didn't think much of him.''

She'd brought him home, sure her father would approve, hoping her choosing a man so much like him—handsome, athletic, the life of the party—would heal the rift between them, bring her absolution for her mysterious faults.

Her father's quick rejection of the All-American had stunned her. His "giving her away" at the wedding had felt more like good riddance. The day that should have been the happiest of her life was indelibly marred by his scowling, drunken sarcasm. Later she wondered if his disdain for her choice of husband had somehow poisoned her marriage from the beginning.

Carlinda shuffled food around on the table, stacking containers until she'd cleared enough space for the two of them to sit down. "Do you know why your father disliked him?" When Marcie didn't respond, she said, "Because Kevin reminded him too much of himself."

Marcie fumbled with the tea bags she'd unwrapped. "He told you that?"

Kevin had, in fact, turned out to be exactly like him—drunken, unfaithful, irresponsible. But it wasn't until he'd become violent that Marcie had left him.

"Not in so many words. He wasn't that honest. But essentially, yes." Carlinda smiled and turned off the gas under the boiling kettle. She looked straight ahead. Her voice was low, almost nostalgic. "It wasn't always fighting and recriminations between us, you know. We still talked sometimes, even confided in each other." She filled their cups. "He was pleased when he found out you were finally getting a divorce and coming home."

The welcome Mason had given her a few days ago had seemed reluctant at best. He never said "I told you so," or called her a fool—though he might have.

But he never said he was sorry she'd been hurt, either. Or that he was happy to see her.

"Maybe…if he'd had more time…" Carlinda murmured.

He had plenty of time, Marcie wanted to counter. But what would be the point? Her one overpowering regret was that she'd never come out and asked her father why he couldn't love her. Now she would never know.

She removed two cups from the overhead cabinet next to the sink and set them down by the stove top. "You didn't tell me Dusty wants to become an actor."

Carlinda stopped, her hand poised over the handle of the steaming kettle and cocked her head slightly to one side. "He had a starring role in a college play, and he's been in a few amateur productions here, but I didn't know he wanted to do it professionally."

Uh-oh, Marcie thought. *I probably just let the cat out of the bag. Dusty's going to be really ticked off at me now.*

"I found him at the orphanage, entertaining the kids there," she explained. "Lula thinks he's serious about an acting career."

Carlinda filled the cups with boiling water. "Your father didn't consider acting very manly."

So that was why Dustin had been so quiet about it. Their father. The he-man, former jock, wouldn't likely have taken kindly to his son dressing up in funny clothes and wearing makeup.

Marcie chuckled despite herself. "Did Dad know Lula was an actress?"

"Oh, yes. The first time she met him she told him what a great dramatic actor Dusty was, but it didn't take her long to figure out Mason didn't approve. She was smart enough to avoid him after that.''

The two women sipped tea.

''Any word from Sheriff Kraus?''

''No.'' Carlinda swallowed the last of her drink. ''And what I'd hoped would be a simple funeral service seems to be turning into a memorial circus. I got a call a couple of hours ago from one of the governor's aides. Apparently, he and his wife want to attend personally, which means the media will be here.''

''We've handled the media before,'' Marcie assured her. ''We can do it again.''

Carlinda carried her empty cup to the sink, diligently washed it and started wiping down cabinets with the dishcloth. Never a particularly meticulous housekeeper, she appeared bent now on straightening and cleaning every nook and cranny of the big country kitchen. When Marcie offered to help, she was quietly shooed away. Understanding that her mother needed time alone, Marcie went to her room.

She craved solitude, too. Maybe a long, soaking bath would soothe away the tension in her neck and back.

The bathroom, like the kitchen, was completely out-of-date. There never seemed to be enough money to upgrade the sixty-year-old house. At the moment, however, Marcie was grateful for the clumsy old pedestal sink with its tarnished brass fixtures, the fading white wainscoting and hexagonal tile floor. Their familiarity formed a comfort zone around her as she stepped into the claw-footed tub.

The scent of gardenia bath oil surrounded her, and she let the silky softness of the hot water seep into her tired muscles. Her decision to come back to Coyote Springs a year after her divorce from Kevin Hayes had not been an easy one. As much as she loved the ranch she'd been born on and the mother who had nurtured her, Marcie knew living with her father would be difficult. But she'd looked forward to the slower pace of ranching. In Houston, where she'd worked as an education therapist for a fledgling company developing computer-based training, everything had felt like crisis management. There'd been little long-range planning or time to think things through.

She heard the phone ring in the kitchen down the hall and knew Carlinda would answer it.

Reluctantly, Marcie rose from the frothy tub, rinsed herself off and stepped onto the oversized bath mat. As she tugged the thick towel from its wooden rack, her mind snapped back to the moment when she'd reached for McGee's hand, the feel of his warm skin and the hard muscle under it.

Yesterday, when they had been riding within arm's reach of each other, she'd caught his sidelong glances, the quick, sensuous appraisals and shy turning away, as if he were embarrassed at having looked at her. If they were teenagers, she could dismiss it as part of the ritual of flirting. But they weren't teenagers, and he hadn't been flirting with her. Not exactly, anyway.

"Damn the man," she groaned, as the fluffy towel brushed between her thighs. Somehow she had the feeling that ignoring this cowboy wasn't going to be any easier in the future than it had been today up at the bowl.

The muffled sounds of a man's voice in the kitchen broke up her reverie. Was it the sheriff…or Tucker?

She shrugged into her blue terry-cloth robe,

clutched the soft material closed above her breasts and crossed the hall. Her room hadn't changed much over the years. There was a laptop on her old writing table where she used to have a typewriter. The walk-in closet wasn't nearly as full of clothes as it had once been. But the pictures of her friends, the posters of rock stars and dream vacations and the ribbons she'd won at barrel racing and pole bending still hung on the pink, floral-papered walls. She looked at them with a fond but forlorn sigh. It all seemed a lifetime ago. Time now to put these things aside. She would. But not immediately. Not yet.

She donned freshly laundered black jeans, an oversized red sweatshirt and threw on a pair of old sneakers without socks. Then she stepped into the hallway, leaving the door ajar, and walked toward the kitchen. She was about to enter it from the dim passage, when she heard the man's hushed tones.

"I'm sorry you have to go through all this, Carli," he said. The intimacy in his voice seemed more than the polite concern of a neighbor. "Does Marcie know?"

"Of course not," her mother replied. "I didn't tell her before, and at this point…there's enough going on in her life. Let's just wait and see what happens."

Confusion shivered through Marcie's veins. For half her life her father had made her feel like an outsider, and now her mother was doing the same thing. What were they keeping secret and why? Who was this man, and what did he have to do with it?

Fingering back her wet hair, Marcie entered the room. Her mother was just closing the door.

"Who was that, Mom?"

Carlinda spun around like a teenager caught smoking behind the barn. "Oh." She put her hand to her heart. "You startled me." She darted to the sink, her movements stiff, self-conscious. "Vince stopped by to offer his condolences."

Marcie rounded the island in the middle of the room, leaned against it and faced her mother. "What haven't you told me, Mom? What are you sure I don't know? What's so secret you have to whisper it in your own kitchen?"

CHAPTER SIX

"YOU'VE GROWN VERY DIRECT," Carlinda said.

"Comes from living with lies, rationalizations, posturing and infidelity for four years. I'm just sorry it took me so long to admit it and do something about it."

Her mother nodded. "It took me longer. Learning the lesson doesn't always make it easier to live with, though."

Marcie sat at the table and observed the one person she'd always felt good about coming home to. "What's going on, Mom?"

Carlinda sat down slowly, avoiding eye contact. "The world's changed a lot since you were born. There were flower children then, a war going on. Two wars really, one over there and one right here at home. Nothing was quite clear to any of us." She paused as if lost in memories; then, with a shudder, continued. "I guess it's time you did know."

Apprehension squirreled down Marcie's spine. Suddenly, she wasn't sure she was prepared for whatever she was about to hear.

"Vince and I...were going steady in college. We'd planned to get married right after graduation, settle on his ranch and raise the ideal family."

Marcie knew her mother and Vince had gone to school together. That they would have dated didn't surprise her, but she'd had no idea they'd been practically engaged. She'd seen them together at church affairs and rodeos and other social events often enough but never noticed any indications of unusual familiarity between them.

"Then Dave Conklin, a guy we'd gone through elementary and high school with, was killed over in Vietnam," Carlinda continued. "He wasn't the first casualty of the war from Coyote Springs, but he was the first one we'd known personally. I got sad. Vince got mad. The next thing I knew he wanted to volunteer. I was furious. Getting himself killed wasn't going to bring Dave back, I argued. But it was no use. Despite all my tears and protests, he enlisted in the army." Carlinda toyed nervously with a spoon on the table. "I was so hurt by his decision, I convinced myself he didn't really love me—otherwise he wouldn't have left. I even talked myself into believing I didn't love him."

The coffeemaker gasped and sputtered, a strangely mournful sound in the sudden silence of the kitchen.

"Vince had hardly shipped out, when Mason started coming around. He'd asked me out on dates once or twice before, but until then I'd always said no. I was Vince's girl. Sounds funny nowadays, but that's the way a lot of us thought of ourselves back then—as somebody's 'girl.' Anyway, I wasn't Vince's girl anymore and Mason…he was the star quarterback on the football team, president of the Student Council, and about the most dashing, handsomest charmer you ever wanted to meet. Elvis Presley, Tom Cruise and Arnold Schwarzenegger all rolled into one gorgeous hunk." She chuckled, her face taking on a happy, faraway look. "I think just about every girl in the school was panting after him."

Did her mother realize how proud she sounded? Marcie wondered.

"A month later, he proposed. I was flabbergasted. I also didn't give him an answer right away." She smiled wryly. "I have to admit, at first I thought his proposal might be his way of getting me into bed."

Carlinda closed her eyes and turned serious. "Then something else happened. I began to suspect I was pregnant, and I got scared. Vince was gone. I knew he wouldn't be coming back for a long time—if at all. Unwed motherhood may be socially acceptable nowadays in some circles, but it wasn't in mine. Abortion certainly wasn't an option. Mason's offer of marriage, needless to say, was the answer to my problem."

Marcie stared at her mother, horrified by what she was hearing. She'd never considered her mother straitlaced, but the revelation that she had slept with someone before she got married had never entered her mind. Now she was finding out she had gotten pregnant...pregnant with her. Marcie's heart started pounding painfully in her chest, and her hands began to shake. Mason wasn't her father. Vince was. Her name shouldn't be Marcie Browder but Marcie Prudhomme.

All this time he'd lived a few miles away, knowing she was his daughter, rarely seeing her, never acknowledging that she meant anything to her. A cold shiver washed across Marcie's skin. What kind of man got his girlfriend, his fiancée, pregnant, then abandoned her—and his child? What kind of man stood by and allowed an abusive alcoholic lecher to raise his daughter?

Marcie's world had just turned upside down.

"So you used Mason. Did he know you were pregnant?"

Carlinda shook her head. "I wasn't far enough along for him to notice."

Marcie was speechless. This was an aspect of her mother she'd never seen before, never suspected. Had she really been as cool and calculating as she sounded?

"Pride and desperation can make us do funny things, foolish things," Carlinda commented, as if reading her daughter's mind. "Though it took a few years before I understood just how foolish I'd been."

Marcie's mouth had gone dry. Her fingers trembled. Her mother, lost in her own thoughts, didn't seem to notice.

"When did he find out I wasn't his child?" Marcie asked.

"Men didn't 'participate' in their wives' pregnancies back then the way some of them do now. Not that Mason would have been inclined to, anyway. It was easy enough to pretend you were premature. My doctor knew, of course, though in my naïveté I'd tried to fool him. But knowing my folks and what revealing my true condition would have meant socially, he played along." She stroked the back of Marcie's hands with coarse, work-hardened fingers. "My shame is not that you're my daughter, but that I didn't merit you, that I don't deserve you. I never even considered putting you up for adoption—which was the only real choice I had."

Marcie felt numb. "So Dad never knew I wasn't his daughter."

Carlinda's shoulders sagged, and she withdrew her hands.

"Not for a very long time. I often wondered if he suspected. But then, guilty people always think other people know their secrets. Actually, the first few years with Mason weren't so bad. He'd gotten picked up as a running back by the Oilers. It wasn't quarterback status, and it wasn't the Cowboys, which had been his dream, but there was still hope that he might make it to Dallas. He wasn't home a lot, either. But I had you, and I enjoyed living here on the ranch, working with my parents." Sadness glazed her eyes. "Do you remember? You were so little. Gramps used to hold you on his lap and the three of us would ride down by the river. You, me and Gramps."

Marcie managed to nod. The knot in her throat wouldn't allow words. Sweet memories of her grandparents tugged at her heart. Good people. Had they known? Had they pretended, too?

"Those were wonderful times for us." Carlinda's voice was soft with nostalgia. "You were four years old when Gran and Gramps were killed in the car accident. That day was the saddest of my life—having to tell you they wouldn't be coming home anymore. By then Mason knew he wasn't going to be picked up the next year by the Cowboys or even the Oilers, so he took over running the ranch."

For a moment Carlinda seemed to lose herself in yesterdays. "It became obvious very quickly, however, that he wasn't cut out to be a rancher or a homebody," she finally went on. "Oh, I'd suspected there might have been other women when he was away at games and training camps. But I'd been able to convince myself it was all in my imagination, or that they were mere substitutes because I couldn't be with him. Then he was home with no place to go. Coyote Springs isn't a place you can lose yourself in. It's certainly not big enough for a man of Mason's stature to fool around and not be found out. I knew then that I had been deceiving myself."

She rose impulsively from her chair and faced the window over the sink. "I confronted him, of course. The self-righteous, wounded wife. He promised to reform, and maybe he even tried, but by then I was pregnant with Dustin. It wasn't an easy pregnancy, which only added to the tension between us." Carlinda folded her arms. "So he found consolation elsewhere. I closed my eyes to it for a while, told myself it was my fault."

"No," Marcie cried out, remembering how for so long she'd blamed herself for Kevin's infidelity. "It wasn't your fault, Mom. He was responsible for his own actions."

Carlinda turned around, a vacant kind of smile on her face that told Marcie her defense was appreciated but misplaced.

"And I was responsible for mine." She resumed her seat opposite her daughter. "We fought a lot more after that. It was in one of those moments of hurt and anger that I blurted out that you weren't his daughter but Vince's. I said it to hurt him and regretted it the moment the truth came out. But, of course, it was too late. In a few words of bitterness I destroyed any possibility for our reconciliation, any hope of our ever being happy again—though it took me years to realize how irreversible our relationship was."

There was a question Marcie had to ask. "Did you love him, Mom?"

Carlinda rubbed her chapped hands together, looked down at their nervous twirling as if she were surprised to see it happening, and stopped the motion. "There was something about him, the bad boy maybe, a zest for life that always had him living on the edge. It stirred something inside me. We were so different really. When I tried to join his world I didn't fit in, yet I wished I could." She looked at Marcie. "Yes, I guess I did love him."

Marcie's heart ceased beating. "But he stopped loving me," she muttered. "Why? Because I wasn't his daughter?"

TUCKER BACKED AWAY. He'd been in the barn checking feed levels so he could reorder, when he saw Vince Prudhomme drive up. He assumed once the rancher had paid his respects to Carlinda he'd want to talk with him. The two ranch owners were his employers, but Tucker knew from experience that the people who hired him didn't always tell him the truth, the whole truth and nothing but the truth. He tried to overhear what they were saying through the open kitchen window, but their conversation was so low and secretive he'd gotten nothing of value.

A few minutes later, Prudhomme left the house, went directly to his truck, climbed in and drove away.

Tucker lingered at the side of the house, puzzled by the air of conspiracy. He was about to return to the barn, when he heard Marcie's question to her mother. He stayed put.

What he learned wasn't so much shocking as it was disturbing—on several levels. With his back against the wall, he couldn't see the two women's faces, but it wasn't necessary to know how much the revelation of Marcie's paternity hurt both of them. He could hear it in the uneasiness of their responses, in the tense pauses between words and sentences.

He tried to imagine what it would be like growing up in a house filled with acrimony and wounded pride, to have a parent you love turn against you. His own upbringing had been so different. There had always been discipline, chores to perform, standards to meet. The structure itself had been reassuring. He never doubted that his parents loved him. He'd tried to bring that same stability and affection to his own family.

It was clear that Marcie had done nothing to deserve the emotional turmoil she'd been subjected to. Where had she gotten the strength to rise above it? A weaker person would have retreated into self-pity. Marcie Browder had not.

As he stepped away, he wondered how this might fit in with Mason's murder. It gave the deceased good reason to kill Vince and even Carlinda. But did it give them reason to kill him?

MARCIE HELPED HER MOTHER clear the table. The silence that loomed between them had grown from uncomfortable to oppressive as each struggled to find words that would bring their world back to normalcy. She glanced out the window as she placed soiled cups in the sink, and thought she saw a shadow dart out of visual range. It could have been one of the dogs nosing around, but something told her this creature had two legs.

"I'm going to check on the horses."

Carlinda nodded. "Good idea. I'm not always sure that new kid, Jim Bob, knows what he's doing."

Marcie wasn't convinced it was true, but it didn't make any difference. They both needed a break from each other, space and time to reevaluate the situation.

She entered the side door of the horse barn between the tack and feed rooms and heard footsteps at the other end of the dark structure.

"Tootsie is a sweet old thing," Dustin was saying. "I learned to ride on her when I was a kid. She's got real smooth gaits, even when she trots, so you shouldn't have any trouble staying on her."

"I wish you wouldn't keep reminding me how clumsy I was the other day," a female chirped. Marcie had no trouble recognizing Lula's voice. "Just because I looked funny getting thrown into that pile of sawdust doesn't mean it didn't hurt."

"Aw, you didn't get thrown, sugar-pie. You just slipped off, that's all." Dustin chuckled. "Actually, I think you looked sort of cute with the shavings in your hair. Like confetti."

"The ones down my back itched something terrible."

"I helped you wash them off, though, didn't I?"

Lula tittered. "Well, yeah, you were kind of helpful and all but..."

"Ahem." Marcie cleared her throat as she approached them from the dim shadows of the barn.

Dustin swung around. Against the bright afternoon sunlight coming in the wide doorway, he was little more than a silhouette.

"Oh," he finally said. "It's you."

Marcie forced cheeriness into her voice. "Who were you expecting?"

"No one," he replied. "That's why you startled me."

He turned back to Lula and gave her a leg up into the saddle, his hand patting her calf reassuringly.

"Dusty, I need to talk to you. I'm afraid I said something to Mom you're not going to be very happy with me about."

"What's that?"

"Mom and I were talking and…I figured she knew about your wanting to be an actor, so I mentioned that I'd seen you miming at the orphanage and how good you were. She seemed surprised, and I realized you hadn't told her."

"Damn."

"I'm sorry. I didn't mean to—"

"You sure have a big mouth, don't you? You've been here less than two weeks and already you've turned our lives upside down."

"Dusty, that's not fair," Marcie protested.

"You're right." He stroked the sorrel mare's neck. "I know it's not your fault Dad went and got himself killed." He adjusted Lula's stirrup and checked the cinch. "I mean it. I'm sorry," he said over his shoulder.

Lula swiveled around in the saddle. "If you want, honey," she said to Dustin, whose right hand had moved up to her thigh, "I'll wait outside. Or maybe you'd like to come with us," she offered Marcie. "Dusty's been teaching me how to ride…or trying to." She giggled softly as she gazed at him. "And he's going to teach me to shoot skeet, and when I learn that, he'll teach me to target shoot."

"He's well qualified," Marcie commented. "He took state champion three years in a row." But as she looked at her brother, she wondered if he had the patience to be an effective tutor.

"We're going down by the tank," Dustin explained without adding his endorsement to the invitation.

The tank was a man-made pond a mile or so from the house. Fed by an old wooden windmill, it was prone to go dry in the middle of the summer. This time of year it would be filled to capacity. The water hole was romantically picturesque, surrounded by fields of bluebonnets and other wildflowers. Years ago Mason had set up a small range there, including a skeet tower. Marcie was amazed it was still functional. So many things on the ranch had fallen into disrepair. Typical, she thought with disgust. Fences can fall down, but the rifle range is maintained.

"Thanks, maybe another time."

"I'll wait for you outside," Lula announced. She clucked at her horse like an old pro, and it moved through the wide wooden doors.

"I am sorry," Marcie emphasized when Lula was gone. "You and Mom seem so close I assumed—"

"Don't worry about it," he muttered as he followed his girlfriend with his eyes. "I'll talk to Mom and get her calmed down. I was getting ready to tell her, anyway."

Marcie didn't particularly like the implication that her brother manipulated their mother, but she saw no use in pointing it out. She followed him into one of the middle stalls and watched as he ran a hand down his favorite gelding's foreleg.

"What's the matter with Duke?" she asked.

"I don't know. He's decided all of a sudden to go lame. You know horses. They don't have to have a reason.'' Dustin straightened and patted the horse's flank, closed the stall door and went to the next one. ''I'll ride Skipper.''

He brought out the sixteen-hand roan gelding, led him down the isle and hitched him to the cross-ties. ''Look, big sister, your plans for fixing up the ranch—'' he threw a saddle blanket over the animal's broad back ''—they're fine, things we should have done a long time ago. We would have, too, if Dad had put me in charge instead of hiring McGee.''

''Maybe when Tux leaves—''

Dustin started to lift the saddle off its peg but stopped in midmotion and looked at her. '''Tux'?'' His voice rose with amusement. ''Sounds like you're getting pretty chummy with the hired help.''

Marcie bit her lip, strangely embarrassed at the comment, as if she'd just said something wrong. Yet she hadn't. Besides, they were two single adults. She almost told her brother Tucker wasn't hired help—in the conventional sense, at least—or even a foreman. But she caught herself in time. She'd let information slip once today; she didn't need to do it again. If her mother wanted Dustin to know McGee was an investigator, it was up to her to tell him.

''He's got a pretty good handle on what's going on around here,'' she remarked, then added with irony, ''more than you do.''

Dustin eyed her sharply. ''What's that supposed to mean?''

''There were no cattle missing from Hawk Ridge. McGee told you he moved them to save you face, rather than embarrass you in front of Mom.'' She didn't bother to tell him that the new foreman's claim that he moved the "missing" livestock was a bluff, too—one she'd called.

"Oh," was her brother's pitiful response.

He rubbed his hand along the neck of the horse he'd finished saddling and walked over to a wall, where he removed a bridle from a peg. With the self-assured movements of someone used to handling horses, he slipped the port bit into the animal's mouth and eased the leather strap over its ears.

"Well, for your information, I haven't been exactly doing nothing." He buckled the throat latch holding the headstall in place. "I've been investigating the rustling."

Marcie stood there, definitely interested. "Have you learned anything?"

"Yes," he said as he checked the cinch. After attaching a rifle scabbard to the right fender of the saddle, he put his foot in the left stirrup and rose, swinging his right leg over the cantle of the western saddle.

"What?" she asked as she stared up at him.

"I've found out Lennie's been selling cattle over at the Cattleman's Trade in San Angelo. A bit curious, don't you think, since he doesn't own a ranch anymore? Dad was royally pissed when I told him, that's for sure."

"Dad knew?"

Dustin smirked. "I just said I told him."

"When?"

"The other day. At the Bucket."

"Is that why he rushed out of there?"

Dustin didn't reply, but his silence was answer enough.

"Why the hell didn't you tell Rudy Kraus when he asked you what Dad was so upset about?"

A slow, satisfied smile creased her brother's face. "For the same reason your friend 'Tux' didn't tell him about the piece of paper he found."

He nudged the horse into a walk and trailed out the barn doors.

"Dusty, wait." But he ignored her. Annoyed, she watched Lula join him and the two of them ride off in the direction of the tank.

"Damn." She turned to take up her chores and slammed into Tucker McGee as he came around the side of the building. His large hands reached out to steady her.

"In a hurry?" he asked. The question was careless, but his look harbored concern and raw need.

She faltered, her heart thudding, not just from the collision, she realized, but from his firm grip on her arms. She'd felt those hands before—at their meeting at the bowl. But this was the first time she'd actually experienced his body against hers. It was...hard and unnerving.

Shrugging away from him and straightening the waistband of her jeans, she was acutely self-conscious of the tightness of her nipples. "What are you doing here?"

"Actually," he admitted, "I was coming to see you."

Needlessly, she adjusted the collar of her pale-yellow shirt, anything to avoid the sea-green depths she could feel studying her.

"A few questions came up today," he said. "I thought maybe we could discuss them."

She wished her heart would stop its vicious pounding. "We can talk while I clean tack."

He walked beside her back into the dim barn. The

redolence of hay and sweet feed mingled with the pungency of leather. Not an unpleasant combination. Marcie always felt calmness settle over her in the barn. Even on the coldest winter nights there was something cheering and reassuring about the smell of the horses, the eternal cycle of nature. But this wasn't winter. It was spring. The time of birth and new growth, of mating and nurturing. And what peace the familiar surroundings brought, the man beside her disturbed.

They moved down the line of stalls, four on each side separated by a wide aisle, checking latches to make sure each was secure. She greeted the animals by name as they munched on hay or grain, and stroked the noses of those who stepped over to the gates to greet her.

Going into the rough-cut paneled tack room, she looked around, very much aware of the man standing at her elbow. He followed her along the row of saddles that hung on wall racks, and the bridles and bits hanging beside them, to a tall cabinet in the corner. After taking out a can of saddle soap and two soft cloths, she handed them to him, removed Sparkle's bridle from the third rack on the left and carried it to the bench near the door. He grabbed Ciska's bridle and joined her. Diligently, they began to clean the brown leather.

"You heard what Dusty said?" she finally asked.

"I guess I've underestimated lover-boy."

"You do a lot of eavesdropping."

"All part of the job," he said lightly. "No extra charge."

She tried to smile, but it didn't work. The situation

seemed to get worse at every turn. "How did he find out about the paper?"

"Probably heard me talking to your mother about it. I doubt she would have told him."

"Do you think he knows who you are?"

Tucker worked soap under a buckle. "I'm going to have to assume he does. If he was listening in on one conversation, he might have overheard others."

A light came on. "Could that be why he tried to fire you the other night?"

Tucker shrugged. "Maybe." He polished leather for a minute. "You know he was arrested for armed robbery last year?"

She didn't look up. "The charge was dropped. He had no part in it."

"Or so your father persuaded his friend to swear. Do you believe it?"

She stopped, and this time she raised her head, but she said nothing.

"He's got a temper," Tucker remarked as he held up the entire bridle to examine it. "And he's a liar."

"He's not a murderer," she insisted, trying to match his coolness. Inside, she shivered.

EARLY SATURDAY MORNING, Marcie drove over to the Prudhomme ranch. Her insides were churning; her fingers sweaty on the wheel. She'd slept little during the night. Her mind kept flip-flopping through a collection of disjointed images: Mason beaming with pride when she got all dressed up as a fairy princess for a kindergarten pageant, his being cold and indifferent at her high school graduation, and that last terrible argument.

Would she have acted differently if she'd known it

would be their final encounter? Undoubtedly. But what else could she have done? She'd experienced physical abuse in her failed marriage, learned unwillingly that there could be no second chance for a wife beater and determined that she would never subject herself to it again. Nor would she allow her mother to be victimized, either.

Carlinda had insisted Monday evening that it was the first time Mason had ever struck her, and in truth, Marcie had never witnessed physical violence between her parents or seen evidence of it. But through her support group in Houston she knew victims of abuse were often ingenious in disguising it. It was another of those unfathomable questions—why victims protected their tormentors.

Or did her mother, having tricked a proud man into marriage, see herself as the tormentor? Had she for years accepted his verbal and maybe physical abuse because she felt she deserved it for her duplicity?

The morning was clear and bright. If only Marcie could feel that way.

Had Carlinda ever truly loved Mason? Had he loved her? How could two people hurt each other so deeply if they were in love? Or did she have it backward? Did they hurt each other so deeply because they were in love? Resentment rose like bile in Marcie's throat. How could Mason reject an innocent young girl? And how could her mother and her real father have let it happen?

She turned off the farm-to-market road to the Prudhomme ranch. She'd been there dozens of times over the years, a neighbor visiting neighbors. Vince's son, Anson, had gone to the same elementary and high school she had. His being three years younger than she made their acquaintance one of association rather than friendship. Her half brother—and she hardly knew him. Did he know she was his sister? Probably not. But it seemed likely he would soon find out.

The Prudhomme ranch was smaller than the Lazy B, fifteen sections versus the Browders' twenty-five. Both had been in their respective families for over a hundred years. Prudhomme's house, older in parts than the one on the Lazy B, was a rambling structure of mixed construction: wood, brick, stone. There was even a section of log. The place was also spotlessly neat, although Doris Prudhomme's bedding plants no longer edged the walk leading from the driveway to the house. The window boxes didn't sport her bright-red geraniums, either. But there was still a welcome hominess about the place.

Vince was standing by the back door when Marcie pulled up. Tall and lean, he had a weathered face, the skin leathery and cracked at the corners of his eyes and mouth—laugh lines that had been etched by sun, wind and time. She'd always liked Vince. Always thought of him as smiling and kind.

The index finger of his right hand was hooked in the handle of a steaming mug. Gray hairs curled above his blue denim work shirt and his well-washed jeans sagged on his narrow hips. He watched her approach.

"'Mornin' Marcie." The smile on his face didn't disguise the wariness behind it. "Your ma called a few minutes ago. Figured you might be heading this way."

Carlinda hadn't been in the house when Marcie got up, probably doing any one of a hundred chores that always needed attention. The ranch life that seemed idyllic to the outsider was constant, hard work. But Marcie hadn't tried to track her down before leaving, just left a note saying she would be back later. She didn't want to discuss, and possibly be dissuaded from, what she had to do. So she'd slunk like a coward to her car and driven away.

"Had coffee yet? I promise I make a better pot than Carli."

Marcie smiled despite herself. Her mother's coffee was notoriously bad. No one could ever figure out how a woman who was so competent in so many ways could mess up a simple pot of coffee, but she did—every time.

"Thanks. I'd love a cup." Bravado, she told herself, trying to sound chipper when her stomach was tied in knots.

Vince opened the screen door, then followed her into the kitchen. He nodded toward the square oak table placed diamond-wise in the bow window and went over to the percolator on the stove.

Marcie sat on one of the slat-back wooden chairs facing the window. Vince poured a second mug and topped off his own.

"You've had a rough homecoming. I'm sorry." He placed the steaming beverage in front of her and sat at a right angle to her. "Oh, did you want something in that?" He gestured toward her coffee.

Marcie shook her head. "This is fine." She stared out the lace-curtained window at the vibrant green patches of rye grass struggling to survive in the shade of three huge live-oak trees. "Mom explained to me last night…" But she couldn't squeeze out the words "that you're my father."

"I know," he said softly. "She told me this morning when she called. It was a shock for you, I reckon.'' He started to bring his hand over toward hers but held back.

Marcie hesitated. Dammit, she wasn't supposed to be tongue-tied like this. Her eyes weren't supposed to burn and her throat wasn't supposed to feel as though she'd just eaten a porcupine whole, tail first. She took a sip of coffee, swallowed hard and bit her lip. ''I don't know what to say.''

''Then let me talk.''

CHAPTER SEVEN

VINCE PRUDHOMME EXTENDED his long arms across the table, the mug at his fingertips. "I fell completely in love with your mother when we were in high school. She was Carlinda Bobrick then. Loved Carli very much, respected her opinions. Of course, that might be because we agreed on just about everything. Except Vietnam. I didn't like opposing her after Dave Conklin got killed, but I had strong feelings, too. Felt there were things I had to do. She was upset with me, but I figured once she calmed down, she'd understand that going off the way I did was right. I couldn't just stand by while people I knew were getting killed."

A man of principles, Marcie concluded, and took solace in the thought.

"Finding out a month later that Carli had up and married Mason nearly drove me crazy. I felt betrayed, angry. I didn't know she was pregnant, and, of course, didn't know the desperation she must have been suffering."

He twisted his heavy porcelain mug with thick, gnarled fingers. His voice when he spoke again was casual, friendly, but Marcie felt his discomfort.

"It wasn't until more than a dozen years later that she told me what had really happened. We'd seen each other in church on Sundays, greeted each other at social events, always been polite and civilized. And

all the time I didn't know she'd borne my child—
you.''

Marcie studied his features. Did she resemble him?
Not the nose. She had her mother's small nose.
Vince's had been broken at least once, its aquiline
sharpness slightly off-center. Maybe a little of the
chin and jawline. It was ironic that she'd always
thought of herself as taking after her dad rather than
her mom.

''When Carli finally did tell me about you,'' Vince
continued, ''it was only because she'd had a fight
with Mason and blurted out to him that you weren't
his. She came to me to explain it so if Mason made
trouble I would understand why.''

What had the secret cost her mother all those years?
And how had its revelation hurt this man? He could
have been bitter, but what she sensed was compassion. He'd lost the woman he'd loved and been denied
the child he'd fathered, yet his sympathy seemed to
be with them.

''Did you tell Doris?''

He nodded. ''Under the circumstances, she had a
right to know. She was my wife, God bless her. She
accepted the situation. Never complained or had a bad
word. I miss her.'' He took a mouthful of coffee, then
paused, his gaze far away, before continuing. ''An
even bigger concern was what I was going to do about
you. Up until then I'd seen you as a cute and happy
little girl. It was a wonderful relief when I realized
Mason wasn't going to make an issue of this. I suppose that sounds selfish, but the truth is your mother
and I didn't want to disturb your happiness, and I had
a family here to protect. So we all stayed mum.''

This time when Vince started to lift his mug, Marcie realized his hand was shaking. He put the mug down without drinking.

"Things changed after that," she reminded him.

Vince pursed his lips. "Yeah. The jolly drinker turned into a nasty drunk."

He reached out and cupped a coarse, callused hand over hers. "Marcie, the hardest thing I've ever had to do in my life was stand by and watch you grow up. I could have interceded. Maybe I should have. But to what avail? Would public knowledge that Mason wasn't your real daddy have made you happier? Your mother was there to protect you, and she assured me you were never in physical danger, and that deep down inside Mason loved you."

He stroked the back of her hand and looked at her directly. "I kept track of you after that, though. You can't imagine how much I wanted to tell you how proud I was of you—proud you did so well in school, proud you were popular and well liked, proud you helped other people. I thought about going to your wedding, but I was afraid Mason might say something and spoil everything. I'm sorry your marriage didn't work out." He smiled a little ruefully. "Someday someone will come along who's worthy of you."

He lifted a hand to her chin and coaxed her face toward him. Reluctantly, she raised her eyes to meet his. They were blue, she realized. A deep, dark blue. And troubled.

"If I made a mistake in not coming forward," he said gently, "I'm sorry. You are my daughter, and I love you."

She hadn't known what to expect when she came here, but she definitely hadn't been prepared for this outpouring of affection. She'd waited in vain for years for Mason to say he cared for her, and now it was coming from a man she hardly knew.

"Marcie, I'm sorry I wasn't the parent you deserved. The decision is yours whether you want people to know the truth. Whatever you decide, I'll support it."

"I don't know yet what I want."

"That's understandable, and I think you're wise in taking time to think it through." Again, he put his rough hand to her chin. "Just remember, I do love you."

Acting on an impulse she hadn't expected, she extended her arm and laid it across his shoulder. It felt absolutely fitting when she leaned over and kissed him on the cheek.

"What you did was right," she murmured. "I didn't know then you were there for me, but I know now. Somehow it makes it easier. Thank you."

Her chair screeched on the linoleum floor when she pushed it back. She rose and moved toward the door.

"Marcie," he called behind her. She turned. "Right now you're not real happy with your ma. But remember, she loves you, too. What she did, whether it was right or wrong, she did for only one reason— she thought it was best for you."

Marcie nodded and stepped out into the sunlight. Tucker was standing there in front of her.

"What are you doing here?" she demanded in a strangled voice. Everywhere she turned he kept showing up.

"I came over to see Unc—"

Temper clawed inside her. Had he been listening? Then it hit her. "Yesterday…when you came into the barn, you entered by the side door, the one closest to the house. It was you I saw from the kitchen window.'' Unsteady annoyance turned to burning outrage. "You listened to Mom and me."

"I didn't intend to."

"But it didn't stop you. You could have walked away."

"I'm an investigator, Marcie. I investigate. That means I watch and listen for information."

"Spy on people," she corrected him. But even the pique she knew she should feel wouldn't cooperate.

"If you like. I'm sorry about what I heard."

She looked up at him, gazed into the intense moss-green eyes that threatened to swallow her. A step toward him, and he'd put his arms around her. How wonderful it would be to be embraced, held, to have his warmth seep its way inside her. She fought to control her breathing, to not let him see how his closeness was affecting her. "You mean you feel sorry for me?"

She took a step toward the parking area, but he reached out, snagged her arm and stopped her. He turned her to face him, his eyes steady on hers, and she felt her nerves becoming even more unraveled.

"Regretting something has happened," he said quietly, "is not the same as pitying the people it's happened to. I'm sorry your parents hurt you. But it's not the end of the world. You'll survive it."

A whirlwind of emotions struggled within her. Bitter sarcasm got in the final punch. "Why, thank you very much, sir. What a consolation. So aside from the assassination, Mrs. Lincoln, how was the play?"

She lurched out of his grasp and strode along the gravel path, though her knees felt weak and wobbly.

"Funny," he said, his long legs easily keeping

pace with her. "I wouldn't have thought of you as the self-pitying, hand-wringing type."

He was right—it wasn't like her. But dammit, she'd just learned her father wasn't her father, that her mother had been dishonest and conniving and that her biological father lived down the road. How calm and accepting was she supposed to be, knowing all those years of confusion and loneliness had been unnecessary?

They turned the corner of the house.

"Marcie, stop." He extended his hand again, but this time he didn't have to hold her. She halted, her head down.

He reached out and drew her into his arms. Her posture stiffened, and he was prepared to release her if she resisted, but she didn't.

He tempered his voice to a near whisper. "What I heard—" he raised her chin with the edge of his finger "—what I heard will never go anywhere."

Her eyes, glassy with tears, remained forlorn. He ached to relieve the grief and sadness in them. A tear trickled, and he lifted a blunt thumb to brush it away.

He snuggled his arms around her shoulders again. This time she melted into his embrace. As her warm breasts pressed against his ribs, heat consumed him. He angled his jaw on her soft brown hair and breathed in her scent.

"I'll never do anything to hurt you," he murmured. "I swear it."

She encircled his waist with her slender arms and rested her cheek against his chest, making his heart pound all the heavier. For a fleeting moment he found contentment, a surge of joy and restlessness.

He looked down. She looked up. There was only

one thing left. He lowered his mouth to hers. In the flash before their lips touched, he saw hope and vulnerability. In spite of the frenzy building within him, in spite of the need, the kiss was gentle. He'd promised not to hurt her.

Desire, awe and lust warred within him and, coward that he was, he surrendered to all of them. The desperation in her grasp, the sweetness of her kiss, awakened a hunger he didn't want to acknowledge. But the feminine allure of her body cushioned against his told him there would be no turning back. The barrage of sensations her gentle response provoked left him gasping for air and defenseless.

"You okay?" he asked a minute later, as she separated herself from him.

She brushed her wet cheek with her fingertips and nodded, a sad-little-girl gesture that stabbed into him.

He followed her to where they'd parked. The hood of his truck was up.

"Trouble with your pickup?" she asked after clearing the huskiness from her throat.

"Fan belt," he said, and removed the offending article from where he'd left it draped like a black snake across the top of the radiator. He showed her the frayed ends. They carried the acrid smell of burned rubber. "If you're going back to the ranch, I'd appreciate a lift. I'll have Jim Bob run into town and get a new belt, then bring me back here to install it."

Without saying anything, she climbed behind the wheel of her Cougar. He got in the passenger seat beside her. They buckled up in silence, glances unnecessary to confirm their mutual awareness. She waited until they had turned onto the country road before she spoke. "You still haven't told me what you're doing here."

"I wanted to check with Uncle Fletch on where he was losing the cattle from."

"Whoa." She slammed on the brake and cut the wheel sharply, veering to the side of the empty road. The car pitched forward, then rocked back to a sudden halt. Her arms were still fully outstretched on the steering wheel as she glared over at him. "*Uncle* Fletch?"

Tucker withdrew the hand he'd braced on the dashboard. His brows arched in humor as he turned to face her. "Fletcher Doggitt's my uncle," he said, as if everyone in the world knew it. "Didn't I tell you that?"

Her arms still locked, she slanted him a scathing look. "No. You didn't."

"Yeah, well, Uncle Fletch was the one who suggested I be called in to investigate the rustling."

"You're full of surprises, aren't you, McGee?" She was beginning to feel like someone whirling through a fun house, except she wasn't laughing. Exhaling through her teeth, she checked the rearview mirror, let off on the brake and pulled into the traffic lane.

"Your uncle, huh?" She'd seen Fletcher Doggitt regularly over the years, at social events, rodeos, 4-H. He'd always struck her as a man's man, not a lady's. Pleasant, hardworking...a loner.

Tucker settled back against the cushy velour upholstery. "Fletcher is my mother's brother. I was ten when my father died, and Uncle Fletch sort of took his place as male head of the family. He didn't live with us, but a picture of him, resplendent in his full-dress Marine uniform, was always on the mantelpiece in the living room.''

Marcie glanced over and caught the faraway look on Tucker's face, the expression of a man experiencing a happy memory. What was he like as a boy? she wondered. What kind of home life did he have?

"He was a war hero, you know. Saved Vince's life during the evacuation of Saigon,'' Tucker continued proudly. "Uncle Fletch carried him out to safety, even though he himself had been shot in the leg. Saved six other people that day, too. By the time he collapsed, he'd lost so much blood, they didn't think he was going to make it.''

That explained Fletcher's limp. It wasn't pronounced, and she'd never given it much thought— just the kind of hitch in his git-a-long that aging cowboys often had. She'd assumed the close friendship between him and Vince was the natural result of their working together for so many years.

"I was a little kid,'' Tucker went on, "but I remember when my parents took me to the White House, where the president presented him with the Congressional Medal of Honor. Mom sure was proud of him and so was dad.'' He rolled down the window the remaining two inches and rested his arm on the frame. "A couple of months later, he was medically discharged. They'd taken him off painkillers by then, said they didn't want him to get addicted. But he was still hurting, so he started drinking.''

Marcie concentrated on the road, not wanting to look over for fear of distracting him. Tucker was telling her about someone pivotal in his life, and suddenly, knowing about him was important to her, too.

"Not long after that, Vince was released and went

looking for the man who'd saved his life. Uncle
Fletch was in pretty bad shape by then. Vince took
him home, got medical treatment for him and weaned
him off the bottle. Uncle Fletch hasn't touched a drop
now in twenty-five years.''

''The man whose life he saved, saved his,'' Marcie
commented.

Tucker nodded.

She didn't doubt that such experiences could bond
men so close they would do anything for each other.
Including kill?

They drove along in silence. Marcie thought about
the difference between the two sets of friends: Vince
Prudhomme and Fletcher Doggitt; Mason Browder
and Lennie Gruen. Selfless war heroes and selfish op-
portunists. Yet both pairs of men had close bonds.
One honorable, the other dissolute. Does time change
people? she wondered. Could a man who'd risked his
own life to save others kill someone he perceived to
be a threat to his best friend?

''How did Vince and Mason get along?'' Tucker
asked a few minutes later.

''They were civil to each other,'' Marcie replied.
''Vince, because I think it's his nature to be friendly.
My father... You have to remember Mason was the
consummate politician, which means there was more
than a little ham actor in him. It used to embarrass
me sometimes when he was campaigning, how he
could be so saccharine sweet with people. I always
expected them to laugh in his face. Instead, they ate
it up.''

She paused to reflect on her brother's interest in
the theater. Was acting in the blood? A smile tickled
the corners of her mouth. She wasn't really a Brow-

der; she was a Prudhomme. It would explain why she had no such ambition or skill.

"I suppose," she went on, "after Mason found out about me, he didn't want to give Vince the satisfaction of acknowledging he'd been used."

Marcie turned off the highway onto the road to the ranch house and pulled into the yard between the house and barn. She was about to open her door, when Tucker reached over and placed his hand on her wrist. The restraint was mild, inviting, not forceful. Except for the raw power his touch had over her.

"If you're blaming yourself for what he became, forget it."

"But it was because of me," she told him.

"No, it wasn't." There was exasperation in his voice. "Alcoholics who continue to drink don't get better, Marcie," he said reasonably. "They get worse." He released her arm and twisted in his seat to face her. "It was because of who and what he was, not because of you. Look," he continued, more patiently, "as an alcoholic, he may not have had a choice about taking the second drink. But every time he sobered up, he was capable of making the right decision. Nobody poured the next *first* drink down his throat. He chose it voluntarily."

She nodded vaguely, knowing he was right, but he could see she still harbored the suspicion that somehow she was responsible for driving her father to the first drink.

"Later, we're going to have to talk more about this, Marcie. But first we've got a killer to find. Any new ideas?"

"I'm not sure." She fumbled with her door handle.

This time he didn't try to stop her. "Wait here a minute. I'll be right back."

She smiled at the quizzical expression on his face and went into the house. Her mother and Shelby were having a cup of coffee at the kitchen table. Carlinda glanced up, her face blotchy, as if she'd been crying, and Marcie recognized in her eyes a plea for understanding and forgiveness. She put her hand on her mother's arm. "Mom, you okay?"

Carlinda nodded. "Did you go to see him?"

"Yes. Everything's fine, Mom. Vince is a good man. You wouldn't have loved him if he wasn't."

Her mother merely bit her lip.

"How about joining us for a cup?" Shelby invited. "Fresh pot. I made it myself."

Marcie shifted her gaze from her mother to her huge companion and paused. "I'd like to…Mom, but first…I need to get the ranch account books."

Carlinda cleared her throat. "They're in the office."

Marcie caught in her mother's voice a sigh of relief that they were still talking. "I know."

"Did you get the computer already?" Carlinda called out. "That was quick."

"No, I just want to check some things."

"Oh. In the desk, second drawer on the left, unless you moved them."

Marcie went into the timeworn room at the end of the hall, where an old rolltop desk sat between two tall sash windows. The room had changed little since her grandfather's death more than twenty years earlier—Carlinda's time capsule in memory of her beloved parents. It was a Victorian room—heavy red drapes, dark-stained woodwork, threadbare Oriental carpet and wing chairs. One of her grandmother's lace doilies, yellowed now with age, cushioned the humidor on a side table. Marcie imagined she could still smell her grandfather's pipe.

She went to the desk and removed two long, green, cloth-covered ledgers, one for the current year, the other for last year.

The two women looked up when she passed again through the kitchen. Not quite sure what to say, she waved at them and announced, ''I found them,'' and went out the door.

Jim Bob's battered pickup was going down the driveway when she stepped into the yard, and Tucker was leaning against the side of her truck, his arms crossed.

''Sent him to get the fan belt,'' he said when she approached. He glanced at the journals. ''What's up?''

''Where's that piece of paper you found on Dad's body?''

''Inside,'' he said, straightening and dropping his arms. ''Come on.''

She walked past him toward the foreman's cottage, aware of him behind her. She was becoming all too preoccupied with his physical presence, all too sensitive to a casual touch, the sound of his voice—the memory of his kiss.

She mounted the two wooden steps to the narrow porch of the weathered, raw-wood-frame building and reached for the doorknob before catching herself. This was Browder property, but these were his quarters. Shifting to the right, she let Tucker move up beside her.

The window-paneled door was unlocked, as were

most of the buildings on the ranch. It was ironic, she realized, that the very fact that doors and windows were left open made her feel secure, safe. The dead bolts and security systems she'd been forced to use in Houston had only added to her sense of paranoia and danger. At night locked doors had meant she was trapped if Kevin grew violent, and she could never be sure he wouldn't.

Tucker ushered her into the front room, which contained a drab, knotty tweed couch, a couple of badly scarred wooden end tables, two soiled, overstuffed chairs and a portable TV on a metal stand in the corner. The mud-colored shag carpet that covered the center of the yellow pine floor had a traffic pattern crushed into it.

He didn't apologize about the place being a mess for good reason. The room was as neat and clean as its shabbiness would allow.

Tucker led her into the kitchen. With its dull, tawny wainscoting, it reminded her of a movie set from the Great Depression. A stained porcelain sink was suspended from the wall, bare pipes visible beneath it. It had never occurred to her that this building, which was supposed to be someone's home, was so ugly and neglected. She'd have to add fixing it up and making it more livable to her list of things to do.

"This place has the ambience of a barracks or a prison," she quipped.

His head jerked, and he stared at her, then broke into a smile. "You'd need to add the bars and a dozen smelly roommates. Thirsty?"

"No," she responded automatically.

He went to an ancient lever-handled refrigerator

and removed a can of root beer. "You sure?" He extended it to her.

"Well, okay, thanks." She accepted it and pulled the tab while he took out another one for himself. Root beer. Was he, like his uncle, a teetotaler?

"Come on over to the office and I'll get that paper," he said, leading the way.

The office turned out to be the bedroom off the kitchen. The single iron-frame bed covered with a faded blue spread, the metal dresser and nightstand were all studies in utilitarian austerity. Light flooded into the room from two windows. Just inside the doorway was a well-used, gun-metal desk that might have come out of an army-navy surplus store. A computer monitor and keyboard took up most of the surface, except in one corner, where Marcie saw framed pictures of a golden-haired woman in her twenties and a little girl of perhaps five or six.

She lifted the hinged set. "Who are they?"

"My wife and daughter." He sat in the wooden swivel chair and used a key to open the middle drawer.

Marcie's pulse went into high speed, yet she had the light-headed sensation it wasn't pumping any blood. She felt suddenly weak, but the only place to sit down was on the bed, and she didn't want to go there. With trembling fingers, she placed the photos back on the desk.

He'd told her he had no family. He'd lied! The looks he'd given her, the kiss they'd shared—were they part of a game? Was he a playboy out for some fun and she nothing more to him than another conquest? Had she learned nothing from Kevin? After all she'd gone through, she should be immune to come-ons, numb to the attractions of handsome men. Apparently, she'd been fooling herself.

Tucker's broad back was arched as he leaned over and removed an accordion file from the lower right-hand drawer.

"They're lovely," she said, hoping he couldn't hear the tears that threatened to choke her voice. "You must be very proud of them."

He'd told her he was from San Angelo but the only relatives he had there were his mother, sister and his brother's family. Did that mean Tucker and his wife were separated, divorced? Or had she completely misunderstood him? Maybe he meant his office was in San Angelo but his family didn't live in the city. Maybe he had a ranch of his own outside town, and that was why he knew so much about ranching. Maybe...

He didn't say anything as he set the file on his knees and focused all his attention on the gray cotton string tied around it.

"You said...you said you didn't have a family. You said... Where do they live?"

His strong, sure fingers were suddenly all thumbs. She noticed they shook when he tried to undo the bow. Frustrated, he dropped his hands to his thighs, took a lungful of air and said in a low, mournful voice, "They don't live anywhere, Marcie. They're dead."

Ice trickled down her neck at the same time heat burned her cheeks. There was no choice now. She had to sit before her rubbery legs gave out completely. After practically staggering to the bed, she all but collapsed onto the corner of it. The iron foot rail felt cold in her hand.

"I'm sorry," she murmured, the words husky, inadequate. He didn't turn to look at her. It was almost a relief. She didn't want to see the pain she knew she would find on his face, or the sadness she now realized she'd seen lurking in the sea-green depths of his eyes.

Her gaze drifted back to the picture. The woman was pretty, her oval face framed in strawberry-blond curls. "I'm happy," her gentle, glowing expression imparted to the world.

And the child. A teal satin ribbon decorated her pale wispy hair. Her smiling, intelligent face reflected love and happiness, but a hint of innocent mischief was there, as well. Her hand lay comfortably in her mother's so that their closeness went beyond physical bonds. *Joie de vivre,* Marcie thought. The joy of living. But they weren't living. They were dead.

"Will you tell me about them?" she heard herself ask.

He raised his head slowly and swiveled to stare at her with begging, pleading eyes. For what? To be left alone? Or to be consoled? She wasn't sure she could do either.

When he didn't answer, she asked, "What were their names?"

Another moment passed. His Adam's apple bobbed as he swallowed. "My wife's name was Beth. Our daughter's name was Ruth."

"How old was Ruth?" Why was she torturing herself this way? Why was she torturing him? She could hear the agony in his voice, see the anguish on his hard, chiseled features. But something impelled her to delve into this man's life. She had no right to stir up old tragedies, yet it was because she could feel

such heartbreak emanating from him that she wanted
to find out more about him.

"She was six when the picture was taken a few
months before…"

They both let the words trail off. No need to say
"she died."

When she at last spoke, Marcie's voice sounded
like a rusty hinge, but she had to know. "What happened to them?"

CHAPTER EIGHT

HE LIFTED THE BROWN ACCORDION file from his lap and placed it on the desk, then swiveled toward her. But he didn't make eye contact. Instead, he rested his elbows on the armrests of the old wooden chair, joined his hands in front of his flat belly and studied his crossed thumbs.

"I'm sorry," she said. "It's none of my business. I shouldn't have asked—"

"I was a Marine," he said.

Like his Uncle Fletch, Marcie thought.

"Training and deployments kept me away from home several months a year." He concentrated on his fingers, watched their tips come together to form a ball. "I knew Beth didn't like my being away so much, but she didn't begrudge me it, either. I loved the Corps. She understood that, and she was proud to be a Marine wife. She had our daughter to take care of, of course, and her community work, so it wasn't as if she was bored. When she got pregnant again, we were both ecstatic."

He looked down at his hands once more, at the thumbs he was nervously twiddling. "But it troubled her, too," he went on in a low, somber voice. "A friend of ours had been injured, another killed on a recent deployment. That brought up fears I guess had been there a long time but she'd never talked to me about—worries that when I went out on maneuvers I'd be injured or wouldn't come back at all.''

He glanced up at the window, his features empty, at least on the surface. Beneath them, Marcie could sense twisted, roiling emotions.

''Were you going to quit the Marines?'' she asked.

''I didn't want to. But Beth was right—our children needed a living father, not a dead hero. I know what growing up without a dad is like. There was no reason I couldn't leave. I'd served my time. So I filled out the paperwork to get out, but I kept putting off turning it in. I kept hoping she'd change her mind.''

He stood up and walked over to the window, which gave a view of the treeless prairie and the broad hills to the south. Marcie was sure he saw nothing of the land.

''Finally, I went out on what I'd decided was my last deployment. One last time, I told her, and then I'd turn in the paperwork.'' He suddenly chuckled soullessly. ''It's always that 'one last time,' isn't it? The last ski run, on which you break your leg. The last lap of the pool, when you get the cramp. But then, if you break your leg or get a cramp, it's got to be the last, doesn't it?''

Marcie smiled with her lips and waited for him to go on.

''We lived in a quadruplex, four apartments in a two-story house. It was winter. One night the heating system malfunctioned and a fire broke out.''

Silence followed, interrupted only by the whistle and chatter of starlings outside the half-open window.

''Ironic, isn't it?'' Tucker said, still with his back to Marcie. ''Beth wanted me to leave the Corps because it was dangerous for me. Yet she was killed staying at home.''

''I'm sorry,'' Marcie said again, and wished there were words to express the ache she felt in her heart for this man and the family he'd lost, wished there were something she could say that would help alleviate the pain she knew would never completely go away.

Yet, she noted, he'd left the Marine Corps anyway. She would have expected him to stay in when there was no longer a reason to leave, become daring and reckless. Or was leaving the profession he loved the penalty he imposed on himself for what he perceived as his sins?

He stood at the window for another few seconds, straightened his shoulders and turned around. He was in control of himself again.

''You any good at untying knots?'' he asked as he resumed his seat at the desk and picked up the accordion file once more.

She reached across the narrow space separating them and took the file from him. Maybe his self-mastery wasn't as great as he tried to pretend. She didn't miss the tiny tremor in his fingers as their hands touched, or the unaccustomed clumsiness in his movements as he gave up the cardboard folder. Had he noticed that her fingers were cold and trembling, too? He'd asked if she was any good at untying knots. If only all the snags in her life were as easy as the one in her hands at this moment. She was getting tangled up with Tucker McGee in a way she wasn't sure she'd ever be able to unsnarl.

After tugging at the center of the knot, which he had not yet pulled too tight, she quickly unraveled the skein and handed the folder back to him. He smiled self-deprecatingly as he accepted it, flipped it open, removed the plastic-protected note and handed it to her.

Forcing herself to do a mental shake, she tried to concentrate on the reason she was there. She rose from the bed and placed the paper flat on the desk, confirmed what her father had jotted on it, then riffled through one of the books she'd brought with her. She referred to the matrix, then to the ledger, again to the scribbled numbers and turned another page of the ranch accounts.

Tucker glanced up at her. "Do they—"

"Yes," she said before he had a chance to finish the question. "They match. At least, the first three columns do. Can you tell me when cattle were rustled from Vince's place, and how many were taken each time?"

"Sure," he said. "I've got it all in my notes."

Again he delved into the accordion file, and this time removed a thin sheaf of papers. "You think...?"

"I'm not sure what I think."

He stood up at her side and peered over her shoulder. She tried to ignore the electrical aura his closeness generated, the energy building inside her. She lined up the documents on the desk. Together, they examined them.

"Here," she said, pointing with one hand to the top row of numbers on her father's matrix and with the other to Tucker's notes and the Lazy B figures.

8   10   2   10

"Eight is the month," she explained. "August. Ten is the day. Two is the number of units that were taken from our place. The last ten is the number taken from Vince's ranch.''

He compared the next line of numbers with the notes and calendar.

9   14   5   15

''September 14,'' he said, his finger trailing across the plastic-coated paper. ''Five units taken from here, and—'' he ran a finger down the page ''—fifteen from the Prudhomme place.''

And so it went, down the rest of the lists.

10	28	6	18
11	17	3	26
12	4	8	22
1	6	10	30
2	15	7	36
3	27	5	18
4	14	6	49

''How did you figure it out?'' Tucker asked.

She told him about Dustin's pantomime at the orphanage. ''There was a date, not a time on the make-believe watch.'' She sat again on the foot of the bed. ''Something was bothering me while I was watching his performance, but I couldn't figure out what it was. Dusty told me he found out Lennie's been selling cattle over in San Angelo. It could be innocent, I suppose. He's been in the business before. He could just be picking up a few extra bucks by acting as someone's agent, but—''

"So you think Lennie's involved in this?" It wasn't really a question.

"Dad and Lennie were two peas in a pod. If one had a deal going, chances are the other was included in it."

"You know what this means?" Tucker asked soberly.

She pursed her lips and looked down at the paper. At the last three lines:

5	3	4	27
6	17	9	34
7	23	12	43

"The numbers go into the future," she said quietly. Moving to the window at the head of the bed, she peered out at the blanket of wild bluebonnets covering the coarse, dry land. "Dad was in on the rustling. He was conspiring with someone to steal cattle from himself and from Vince Prudhomme."

"Why?" Tucker asked.

She thought she might have the answer, but it brought with it a cloud of depression. "I've been doing some thinking... Vince's wife died a little over a year ago."

"Uncle Fletch said he took it pretty hard." Tucker's voice had deepened, and she realized she was dredging up more unhappy memories.

Marcie nodded. "They were devoted to each other. I liked Doris. She was fun to be with. But with her gone, Vince's free to remarry."

He gaped at her, but just for a moment. Obviously, he hadn't thought of it and felt he should have. "Your mother?"

She lifted her shoulders in a reluctant shrug. "I don't know..." She didn't want to consider the possibility that her mother had been unfaithful to the man she married, committed adultery with the man she'd once deserted. "But I imagine that when Doris died, Dad began to worry maybe Mom and Vince would want to get back together again. As I told you, if Mom divorced Dad, she'd take the ranch with her. About the best Dad could expect was half of the Green Valley place, since that was acquired by them jointly after they were married. But the land is worthless as far as making money on it is concerned, and half of zero is zero."

"How does this play into your father's death? It seems to me it would make more sense if your father killed your mother, or even Vince."

"If Dad was afraid Mom was going to leave him for Vince, maybe he began rustling Vince's cattle to ruin him."

"And stole some of his own cattle to divert attention from himself," Tucker concluded.

Marcie agreed. "You saw the numbers, and they're going up. The Lazy B can afford to lose a few head. Vince can't." Then she added, "Besides, if Dad's been rustling our own cattle, we're not really losing them."

"Somebody's been stealing cattle from a couple of the spreads over by Spring Mesa," Tucker noted. "Do you think he was involved in those jobs, too?"

Marcie's glance shot up. She'd forgotten about the rustling going on in other parts of the Coyote River valley. "When did it start over there?"

"According to Uncle Fletch, it's been going on for a couple of years."

"Since before Doris died, then."

"Yes. By at least six months."

Marcie breathed a sigh of relief. If her notion was right, her father's treachery was focused on just one victim for a very particular reason. That was bad enough, but at least it made sense in a twisted sort of way.

"It's more likely the thefts over in Spring Mesa are what gave Dad the idea."

"Do you think your father was personally involved in the rustling?"

"You mean did he actually go out and round up cattle, load them into trucks and take them to market?" She laughed. "Not likely. About the heaviest work Dad did in the last twenty years was twelve-ounce curls at the bar."

Tucker grinned, then turned serious. "So who did it for him?"

"There's only one person he would trust with that kind of dirty work."

"Lennie Gruen," Tucker said, shaking his head. "But I can't see him roping steers, either."

She pictured the flabby corpulence of the man; the bulbous nose; the soft, clammy hands. "No," she agreed, "but he was a good chief of staff when Dad was in politics. Senator Browder had all the connections in high places. Lennie's contacts were a little lower on the food chain."

"You figure that's why your father went up to the bowl—to meet Lennie?"

"I don't see why. They saw each other all the time at the Beer Bucket and other watering holes. If they wanted to have a private conversation, they could have gone to Lennie's house, or any open field for that matter. Why go to that out-of-the-way location?''

"Unless someone else insisted on meeting him there,'' Tucker offered.

"But who? And again, why there?'' Marcie paused to consider her own question. "How about, because there was something there that one or both of them had to see.''

"Like what?''

"Like cattle that weren't tagged with either Browder or Prudhomme marks.''

Tucker rubbed the bridge of his nose and tried to comprehend what she was getting at.

"You saw the marshaling area up at the bowl,'' she reminded him. "Plenty of room for several hundred head of cattle, and convenient access to a public road. Suppose someone else's cattle were there, too.''

"You mean somebody else was using your land as a staging area? Why? It's not convenient to anyone else's grazing pastures, except Vince's.'' Then the light dawned. "You're not suggesting Lennie, or whoever was doing the actual stealing, took some of the cattle off Vince's place and found they weren't Vince's?''

"Maybe they were some of the cattle from over near Spring Mesa.''

"Vince stealing cattle?'' Tucker chuckled.

"Or someone working for him,'' she offered, a trifle miffed at his easy rejection of her idea. "Okay, I know I'm grasping at straws. But somewhere in my father's trip to the bowl is the answer to his death, if only we could figure it out.''

"Fair enough. But let me give you two reasons this theory won't wash,'' Tucker said earnestly. "First,

Vince was the one who asked me to come here and investigate. Why do that if he's the guilty party? Even if he thinks himself pretty slick—and he doesn't strike me as a devious man—why take the chance that I might hit on the truth?''

With a stab of conscience, she realized they were talking about her father. As a young girl, she'd always called him "Mr. Prudhomme." Later he became "Vince." Neither sounded appropriate now. Would she ever address him as "Dad"?

"Unless he thought you weren't smart enough to figure it out," she taunted the man sitting at the desk.

"There's that, I suppose." His jaunty grin quickly faded. "The second reason is Uncle Fletcher would never be a party to such a scheme."

"It doesn't seem likely," she admitted in frustration. "But there's some reason Dad was up at the bowl. What is it?"

WHEN MARCIE RETURNED TO the house to put the account ledgers back where they belonged, she found Shelby alone in the kitchen, wearing a red-and-orange muumuu that was one shade shy of being garish. "Where's Mom?"

Shelby pulled a square plastic container of lettuce and tomatoes from the refrigerator. "In town. She needed to get her hair done for the memorial service, so I made an appointment for her with Ethlene to get a perm."

Marcie started for the hallway leading to the office. "Good idea. She could use a break." She continued on and returned a few minutes later to find the table set for two, a variety of cold cuts, salads, breads and condiments on the counter.

"Sit down," Shelby invited. "It's past lunchtime, and I bet you haven't eaten a thing."

"I'm really not—"

"Do you want coffee, tea or pop with your sandwich?"

"I...I'll get a Coke."

"Good. Get me one, too. You want roast beef, ham or chicken? Swiss, cheddar or provolone? Mustard or mayo? White, rye or wheat?"

Marcie retrieved two cans from the refrigerator, popped their tops and surveyed the counter. "Beef, I guess. On wheat. No cheese. Just lettuce and tomato. A little mayonnaise."

Shelby prepared the sandwiches with the speed and dexterity of an old pro—which, of course, she was—garnishing the two halves with black olives on toothpicks. "I thought this might be a good time for us to sit and visit. I haven't really had a chance to talk to you since you got back. Been a while since we've seen each other."

Marcie always enjoyed her chats with Shelby, catching up on local events and the lives of her friends. But somehow she didn't think this discussion was going to be about the interval since her last visit. She bit into the sandwich. Why did salads and sandwiches always taste better when someone else fixed them?

"Your ma's going through a rough time right now," Shelby said as she worked at the counter on her own lunch.

Marcie nodded. "I know."

"I'm not talking about your daddy's death. That's bad enough, but she's been prepared for it for some time."

Marcie swallowed. ''You mean she knew he was sick?''

Shelby set her own plate on the other side of the table. Her sandwich was twice the size of Marcie's.

''No. That came as a shock.'' She took a generous bite of food and talked around it. ''What I mean is that she was aware the situation couldn't go on indefinitely without something happening—an accident with his truck, maybe a heart attack or a stroke. It was pretty obvious his health was deteriorating.''

Marcie couldn't decide what to say, so she took another bite of her sandwich.

''What's got your ma upset is what this has done to you. She loves you very much, you know?''

''And I love her…''

''But you're disappointed in her.'' Shelby took a huge chomp out of her sandwich, chewed and observed Marcie. ''You found out yesterday she's more human than you'd realized, that she's got some flaws and weaknesses you wish she'd kept hidden from you.''

Marcie finished half her sandwich and pushed the plate aside, the food suddenly tasteless.

''Honey, she wishes she could have kept it from you, too. She's been afraid from the day you were born that you'd find out. And now that you have, she's afraid you hate her.''

''Oh, Shelby, I don't hate her.''

''No, but right now you don't like her very much, and you've lost respect for her.''

''That's not true, either.''

Shelby smiled softly. ''I think it is.'' There was no acrimony in her words, just quiet sympathy. She took a sip of her Coke and rested back, making the wooden chair groan. "Let me tell you some things you don't know, things that might surprise you."

Please, no more surprises, Marcie wanted to cry out. *I've had enough surprises for a lifetime.*

"Your mother and Vince had been going together on and off since high school. If they'd gotten married right after college like they planned, I suppose they might have been happy. But there was always a certain amount of friction between them. Believe me, the argument they had over his going into the service wasn't the first one, and I don't think it would have been the last."

Funny, Marcie thought, Vince said they saw eye to eye on everything—except the war. Which one, Vince or Shelby, had the flawed memory?

"I've always suspected your ma never told Vince she was pregnant," Shelby continued, "because she knew deep down inside they weren't really meant for each other."

"And she and Mason were, I suppose?" Marcie retorted, eyebrows raised in disbelief.

Shelby smiled broadly at her. "Yep." She eyed Marcie's half sandwich. "You going to eat that?"

Marcie shook her head.

Shelby reached across the table, picked the sandwich up and took a healthy bite. The conspiratorial smile returned to her face. "I told you you'd be surprised. Truth is, your mother loved Mason more than you know."

Marcie remembered the wistful expression on her mother's face when she'd talked about the star quarterback courting her.

"God, he was beautiful back then." Shelby sighed. "Had the hots for him myself for a while. That body…'' She plunged the last corner of the sandwich into her mouth, chewed and swallowed. ''Oh, he and Carli used to fight, but your ma told me once that making up made it all worthwhile. She didn't like his playing around, of course, especially with those young girls. It became the major issue once he quit football. But before then, when he was away, she could pretend it didn't happen. It was only when word spread in Coyote Springs about his fooling around that she made her big mistake. You've got to realize how humiliated she felt. That's when she blurted out about you.''

Marcie could feel her heart sink. She understood the shame in knowing a husband was sleeping with other women. She also knew her mother had used her to humiliate the man she supposedly loved.

''Didn't you ever wonder why your ma never divorced him?''

''Because of the ranch…''

''That's why he didn't divorce her,'' Shelby pointed out. ''He'd lose everything. But why do you think your ma didn't throw him out?'' When Shelby received no immediate answer, she said, ''Because she loved him. She wasn't going to split up the ranch, but she couldn't turn him out without a penny, either. She loved him, Marcie. Not wisely but well, as the saying goes.''

Marcie twirled the Coke can in her hand. What kind of love is it that destroys people's lives?

''She made him promise never to tell you what she'd told him, and he kept that promise. I wish to God he hadn't. Maybe things would have been different, better, if it had all come out in the open. But who knows. It might have been worse.''

She rose from the table and picked up their plates. "Something snapped in Mason after that," Shelby said, standing by the counter. "The way he saw himself and Carli, and even you, changed. It was as if, in a moment of bitterness and pain and temper, your mother had put a knife in him and twisted, and when she did, she let out all the warmth that was in the man. Neither of them ever recovered. All these years your ma's had to live with the knowledge that she'd forfeited his love. And now she's afraid she's lost yours, too."

"She told you all this?"

"Over time." Shelby started to carry the dishes to the sink but turned back. "Don't hate her, Marcie. I know you're hurting right now, but she's hurting more. And she's been hurting for a long, long time."

CHAPTER NINE

AFTER LUNCH MARCIE SADDLED Sparkle and went riding, not into the heart of the Lazy B ranch, but along the fence line that paralleled the public road. The sun was warm and soothing. By late afternoon it would be hot and, unless a breeze was blowing, could become uncomfortable. She hadn't mentioned where she was headed when she left the house. Shelby didn't ask, and no one else was around to question her. It had been a couple of hours since she'd been with Tucker. His pickup was back in its usual spot by the foreman's cottage. She wondered if he was still inside but was oddly grateful when he didn't materialize. She needed time alone, time to think.

The Beer Bucket was some five miles down the road. Her father's favorite tavern wasn't her destination, however. More like a starting point. She should have thought of making this excursion sooner.

The last place her father had been seen alive was at the saloon. From there he'd taken Dusty's dune buggy and driven off. Where to? Certainly not home. If he'd been planning to return to the ranch, the fastest, most direct way would have been west along the road Marcie was paralleling. Besides, he took the buggy because his pickup was almost out of gas. The service station was on the way home, which meant he must have been going in the opposite direction.

That seemed clear enough. But what was so all-fired important that he didn't have time to go a mile out of his way to gas up?

There was one obvious destination. Lennie Gruen's house was a good ten miles east by road. As the crow flies, however, across a corner of the Browder ranch, it was probably less than five. Could her father have been going to see Lennie? Why? Because Dustin had found out about the cattle being sold in San Angelo?

No other plausible explanation had occurred to her by the time the low, tin-roofed beer hall came into view on the other side of the road. She kept to the trail. The barbed-wire topped fence was in good repair—no gates, no breaks. Her father couldn't have entered the Lazy B in the immediate vicinity of the bar. But she remembered there was a padlocked gate about a mile farther down the line.

At a moderate walk, Sparkle reached it in a matter of minutes. The heavy chain was still in place, the padlock secure. The wide gravel shoulder of the highway that gave access to the rusty steel pipes of the cattle guard offered no hint of recent traffic. She followed the hard-packed caliche roadway inside the fence line as it wended its way through mesquite and cactus to a low draw that would turn into a muddy stream when it rained. The last rain had come less than a week earlier. The ground was barely damp now, but it had obviously been muddy and slick when a wheeled vehicle went through it last, for tire marks were deeply etched in drying curls of mud. If looks weren't deceiving, the tread pattern was the same as the one up at the bowl where the buggy had been found.

Marcie's pulse quickened and a chill crept up her

spine. She had the same eerie feeling of being watched she'd had when she was at the Green Valley place looking for her father. Sitting straighter in the saddle, she scanned the land around her, but the young mesquite saplings gave nothing away.

What was she looking for? Perhaps a clue that could lead her one step closer to her father's murderer.

Had the sheriff been here? Had he found this spot the same way she had? For that matter, what was the sheriff doing to find the killer? She'd heard nothing from him since his early-morning visit Wednesday.

She dismounted in a little cove of spring grass and dropped the reins, knowing the mare would be content to munch the sweet shoots. Then she trooped around to the drying mud hole. The area was surrounded by spidery clumps of poisonous Johnson grass, tiny sprays of rye, the pervasive thorny sprouts of mesquite and an occasional patch of wildflowers: yellow snakeweed, lavender powderpuffs, wild onions and tiny primitive daisies. The colors were dazzling now, but over the next few weeks and months they would wither into dry tangles of ocher and brown, tan and dull pewter.

Even in this jumble of color, something caught her eye, something metallic. She approached the base of a waist-high gray rock and paused over the object, then squatted to get a better look at it. A brass casing.

A shiver slid down her backbone. It took a moment for her to realize it wasn't the piece of metal on the ground that had her heart pounding but the feeling again of being watched. Near panic, she sprang to her feet and spun around.

Tucker stood a few yards away, facing her. The

grin on his lips did nothing to relieve the thudding in her chest. Just intensified it, momentarily draining her willpower. She stood as motionless as he, their eyes locked.

"Do you always sneak up on people?" The words were soft and timorous at first, but the sound of her own voice made her more assertive. "And how did you manage to do it without my hearing you?"

His humorous expression relaxed into a reassuring smile. "You were so intent on your quest you didn't hear me."

As if to emphasize his point, a crow cawed overhead and a bee buzzed around a clump of young broomweed at her feet—sounds she hadn't heard a few moments earlier. Was he telling the truth? She looked at him. The afternoon sun cast the planes and contours of his shirt and jeans in distracting relief. Marcie realized she'd again stopped hearing the sounds of nature.

Hooking his thumbs in his belt loops, Tucker took a step toward her. "Sorry. I didn't mean to startle you."

"You haven't told me why you're here." The man's presence disconcerted her, unraveled the already frayed edges of her composure. Except now it wasn't fear that kept her pulse throbbing. She wasn't afraid of him, not physically. In spite of his imposing size and obvious strength, she felt no threat of violence in Tucker McGee. Kevin Hayes had been strong, too, but in him she'd mistaken ferocity for determination, obsession for strength of character. The truth had been in his eyes all the time, she now realized—if only she'd known how to read them. Tucker's were powerful, captivating, but they were also caring. His eyes, she saw, spoke of a will to heal, not to hurt.

Another reality occurred to her, but one she was far more reluctant to acknowledge. She was falling in love with Tucker. The idea, exciting and ungovernable, taunted and frightened her.

He moved to within arm's length of her, and for a fleeting moment she was sure he was going to reach out and brush his hand against her cheek. The mere anticipation had warmth capering through her.

"Probably for the same reason you are," he commented, his gaze continuing to hold hers. "To find out where your father went after he left the bar."

She glanced around for a horse or a vehicle but saw nothing. "How did you get here?"

"I left Cisca just past the boulders there, with your mare." He pointed to the coarse, dull gray rocks sticking out of a dense field of prickly pear cactus. "I saw you cut through here—"

"You followed me?" Ever since she'd reached the gate, she'd felt someone watching her. Now she knew who it was. This time. He said he hadn't been the one observing her at the bowl, but...

The corners of his eyes webbed with amusement. "Only if it's possible to follow from the opposite direction." He gazed at her and a certain solemnity returned to his demeanor, though the smile didn't completely fade from his lips. "I followed you only from the gate, Marcie."

"Why didn't you call out?"

"I could have," he admitted. "But I wanted to see where you were going."

"Spying again."

He didn't respond. He only stared. To keep her

hands from fluttering, she jammed them into her pockets. Unable to bear the intensity of his scrutiny, she looked away.

"Are you afraid of me?" he asked boldly, yet in a voice that was solicitous and vulnerable at the same time. "Do you think I want to harm you?"

"No!" she shot back. "No. I...I don't—"

"Then what?"

She realized she was hunching her shoulders but couldn't tell if it was by an act of will or defensiveness. She let them sag. Her knees had suddenly grown weak. Glancing around her, she took a small pace back to one of the boulders on her right.

Tucker sprang forward and circled her shoulder with a warm, firm hand. He eased her onto the natural seat of the cool stone.

"You're shaking," he said, sitting beside her, clasping her all the more tightly. "What's the matter?" he asked. "I would never hurt..." He loosened his grip on her.

She countered by leaning deeper against his hard chest. "Just hold me a minute."

This time he wrapped both arms around her. It was impossible not to curl into the shelter of his embrace. She snuggled against his shoulder. He stroked her hair.

Eager to see the reassurance she knew she'd find in his eyes, she lifted her head. But her search didn't get past his lips.

He brought his mouth down to hers. A gentle touch at first. Warm flesh against warm flesh. The softness quickly turned to hardness. His tongue probed until it came in full, moist contact with hers.

There was no denying him. She had no will to resist, no desire to push away. She wanted to experience him as much as he did her. She could feel the tension in his body, taste the desperate need in the passion of his kiss, in the way he explored her. His warmth flowed into her, as she knew it would. She responded to his demands, an eager partner in his exploration. She wanted him as much as he wanted her.

They separated and he climbed to his feet, his back arched, rigid, powerful. But it was the sensation of his kiss, strong, gentle and vulnerable that lingered on her lips, on her mind. Tucker's embrace renewed a hunger too long unrequited. When he turned, she contemplated his somber face, the dark brooding expression.

Did he see Marcie Browder sitting before him or a woman called Beth? Did he desire a living woman or, in touching her, only mourn more deeply a dead one? Whatever the answer, Marcie knew they weren't ready to go forward. Not yet. Almost with relief she backed away from the promise his touch had offered. She wasn't yet sure of herself, either.

"You came here for a reason," he said a minute later, his voice almost level, "and you found something. What was it?"

She got up from the now-warm stone, walked to the spot where he'd found her and pointed to the shell casing on the dry ground.

Slipping the tips of his long fingers into his jeans pockets, he strolled toward her. She wasn't fooled by the careless stride. His set features didn't quite mask the war of emotions battling beneath them. He peered down to where she pointed, still keeping a couple of feet between them, and Marcie realized this time he was afraid of her.

He bent to pick up the shiny brass object. A commanding voice behind them ordered, "Don't touch that."

They both spun around to find themselves facing Rudy Kraus.

Tucker took a deep breath, held it, then let it out slowly. Like Marcie a few minutes earlier, he'd failed to sense someone lurking. But in his case he didn't have the excuse that he was intent on an investigation. He'd allowed himself to be distracted by a beautiful woman, lured by the betrayal of his body. That kind of carelessness, he reminded himself, got people killed.

"Sheriff!" Marcie exclaimed breathlessly.

The white-haired man shifted his attention from Tucker to her. "What did you find?"

"I'm not sure," she answered, her voice shaky, uncertain. She pointed to the clump of cactus. "It looks like a cartridge shell."

"It is," Kraus confirmed, though he was still standing more than a dozen yards away in a cleft between two vertical rocks.

"But—" Marcie began.

Tucker let a slow smile creep across his face. "You've been here all the time." What a careless idiot he'd become. To an old-timer, familiar with the land and people, this would be an obvious target for investigation. He should have known from the lawman's reputation that he'd check out details, lay traps.

Marcie pulled her lips between her teeth, and Tucker knew exactly what she was thinking. He could almost hear her mind working: had the sheriff overheard their conversation? Had he seen their kiss?

Rudy Kraus didn't say or do anything to confirm

Tucker's observation. He just looked at him with a kind of aloof confidence.

"Why d'y'all come here?" he asked Marcie.

She surveyed both men. "We…I've been trying to figure out where Dad went after he left the Beer Bucket the other evening."

"And you?" he addressed Tucker.

"Checking fences, when I saw Marcie."

"The two of you just happened to be in the same place at the same time?" Kraus's brows arched pointedly. The incredulous expression confirmed that the old man didn't expect an answer and might not believe one if he got it.

How much had he been able to hear from his hiding place? Tucker asked himself. Did he think they'd met here as lovers? Or perhaps as conspirators?

Kraus looked at Marcie again. "So what did you decide?"

She shuffled uncomfortably. "We've been testing out theories."

"Go on." She hesitated, so he added, "I need all the help I can get, Marcie. I know you and your daddy didn't get along real well, that you even threatened him." He paused to let the words sink in. "But we're both after the same thing, your dad's killer."

Marcie lowered her head for a moment, duly chastised. "Dusty said Dad took the dune buggy because the truck was low on gas."

"You have a problem with that?"

"No, but Dad may have been only using it as an excuse. After all, the gas station was on the way home, and Dusty obviously didn't run out of fuel."

"I'm sure you've already thought of that, Sheriff,"

Tucker intervened. "Have you been able to verify it?"

"The attendant confirmed Dustin drove in just as he was closing and filled up both tanks," Kraus acknowledged. "The guy remembered because it took a few minutes and he'd already closed down the cash register. Dustin had to use his credit card."

That made checking times convenient, Tucker thought. "Did he say which way Dustin went when he left?"

"Back the way he came," the old man replied.

Toward the Beer Bucket, Tucker noted. But he could easily have driven past it and returned later. "How long was he gone from the bar?"

Kraus massaged the back of his neck. "Depending on who you talk to, anywhere from fifteen minutes to an hour and a half. No one was paying close attention." He turned to Marcie. "You were saying…"

She pulled on her earlobe as she replied. "I got to thinking that maybe not having gas in the truck was an excuse to take Dusty's buggy. It's the type of game Dad would have enjoyed playing."

"And you think he came here with it? Why?"

"This is the only place, or at least the nearest place, with the kind of rough terrain where he could really get the thrill of it, check it out."

"So you think he took it for the fun of it." Kraus glanced down at the ground. "Looks like he did a bunch of slippin' and slidin'. But it still doesn't explain what he was doing up at the Green Valley bowl."

Marcie shrugged. "Maybe when he left here he decided to go for a long ride, feel the wind in his face."

The sheriff looked off into the distance, rubbed one cheek, pursed his lips and rubbed the other one.

Tucker had a sudden picture of Marcie's chin upraised to the sun, her auburn hair longer and tousled in a crisp breeze. "Did you ever ride a motorcycle?"

The question, seeming to come out of nowhere, caught her off guard, but the confusion lasted barely a split second. She ran her tongue across her teeth. "I had one in college for a little while, in my rough-and-tumble phase."

"I hope you wore a helmet."

"Most of the time. But there is something exhilarating about letting the wind ruffle your hair."

At a gently intruding "Ahem," they both looked over at the sheriff.

"So you think your father just happened to decide to go to a remote corner of his ranch to watch the sunset," Kraus said, "and when he got there he just happened to meet someone who wanted to kill him?"

Tucker knew it didn't sound particularly convincing, and clearly the sheriff wasn't buying it, but the conjecture held a certain appeal. It also put a great big hole in the theory he and Marcie had been concocting that her father had gone there to meet someone.

"Sheriff, I'm sure you noticed the other day that livestock had recently been corralled at the bowl," Tucker observed.

Kraus let out a weary breath. "Yes," he drawled.

"Marcie and I did some checking around the area a couple of days ago. We think that's where stolen cattle are being marshaled to be shipped out to wherever they're being sold."

"Go on."

"Browder may have gone up there and surprised the rustlers."

"And they killed him." Kraus made the statement sound like a question.

Tucker nodded.

"Pretty drastic action on the part of sneak thieves."

"What if my father recognized them?" Marcie asked.

"Possibly," he concluded without conviction.

Tucker studied the lines and folds of the aging peace officer's weathered face. "You don't buy it. Why?"

Kraus shook his head. "That dune buggy of her brother's. It's pretty noisy as I recall. It would be mighty difficult to sneak up on someone in it, especially people who were on the alert. Seems to me they'd have plenty of time to either hide or skedaddle."

"So what's your theory?"

"If he went up there voluntarily, it seems more likely it was to meet somebody."

Tucker and Marcie exchanged glances.

"Meet who? And why?" she asked.

"I reckon when we figure that out, we'll know who killed him."

Kraus walked across their path directly to the shell casing on the ground. "I wondered who would come looking for this."

So Kraus had already found it and staked out the place in anticipation of someone showing up to retrieve it. The grandfatherly old-timer was indeed sharper and more wily than he made himself out to be.

The sheriff removed a small plastic bag from his

hip pocket, bent a little stiffly and with a gloved hand placed the piece of evidence in the bag. He held it up in front of his face and examined the shell.

''What do you make of this?'' he asked, not specifying which of the two people he was talking to. Tucker wasn't fooled by the seemingly casual way in which he posed the question. Rudy Kraus had already reached his own conclusions. When neither of them said anything, he went on. ''There's no corrosion on it.'' He rolled it around in the plastic. ''So it hasn't been here too long. I'd say since the rain we had a few days back.'' He slipped the package into his breast pocket, adding casually, ''It's also a 9 mm, the same caliber that could have been used on your daddy.''

Marcie took a step backward. ''You think Dad was killed here?''

An out-of-place piece finally fit. Tucker had been uncomfortable about something when he found Mason's body up at the bowl, but he hadn't been able to put his finger on it until now. Caliche. The sticky, cream-colored substance had not only been crusted on the backs of Mason's boot heels but embedded on the bottom side of his shirt and pants. It was out of place because there was no caliche at the bowl, only rich, brown soil.

''Could he have been shot here and transported to the bowl in the buggy?'' Tucker asked.

''It's a possibility,'' Kraus confirmed.

Marcie looked from one man to the other and asked what was on all their minds. ''Why?''

The question hung in the air unanswered. Finally, Kraus repositioned his white Stetson on his head.

"Not much point in hanging around here anymore. I've got other leads to follow."

"Do you have a suspect, then?" asked Marcie.

"Everybody's a suspect."

"Everyone?" It gave her a queasy feeling to realize this kind old man, whom she'd known all her life, might actually regard her as a potential murderer. "You don't really think I killed him, do you?"

Kraus scratched his head and looked at her with basset-hound eyes. "No, Marcie. I don't. But I can't exclude you as a suspect, either. I've got to do my job. The fact is, most murder victims are killed by people they know. Domestic violence—mayhem by family members or close friends of the victim—is still the most lethal form."

Except he wasn't my father, she almost blurted out. Would awareness of that fact relieve her of suspicion, she wondered, or increase it?

"I think you had a very good reason," he went on, "to be angry with your daddy after what he did to your ma. Your last words to him, as I recall the report, were that you'd kill him."

Her stomach was in knots, the sound of panic in her voice. "Rudy— Sheriff, that was an expression. I didn't mean it literally. Besides, I threatened him only if he attacked me or my mother again."

"How do I know he didn't?"

"But—"

He held up his hand in a silencing motion. "And you knew his routine, where to find him."

"Sheriff," Tucker interjected, "Browder didn't follow routine the night he was killed. He took his son's off-road vehicle, and as far as we know, that was the one and only time he ever did."

Kraus listened in thought, his lips pursed. Then he said, ''The two of you came directly to the spot where he may have been ambushed. Coincidence? Maybe. But I got to tell you, I'm mighty leery of coincidences.''

''She couldn't have done it,'' Tucker nearly barked.

''Why's that?'' the old man inquired coolly.

''Because she was with me at the ranch the entire evening.''

CHAPTER TEN

MARCIE REALIZED ALMOST too late that her mouth was hanging open. She managed to clamp it shut before the lawman turned to her.

"Is that right?" It wasn't a question as much as a challenge.

Why in the world had Tucker said they were together? It certainly wasn't true. Not that the idea was so terribly abhorrent. She enjoyed his company and found herself looking forward to it more and more when they were apart. That she did made her wonder why. After her divorce last year, she'd had no desire for male companionship. She hadn't sought it and had rejected it when it was offered.

Until she'd met Tucker McGee. What was it that made him different?

For one thing, she didn't feel threatened by him. There was none of the male posturing her ex-husband had been so fond of. None of the psychological muscle flexing Kevin had liked to indulge in, mind games that left her feeling useless and ungrateful. Tucker, on the other hand, not only respected her opinions, he wasn't intimidated by them. He didn't perceive her strengths as an indictment of his weakness.

Clearly, he felt grief for the loss of his wife and daughter, and on the emotional level he blamed himself for what had happened to them. But he was also intellectually honest with himself. That integrity of character, she was confident, would eventually help him find closure. He didn't wear his pain on his sleeve, though he couldn't keep it completely from his eyes. For beneath the torment and remorse for a lost family, Marcie sensed a man who was essentially at peace with himself. And that made him easy to be with. Desirable.

She felt him watching her, waiting for her reply, and she remembered the sheriff had asked her a question. Then a second thought intervened. Was the lie to protect her or to give himself an alibi? Where had he been the night her father was killed?

"I was at the ranch all evening," she equivocated. "And all night."

"I see," Kraus said in a lowered voice, as if he were disappointed. It took a moment for her to realize he'd misinterpreted her last remark to mean she and Tucker had spent the night together. She glanced at Tucker, saw a flicker of amusement that made her feel even more guilty.

"Did you check the buggy's fuel tank?" he asked hurriedly.

The sheriff hitched up his belt, a sour expression on his face. "It wasn't out of gas, if that's what you mean. Running low, but there was probably enough to get back from the Green Valley place."

Tucker shrugged. "Just an idea."

The sheriff gave him a distrustful glance before walking through the rocky passage he'd come through earlier. A moment later, Marcie recognized the rumble of his four-wheel-drive Cherokee. He'd hidden it well.

Immediately, she looked at Tucker standing a few

feet away. He was watching her, waiting for the inevitable question.

"Why did you lie just now?"

"I didn't." He sauntered away, trying to be casual, not quite succeeding.

She took three strides, reached out and grabbed his arm, forcing him to face her.

"You said we were together the other night."

"I said we were both there at the ranch. It's true. You were in your room. I was in mine."

She could feel the corded muscle of his forearm. "How do you know where I was?"

"I can see your bedroom window from mine. I was reading that night and noticed your light on. You passed in front of the window several times, so I know you were there."

He sounded like a Peeping Tom, but the angry—almost frightened—coldness in his response wasn't that of a voyeur. This wasn't a man to stand by and watch. He was rattled about something. What?

"You want to know what book I was reading?" he asked, trying to make light of it. "Tom Clancy's *The Cardinal of the Kremlin*. You'll find it on my bedside table."

He did an about-face and started toward where they'd left the horses.

She followed him. "Why did you ask about the gas in the dune buggy? Did you really think Dad went up there and got shot to death because he ran out of gas?"

He spun around, regarded her with eyes that seemed infinitely capable of surprises. One moment cold and impersonal, the next warm and caring. Now they seemed distant, as though his mind were somewhere else. He crossed his arms and leaned his hips against a boulder. Not the one they'd sat on when he kissed her, she noted, as if now that one were somehow special, sacred.

"Of course not," he said. "Based on the shell casing you found, it's pretty clear someone fired a gun here in the not-too-distant past. On that little bit of evidence, we're all jumping to the conclusion that your father was killed here."

"There are the buggy tracks," she pointed out.

"They could have been made earlier by your brother."

"True," she conceded. "If the sheriff has the bullet that killed Dad, he can perform a ballistics check on the shell to see whether it matches the one—"

"It wouldn't be conclusive. You can match bullets to gun and rifle barrels but not to shells."

"You seem to know a lot about the subject."

"I was an expert marksman in the Marines."

"And they taught you ballistics?" She slanted him an incredulous glance. "I've won my share of trophies at target shooting as well as skeet, but I never learned anything about ballistics."

"It spurred my interest, so I studied up on it."

"That still won't prove anything, will it? Even if the shell and bullet match?" she asked after a moment's reflection. "The casing will only suggest Dad was threatened here—"

"And forced to drive up to the bowl," Tucker completed her thought.

"So we come back to the same question—why go to the bowl?"

She leaned against a sloping rock, facing him, distracted by the way sunspots, penetrating the frilly canopy of mesquite trees, danced across the jeans molded to his thighs. His facial features were muted in the shade cast by his wide-brimmed Stetson. It didn't make him less attractive, only more mysterious.

"Maybe we've been looking at this backward," Tucker said. "Our assumption is that someone was threatening your father, confronted him and shot him. Suppose it was the other way around. Did your father own a handgun?"

She shook her head. "There are several rifles and shotguns in the gun case in the study, but no handguns."

Tucker was surprised. Most ranchers owned one or two pistols or revolvers for protection against varmints, though few ever used them.

"Dad didn't like handguns. He thought they were more dangerous than useful. When he was a kid, one of his playmates found his father's .38, accidentally discharged it and killed himself. Why do you ask?"

"My 9 mm Beretta is missing."

She gaped at him, trying to comprehend the implications of what he had just said. "You own the type of gun that killed my father, and now it's missing?"

He kneaded the back of his neck. "After the sheriff said your father might have been shot with a 9 mm, I went and checked on mine. I kept it in the bottom right-hand drawer of the desk. It's gone."

She remembered the funny look Dustin gave Tucker when the sheriff speculated on the type of weapon that might have been used. At the time she'd dismissed it as a symptom of her brother's hangover. But it hadn't been that at all. Dustin knew. Marcie's whole body began to tremble. She pushed away from the rock. Crazy thoughts were beginning to roar through her head. Tucker McGee had been secretly hired by her mother and biological father, supposedly to investigate cattle rustling. Two weeks later, Mason was killed by the same kind of weapon the investigator owned.

It was absurd to think…she didn't like the suspicion bouncing through her head. It was a ridiculous notion, not worth a second thought. She wouldn't even consider the possibility that Tucker had been hired to kill Mason Browder. It was too far-fetched, too outrageous. There was no way the man she was falling in love with could be a hired gunman, a murderer.

"You didn't report it to Kraus. Why?" But she didn't bother to wait for a response. "When was the last time you saw it?"

"When I moved into the foreman's place."

"Who knew you had it?"

"Jim Bob helped me move my things into the cottage. He dropped the box the gun was in. At least three other people saw it—your mother, Dustin and his girlfriend. Your brother seemed fascinated by it. He even asked to examine it."

"And you let him?"

Tucker nodded.

Marcie took a long breath. "Which means if they find it and it turns out to be the murder weapon, his fingerprints might still be on it." A chill shivered down her spine.

"Possibly, but it doesn't prove anything. There are enough witnesses to testify about the circumstances under which his prints got there. Besides, we can't be sure Jim Bob didn't tell his buddies about it, or that Dusty or Lula didn't mention it to other people. Anyone could have known I had it. Figuring out where I kept it wouldn't have been hard, either.''

Marcie bit her lip, while her mind raced to images of her brother in the dock, accused of murder.

"So you don't know when it was stolen. Do you know how? Did whoever take it break into your desk?''

Tucker shook his head. "Either the thief had a key or was very good at picking locks.''

She pictured the old metal desk in his room, the kind that had a single lock on the middle drawer, which, when opened, released the other drawers. Was it possible to crawl under the desk and trip the mechanism without using a key? Who would know how to do it?

Tucker brushed the hat back off his forehead. "Let's try this a different way. We've been going on the premise that your father, aided and abetted by his pal Lennie, was stealing cattle from the Prudhomme place to ruin Vince, and that they were taking a few from the Lazy B to divert attention.''

"Yes…''

"Suppose they weren't partners. What if Lennie was doing it on his own, your father caught on when Dusty told him about Lennie selling cattle in San Angelo and he went to confront him. They had a discussion, an argument, and it turned violent. Your father…Mason pulled a gun, fired a shot—either in a struggle or as a warning—and forced Gruen to get into the buggy with him. Then he drove him up to the bowl.''

Marcie took a step away from Tucker, hand upraised as ideas stampeded through her mind. Revers-

ing course, she stood in front of him. "It makes a bit
of sense, although Dad carrying the gun bothers me."

"Maybe he didn't," Tucker suggested. "Maybe it
was already in the buggy."

"Dusty took it?" She didn't like that idea, either,
but couldn't completely ignore the possibility.

"Not necessarily with evil intent," Tucker tried to
assure her. "Maybe he just 'borrowed' it to try it
out."

Borrowed certainly sounded better than stole, she
mused. Was Dustin a thief? She thought about the
liquor-store robbery he supposedly hadn't had a hand
in and her brother's acting ability.

Marcie felt suddenly overwhelmed. All the doubts
she'd had about anyone seemed to be coming to the
surface. Tucker, Dustin, her mother, Vince.

"I don't imagine Lennie's very well fixed anymore," she went on. "From comments I've heard my
mother make, he went though most of the money he
got for the Green Valley ranch pretty fast. Whether
he and Dad were partners in this cattle thing or not,
I imagine he needed a steady infusion of cash." She
returned to her hard seat across from Tucker. "There
are still a few problems, though. Where did they
meet? Why come here? And why go up to the bowl?"

"I might be able to answer the last one—why they
went up to the bowl."

She eyed him, waiting for his answer.

"My guess is that Lennie's first reaction would be
to deny his involvement, in which case your father
might have taken him there to show him the proof
he'd found. But I think there could have been another
reason, too. To strand him there as a punishment. To
make him walk home. Teach him a lesson."

Marcie couldn't help but laugh at the rightness of it. "God, that would be just like Dad. And then have the sheriff waiting for him when he got back."

Tucker watched thoughts and emotions scatter across her face. There was the satisfaction of solving a puzzle, of course, but something more, too. Was it the hope that her father might not have been the vindictive, dishonorable thief she'd earlier considered him to be?

"But the plan went wrong," she finally said. "Somehow Lennie managed to get the gun and shoot him."

Tucker nodded. "Have they been known to fight before?"

She shook her head. "They were more likely to gang up on somebody else. Besides, even in his cups, Dad wasn't a violent man." Then she froze. "Until recently."

He placed his hand on her back. "He was sick, Marcie. The doctor said he was dying. Maybe he didn't know that, but I'm willing to bet he sensed something was wrong. He was lashing out—"

"Dammit, he was drunk." She lowered her head, her mind reviewing all the times she'd seen him intoxicated. It made her sad to think those incidents might be her most lasting memories of him: smelling of beer and liquor, slightly unsteady on his feet, eyes bloodshot, speech slurred. She'd loved him once. She wanted to remember the good times they'd had together. There must have been some—times when she felt safe and secure in his presence, proud of his being her papa. But for the life of her she couldn't remember any of those occasions now. Her insides tumbled as she tried to hold back the tears that were suddenly too close to the surface.

Tucker watched her with a familiar ache of helplessness. He had disliked Mason Browder, seen him for what he was, a drunkard and a bully, who apparently was also a lecher. But as he observed the emotions creep like the gloom of storm clouds across Marcie's face, darkening the natural brightness of her eyes, turning down the corners of her mouth, he began to hate the dead man.

But he hated the person who'd killed him more. Mason's murderer had robbed his daughter of her last chance to find reconciliation with her father. Now she'd never be able to come to terms with the man who, for better and worse, had brought her up.

She straightened and resumed her walk toward the area where she'd left her horse.

"I don't think Lennie was in it by himself," she commented. "I think we were right the first time. They were in it together."

She took a few more steps, trying to decide if this revised version of what might have happened had any real credibility. What would the next move have been if her father had succeeded in stranding his old drinking buddy up at the bowl? What would Lennie have done in retribution? Would they have laughed about it the next time they met at the Beer Bucket and called for another round of drinks for all their friends?

Tucker was following her with his eyes. The look of concern she saw in his quiet gaze disturbed her, as if he were seeing into a part of herself she didn't want exposed.

She turned to leave, but his hand on her arm stopped her. He moved his other hand up to the bottom of her jaw and lifted her face to his. "None of this is your fault, Marcie." His words were soft and soothing and filled with caring. "If you're blaming yourself for what happened, don't."

"It's just that…the last time I saw him—" Tears of regret misted her vision as his thumb stroked her chin.

"You were angry with him for good reason."

He closed the few remaining inches between them and extended his arms. She accepted them and pressed herself to him. He couldn't control the response of his body to hers. *Don't despise me,* he wanted to say, *for needing you the way I do.*

"WHAT HAVE WE ACCOMPLISHED?" she asked later. "Have we eliminated anyone? Except maybe each other?"

They were sitting on the porch of the foreman's cottage. The ride from the arroyo had been quiet. Marcie's thoughts had been focused elsewhere, and judging by the glances she caught from the man on the pinto, so had Tucker's. She kept reliving the sensation of warmth melting through her when he'd rested his hand on her back, when he'd thrown his arms around her protectively. She couldn't deny the sense of well-being and security his touch gave her, and she couldn't dismiss the recollection of his physical response to their embrace. As for the kiss…

"Is that what you think I was doing," he interrupted her reverie, "trying to establish an alibi for myself?"

He said it humorously, but she sensed the same outrage she'd felt when she realized the sheriff considered her a suspect.

"Well, if you were," she conceded, "it worked. I was home all evening, and I'm sure I did pass in front of my window periodically. Spring cleaning. Mom gives my old room a lick and a promise once in a while, but it hasn't really been lived in since I left eight years ago." She looked at him and smiled. "I guess I'll have to draw the drapes in the future if I don't want people watching me."

He grinned.

Just how casual had his observation of her been? she wondered. The idea of him lying in bed watching her though the open window disturbed her, but not the way it would have even a couple of days ago. She would draw the drapes next time, she decided, but when she did, it would be very, very slowly.

Restless, she jumped to her feet and paced in front of him. "So who can we eliminate from our list of suspects?" she reiterated.

"Potentially no one." He propped his elbows on the top step and leaned back, his long legs angled to the ground. "Your brother had ample opportunity to steal my gun. He said your father was upset the other night before he ran off in the dune buggy. But we have only his word their argument was about Lennie's selling cattle. Could your brother have been involved in the rustling?"

"Dusty?" Her voice went up. She'd said herself he was just like his father, a chip off the old block. But was he? She couldn't get the picture out of her mind of her kid brother dressed up as a mime, entertaining parentless children at the orphanage. "He's impulsive and occasionally stupid," she admitted, a bite in her words. "But I don't think he's bad. And don't remind me about the liquor-store holdup," she added with a wave of her hand. "He was in the wrong place at the wrong time in the wrong company."

"All right," Tucker agreed after a moment's pause. "Let's forget about your brother for the time being. If Jim Bob has a big mouth, anyone at the ranch could have gotten the gun, including half a dozen ranch hands." Then he added, as if casually, "By the way, I know where you were the evening your father was killed, but I don't remember seeing your mother."

"Mom? Surely, you don't think—"

"Just asking. At some time the sheriff's bound to. Do you know where she was?"

"She went out right after supper."

"Where to?"

Marcie wasn't even sure when Carlinda had gotten home. "I haven't asked her."

"How about Lennie?"

"What? Oh, you mean did he have a chance to steal the gun? Yeah, I guess so. He came here a couple of times a week to see Dad. Sometimes they'd go drinking together, and he'd drop him off later."

"Designated driver?"

"Dad had his license suspended a couple of times for DWI. Rudy Kraus told him if he got picked up one more time for drunk driving he was going to have his license yanked permanently. Dad was a lousy driver even when he was sober, but the humiliation of a former state senator having his license revoked…well, you can imagine."

She took a few paces, her fingers stuck in her back pockets. The seemingly casual posture drew her shoulders back and pushed her breasts in generous relief against her cotton plaid shirt. Tucker swallowed deeply.

"Lennie, on the other hand," she continued, "is actually a very good driver, even under the influence, which is probably why the highway patrol and the sheriff's department have never picked him up. So as often as not, Dad would let him chauffeur him around."

"Except the other evening. Apparently, your father was going to drive the truck to wherever he was going, until he realized it was low on gas. Interesting," Tucker commented distractedly, his attention still riveted on the tug of her shirt buttons.

"I wonder what Lennie's alibi is for the evening in question," Marcie commented.

"Maybe we should go talk to him, see if we can find out anything," Tucker replied. "Maybe even scare him a little."

CHAPTER ELEVEN

TUCKER PULLED OUT OF THE ranch road onto the public highway.

"You said your mother moved into town after your father died," Marcie commented, not quite sure why she was raising the subject, except she wanted to know more about the man sitting next to her.

He slipped the gearshift lever from third to fourth. "Mom was born and raised in town and considered herself a city girl. She didn't mind living on the ranch, but that was because Dad was there. Ranching was his life. He loved the hard labor, the constant activity, the outdoors. I remember his hands most of all. Big, strong and hard with thick calluses."

Marcie looked over at Tucker's hands curved around the steering wheel. They were big and strong, too. She could easily imagine them becoming crusty like his father's. But even more than his hands, she was aware of the love she heard in Tucker's voice when he talked about his dad. What kind of father had Tucker made? She pictured him holding his daughter on his lap, reading her bedtime stories, brushing back her hair in a gentle caress. Would he have rejected his little girl because of something her mother had done?

"After he died, Mom decided to move back into town." Tucker glanced in the rearview mirror, though the road was empty. "My brother was starting high school, and it made more sense to be close to things."

"Made sense to her," Marcie repeated. "How about you? How did you feel about it?"

For just a moment, his lips tightened. "I loved the ranch as much as Dad did. I used to trail after him whenever I could." Tucker chuckled. "Helping him, of course. I was probably a terrible pest, constantly asking why, wanting to do what he was doing. But he was always patient, always willing to show me things, teach me." His voice had gotten softer and there was a wistfulness in it that had Marcie studying his profile.

"You still miss him, don't you?"

"Yeah," he said quietly, "I guess I do."

He checked the mirror again, flipped on his signal and turned to the right. "I was pretty upset with Mom for a while. It felt like I was abandoning Dad."

"It must have been very difficult for a ten-year-old boy."

He nodded. "Tougher on her, I think. She was in her early thirties with three kids and no husband and no marketable skills, as far as she knew."

"So how did she support you?"

Tucker let out a chuckle. "The old-fashioned way. She worked. Took whatever job she could get. Waited tables, cleaned houses. The one thing she did know how to do was cook. She got a job as a short order cook in a bar, then catered a couple of small parties." He smiled. "That's sort of an exaggeration. Actually, it was making sandwich trays for a bunch of good old boys for their Saturday-night card games. But it was a start. Her reputation grew, and within three or four years she was earning more money in private catering than her regular job. I remember when she quit the restaurant. I was just starting high school myself. She never said it, but I could tell she was scared.''

''But she did it.''

''Yep.'' Tucker's smile was one of absolute pride. ''The rest, as they say is history. She's got a dozen employees now and complains constantly about all the time she has to spend supervising them instead of cooking. Actually, though, she loves it. There are still a few dishes she insists on preparing herself, what she calls her secret recipes.''

''And you? How did you get into private investigating?''

Tucker stroked his hands along the top curve of the steering wheel, and Marcie had the impression of him changing mental gears. The sweet nostalgia of a few minutes earlier had slipped into the hard present.

''After I got out…I had to do something, and my brother had an opening. It was as simple as that.''

''So being a sleuth, a private eye, wasn't something you've always dreamed of doing?''

He laughed, as she'd hoped he would. She liked the sound of his laughter. It started as a light rumble and matured into a full-bodied drumroll. ''No, being the world's greatest private eye wasn't my first ambition.''

''What was, besides being a Marine?''

''Ranching. I guess I've never gotten it out from under my skin. But there aren't many cowboy jobs open these days, and I've never been a rodeo rider.''

Too bad, she thought, recalling his imposing image in the saddle.

''Have you ever been to Lennie's house?'' he asked.

Marcie sighed. "Once, about ten years ago. Dad had just won reelection to the state senate and Lennie invited all of us, Mom, Dusty and me, out to dinner. We stopped off first at Lennie's place for what he called cocktails. I remember Mom's disgust when she met Lennie's 'hostess of the week.' She could have been his granddaughter. She looked about two years younger than me."

"How'd he get away with playing around with underage girls?"

Marcie laughed. "How often do you hear of a girl yelling 'statutory rape'? Besides, Dad insisted she was of legal age."

Tucker accelerated, and they sped along the empty county road.

"You may not believe it now," Marcie continued, "but Lennie was a charmer once, just like Dad, and a smooth talker. Besides, he was also a slick politician's chief of staff, a power to be reckoned with in his own little world. He took better care of himself in those days, too, didn't look quite as dissolute as he does now. But he already had a reputation for liking 'em young."

Tucker glanced at her out of the corner of his eye. "Did he ever put the make on you?"

"Even Lennie Gruen wasn't that stupid." She shook her head. "No, he never actually made a pass, but I was always aware of him ogling me, wishing he could."

Tucker's hands tightened on the steering wheel, his knuckles straining white. "That son of a—"

She reached over and rested her hand on his wrist. "I don't think he was ever a real threat to me," she assured him. "I just stayed away from him and didn't give him a chance to exercise his fantasies."

"That son of a bitch," Tucker repeated.

"Turn here," Marcie instructed him. "It's down at the end of this road. Hmm. I see they finally paved it. This was just caliche last time I was here. I wonder if Dad had anything to do with it." Then she commented with wry humor, "But why else would the township go to the expense of paving a road to a single house on a remote edge of the city limits?"

They drove around a sweeping curve. "As I recall," Marcie added, "it's a pleasant little place. Originally, it was his family's Sunday house."

"Sunday house? I didn't know there were any left around here."

"It's got to be one of the last," she agreed. "As I recall, while Lennie was chief of staff, one of Dad's constituents offered to improve the place."

"Corruption," Tucker mumbled.

"Sir, you shock me with such a suggestion." She grinned over at him, turning his scowl into a smile. "Anyway, Lennie expanded it. Then, after Dad bought the Green Valley ranch, Lennie moved in permanently. Actually, the place was very tastefully done."

Tucker's brows knitted. "Hold it. Sunday houses were supposed to be in town. The families of well-to-do ranchers would journey in, pick up supplies and trinkets on Saturday, spend the evening socializing and stay overnight in their Sunday houses. After church the next morning, they'd make the long trips home to their ranches for another week or month. So what's this one doing way out here?"

Marcie emitted a soft chuckle. "The town was

mostly on this side of the Coyote River until the flood of '96. That's 1896. Then it shifted to the other side. According to Lennie, the original structure was washed away in the flood, but his grandfather refused to go along with the town's migration and insisted on rebuilding in the same spot.''

Tucker grinned broadly. ''You've got to admire that kind of persistence, even while you're scratching your head wondering where the man left his common sense.''

''Bullheaded stupidity, you mean,'' she said with a laugh.

He slowed as they approached a lone residence huddled under a pair of huge live-oak trees. Tucker could barely make out what was probably the original house, a narrow, story-and-a-half stone affair that typically contained one or two rooms and perhaps a loft where the children would have slept. It was sandwiched now in between well-proportioned frame-and-glass additions that complemented rather than clashed with the simplicity of the central structure.

''Looks like we caught him at home,'' Marcie said, pointing to the mud-spattered Mercedes sitting at the back of the driveway. Vines covered the doors of the detached two-car garage.

Tucker left the keys dangling in the ignition when he shut off the engine. Not much chance of anybody stealing the battered old pickup in this neighborhood. Marcie unbuckled her seat belt and climbed out of the truck, then walked around the front of the vehicle to join him.

They stood silently next to each other. His hand reached out for hers. She took it without thinking, then looked up at him. His face was grim, his jaw muscles flexing as he stared at what should have been a front lawn but was, instead, a maze of uncut, raggedy weeds.

"What a waste," he said with a sigh. "There should be a rubber tire hanging from that limb." He pointed to the thick bough of a live oak that extended almost parallel to the ground, then he waved toward a flat, multilimbed crotch in the opposite tree. "And that's perfect for a tree house."

His eyes had taken on a bemused sparkle and she wondered what sweet memories were playing peek-aboo in his mind.

"Did you have a tree house when you were a kid?" she asked, holding on to his arm with both hands.

The laugh lines deepened and his face lit up. "No, but my best buddy did. We used to race there from school and fill water balloons to drop on the girls when they came strolling home from their club meetings."

"Nice guys," she teased, trying to picture him as a lanky adolescent up to mischief. The image came easily, almost making her giggle.

"Well, they deserved it," he proclaimed, momentarily reverting to a self-righteous teenager. "They were saying things about us."

I bet they were, she thought.

"Besides, it was harmless. None of them drowned, as I recall." He chuckled over the fond memory, adding, "Though from the unholy shrieks coming out of them, you'd think they were going to."

She laughed with him, visualizing it all too clearly, like something out of Tom Sawyer and Huckleberry Finn. Innocent pranks by boys against the very girls they would later try to steal kisses from behind the

lockers in the hall. And, of course, the feigned hurt
feelings by the girls, who secretly dreamed of the
jerks doing just that. She was enjoying the imaginary
play under the shady oak trees, when Tucker interrupted with reality.

"I doubt the front door's been used in a while."
Even the flat stone walk going up to the door had
crabgrass and winter rye sprouting between the
cream, orange and rust-streaked pavers. "Let's check
the back."

There was no fence around the house or the property. The driveway showed similar neglect, with purs-
lane and dandelions poking their way up through a
network of cracks in the concrete. A path had been
clearly worn, however, from where the aging luxury
car was parked to the back door. Tucker mounted the
two stone steps and knocked moderately hard.

There was no response.

"He might be sleeping," Marcie suggested.

Tucker rapped on the door a little harder. "Mr.
Gruen? It's Tucker McGee and Marcie Browder.
We'd like to talk to you."

Still no answer.

"Could he be out with someone?" she asked dubiously.

Tucker grasped the doorknob. It turned easily. He
expected the dead bolt above it to resist. It didn't.
Cautiously, he pushed the door open, Marcie at his
elbow.

"Hello? Anybody home? Mr. Gruen?"

No answer.

Tucker mounted the final step into the kitchen. The
room was dimly illuminated by the filtered light coming through a small window between faded metal cab-

inets on his left. The sink and Formica counter were cluttered with dirty dishes.

He moved farther in, Marcie right behind him, clinging to his arm. For a silly moment, he felt like one of the Hardy boys with Nancy Drew on his tail. He swallowed the smile the image conjured.

"Lennie?" Marcie called out. But there was still no answer.

The room smelled of uncollected garbage, dust and something else, a pungent sour sweetness. Tucker felt a familiar tingling in his nose. His stomach began a slow roll. Straight ahead of him was a closed door, which he suspected led to a dining room.

"Wait here," he muttered, and disengaged her fingers from his arm. But as he approached the door, he felt her warm hands on his back. He should have known she wouldn't stay put. He almost turned on her, nearly lashed out at her to listen to him, that it was his job to make sure she was safe. Instead, he breathed deeply from the diaphragm and pushed on the swinging door.

Spring-loaded, it swung forward, then back. He stopped it with his extended palms. Marcie moved up beside him. She stood stock-still in the doorway for a moment before moaning, "Oh, God."

Tucker looked at the man sprawled across the oval oak table in the middle of the dining room, his broad back to them, arms outstretched on the bare wood. Within inches of his left hand was an open whiskey bottle. Clasped in his right was a gun.

Tucker moved a little to one side to get a better view. Blood had pooled under Gruen's head, or what was left of it.

Marcie's exclamation was more forceful this time,

and more ragged. "Oh, God. Oh, God." She covered
her mouth with her hands and backed up against the
wall beside the door. Tucker felt his own gorge rise.
Forcing it down, he studied the mortal remains of
Lennie Gruen. A wave of relief swept through him
when he realized he didn't have to touch him to verify
the last thread of life had fled. He'd gathered too
many friends and pieces of friends while he was in
the service. The mystery of death held no allure, no
fascination.

He turned swiftly to Marcie, blocking her view of
the dead man. Firmly placing his hands on her shoulders, feeling the tension tightening her soft muscles,
he led her out of the room. She started to turn back.
"He—"

"There's nothing we can do for him." Gently, he
propelled her forward.

"How do you know?" she asked, her voice husky.

"The blood's dried. I'd say Gruen's been dead for
at least six or eight hours." Away from the sight of
the corpse, she began to regain her color.

"What are we going to do?"

He'd have more options, he knew, if he were alone.
More opportunities to explore this latest tragedy. *How
tired I am of death,* he thought, then looked with startled awareness at the woman within his reach. *And
hungry for life,* he added to himself, resisting the
temptation to touch her.

"You're going to go out to the truck," he said
more sharply than he intended, "and use the cell
phone to call the sheriff while I wait in here."

"But—"

"Just do it, Marcie. Please."

The entreaty beneath the command convinced her

far better than his words. She'd been unnerved by the sight of the dead man, but she had a feeling Tucker was even more shaken. Was the gory sight bringing back other memories? she wondered. He'd seemed calm enough when he found her father's body. But then, her father's remains hadn't been so mutilated.

"Come with me," she begged him.

"No," he said, taking a deep breath. "I have to check on something."

She wanted to ask him what, but he turned away. With dejection bordering on numbness, she walked over to the cab of the truck, climbed in behind the steering wheel, leaned across the bench seat and removed the cell phone from the glove compartment. She punched in the all-too-familiar number.

Tucker retraced his steps through the musty kitchen into the dining room. Venetian blinds covered the double-sash windows on the left. He didn't want to touch the light switch for fear of disturbing any fingerprints there might be on it. Pulling the thin control cords of the blinds, he flooded the room with daylight. And wished he hadn't.

Stark whiteness poured in, exposing the room's full horror. With it came awareness of the sickening stench of blood and corrupting flesh.

He breathed shallowly, but it didn't keep his stomach from contracting, his skin from crawling. He steeled himself to touch the sleeved arm of the cadaver. The man's body was in rigor mortis, as cold and solid as stone, which meant he'd been dead for at least eight hours but less than twenty-four.

Tucker straightened, involuntarily caught a glimpse of the mottled pink-and-white mush of brain tissue, and clamped his jaw against a sudden wave of nausea. He turned away and compelled himself to think.

None of the lights was turned on when they came in. Did that mean he'd died before sundown or after sunrise? It was possible, of course, that he had died in the dark, but it didn't seem likely. Lennie Gruen, he had a feeling, was partial to doing things with the lights on.

There were two other things Tucker needed to check at this point, and it took only a moment to confirm the first.

The gun in the corpse's hand was a 9 mm Beretta automatic.

He didn't have time to check the second before Marcie reappeared in the doorway. She spared him hardly a glance before her eyes locked onto the hulk at the table.

"From here," she said in a voice still uneven, "he looks passed out."

"He's out, all right," Tucker replied somberly. "Permanently. His hangover this time is divine."

Gallows humor. "What have you been looking for?"

"I wondered if he left a suicide note."

She remembered the piece of paper he'd pilfered from her father's body and kept from her. "Have you found anything?"

"No."

Maybe because she'd seen the way the sight of the dead man had affected him, she believed him. "Did you expect to?"

"A confession would have been nice, too, especially since he used a 9 mm to kill himself."

She gaped, and her heart stopped. "Is it your gun?"

"I don't know. It's a Beretta just like mine. But there are thousands of them in circulation. We'll have to wait for a positive ID after the sheriff gets here. Mine was registered."

"You think it's yours, don't you?" More statement than question. Her chest was pounding.

"Unless he had a gun collection of his own."

Trying to ignore the corpse, she strode past the table to the door at the other end and stepped into the living room. Her memory had been correct. The house had been remodeled with a certain understated elegance. The good taste, however, had apparently been limited to the interior decorator, not the inhabitant.

"*Sloppy* would be too generous a term to describe this place." Tucker came up beside her.

"Pigsty comes closer," she agreed, remembering the cleanliness and order with which the living man by her side kept the foreman's cottage.

They surveyed the place. To the left were two medium-sized rooms separated by a small bathroom. One was obviously used as an office; there was no gun case in it. The other, a spare bedroom, appeared almost pristine compared with the rest of the house.

"It doesn't look like he had many overnight guests," Marcie commented.

"Not in this room, at least. Let's see what else we find."

On the right, off the living room, the large master suite was best described as sybaritic: deep-pile maroon carpet, circular bed on a white pedestal and mirror-tiled ceiling.

"Depraved," she commented without humor.

The bathroom was no less decadent. Gold-plated fixtures and a sunken whirlpool bath big enough to entertain two or three intimately. The lower halves of the shower stall's three clear glass sides were milk-white from calcium deposits left by the city's notoriously hard water.

"I think it's safe to assume," Tucker said, "that our late friend didn't have maid service."

He didn't have to use his knuckles or a handkerchief to open the accordion doors to the closets that lined one wall of the room. They all stood half or fully opened. One, off its track, hung precariously at an angle. Tucker poked around.

"What are you doing now?" she asked.

"Checking his shoes and boots," he mumbled as he brushed back clothing that reeked of nicotine and body odor. He examined the few pieces of footwear neatly displayed in a rack. The dust indicated they hadn't been touched, much less worn, in a long time. Several more pairs of boots had been tossed in a pile in the corner next to the end closet.

Marcie walked over to them and looked down. "I bet these are the ones he wore regularly."

Tucker jostled them around with his foot. "No mud or caliche caked on any of them."

"Meaning he didn't walk back from the bowl."

"Meaning he wasn't wearing any of these if he did." Tucker surveyed right and left. "There could be another pair around here somewhere, or they might be the ones on his feet now, or he could have disposed of them."

"Why would he do that?" She supplied the answer before he had a chance to reply. "Bloodstains."

She shivered, though the room was far from cool.

In fact, she realized, it was downright warm. "He doesn't seem to have turned on his air-conditioning yet."

The irritating shrill of police sirens suddenly grew louder, then stopped abruptly. They had barely retraced their steps to the living room, when they heard the kitchen door slam and saw the sheriff enter.

CHAPTER TWELVE

THE SHERIFF'S EXPRESSION was grim, his stride heavy and determined, as he crossed the kitchen. He got as far as the dining-room doorway before coming to an abrupt halt. Beneath the rosy cheeks, tanned creases and leathery wrinkles, Marcie detected something she could only describe as pity. She didn't imagine Sheriff Rudy Kraus liked the deceased or had much respect for him as a man. But regardless of his moral failings, his wasted talents and ignoble end, Lennie Gruen had still been a human being.

Barrel-chested, bull-necked, Rudy Kraus stood there for a long minute before inching closer. He removed his hat, and for a moment Marcie thought it was out of respect for the dead, but then he took a red bandanna from his back pocket and mopped his brow and sweatband, while he stared down with a look of disgust at the still form.

The faint murmur of men and vehicles moving around in the bright, colorful world outside, seemed totally at odds with this dingy, gray realm. The three of them stood in profound silence.

The old man replaced the Stetson on his white-streaked head and, without saying a word to the people nearby, began looking around the room, studying the setting. His brow furrowed under the curled brim of his hat, he bent over the dead man with his hands clasped behind his back, as if unwilling to let them touch the corpse.

A uniformed deputy appeared in the doorway.

"Ben," Kraus addressed him sharply, "I want you to escort these two people out of here. Keep them in front. I don't want them getting in the way, and I don't want them talking to anyone. Is that clear?"

"Yes, sir." Ben looked across the table at Marcie and Tucker standing in the opposite doorway. "Come with me."

The relief Marcie had initially felt at the appearance of the sheriff had already tripped into discomfort. Now it tumbled further into distress. She started forward. "Rudy—"

"Outside," was all he said.

"But—" she began to protest.

"Now!"

Tucker took her elbow and steered her toward the kitchen doorway. "He's got things he has to do in here," he said softly.

She followed with a backward glance, stung by the lawman's hostility.

Two more uniformed deputies, holding clipboards, stood at the bottom of the steps, waiting for them to descend, then rushed past.

Marcie heard the sheriff tell them, "I want the gun's serial number before the body leaves here."

The same justice of the peace who'd come to the bowl to officially declare her father dead strolled past them on his way to the house. He nodded a brief acknowledgment to Marcie, but it was almost surreptitious, as if he were cheating by doing so. *Surely he doesn't think we had anything to do with Lennie's death*, she told herself. *He couldn't. It's obviously a suicide.*

Ben waved them around to the front of the house where sheriff's department cruisers were parked beyond the shade of the giant oak trees. Marcie and Tucker were ushered well outside the path other deputies and medical personnel were cutting from their vehicles to the rear of the building.

She looked at Tucker for moral support. He gave a reassuring smile, then extended his hand. She found hers slipping into it without hesitation, as if it were the most natural thing in the world. Judging from Ben's sidelong glance, however, the gesture might have been the special handshake of conspirators.

It was several minutes before the county's chief law officer reappeared. He advanced toward them, stopping another deputy to tell him something along the way. Finally, he faced Marcie.

"What were you doing in there?"

Marcie almost flinched at the harshness of the question. "We came to talk to—"

He shook his head impatiently. "We'll discuss why you came to visit your father's drinking buddy in a few minutes. What I'm asking you now—" he pinned her with angry gray eyes "—is what you were doing in the house with a dead man. A rather ugly and messy dead man. How come you weren't waiting for me out here?"

Embarrassment surged through her. The springtime sun suddenly blazed burning hot, while the old man's tone had turned icy cold. She was grateful for Tucker's hand, for its warmth and sturdiness, something solid to hang on to. Marcie felt anxious, though

Tucker seemed passive, which she found both reassuring and perplexing.

"We got here about thirty minutes ago," Tucker answered calmly. "Knocked and called out, but got no answer. I tried the door. It wasn't locked." He lifted a shoulder. "We found him just as you saw him and called you a few minutes later."

"You're pretty good at finding dead bodies, McGee."

Marcie's mouth fell open. "What's that supposed to mean?"

Kraus ignored her.

Tucker released his grip on Marcie and leaned against the fender of the car. Hooking his thumbs in the pockets of his jeans, he studied the sour visage of the lawman. "What is it that's bothering you, Sheriff?"

Kraus planted his ample rump against the opposite car's door a few feet away, crossed his arms and faced him squarely. "You were obviously looking for something in there. I want to know what it was."

"A suicide note."

"Did you find one?"

"No."

"Or is there none that you'd care to share with me?" Kraus asked pointedly, glaring all the while at Tucker. When he got no reaction, he asked, "Why wouldn't a suicide note be by the body?"

Tucker shrugged. "Drunks don't always do things logically."

"What did you expect a suicide note to say?"

Marcie spoke up, hoping she could defuse the confrontation she saw building. "I thought he might express remorse over Dad's death."

"Is that all?"

"Maybe that he had killed him."

Kraus frowned skeptically. "Why would Gruen kill his best friend?"

"It's complicated," Tucker answered.

"Well, McGee, you're pretty good with words. Why don't you see if you can put it in nice easy terms that a simple country boy like me can understand. I've got plenty of time."

The sheriff's open hostility was beginning to frighten Marcie. "I think Lennie might have been behind the rustling that's been going on."

"Now, why would you think that?" Kraus asked in a sarcastic drawl.

"The other day my brother found out Lennie's been selling cattle. As far as we know, he hasn't owned any since he sold us the Green Valley ranch. Where did he get them? That was one of the questions we wanted to ask him."

"Maybe he was acting as your daddy's agent. After all, he used to be his chief—"

"We thought of that," Marcie countered.

"We checked the records," Tucker contributed. "The Lazy B hasn't sold any cattle in nearly a year."

"So you figured Gruen was stealing them from the Lazy B and Prudhomme's place and selling them." It was a statement, but the tone suggested incredulity. "If he was stealing, it seems to me it would give your daddy a reason to kill him, not the other way around."

"Maybe they had an argument, struggled and Lennie got the best of him," she offered.

"And he killed his best friend?" Kraus's jaw tightened and he took a deep breath, his crossed arms rising higher above his round belly.

"It would explain his suicide," Tucker pointed out.

Kraus rubbed the side of his face. "It still doesn't explain why he would steal from his best friend in the first place."

"As a cover-up," Marcie told him. "From what I've heard, Lennie's run through all the money he got from selling his place. If he was stealing cattle from Prudhomme and the ranchers over by Spring Mesa, he couldn't very well not steal from us, too, not without raising suspicion. He wasn't stealing many of our cattle, just a few."

The lawman's expression relented for the first time, the sneer of ridicule suspended. Marcie saw hope she might be able to keep the relationship between her mother and Vince Prudhomme out of it.

"You said you were checking for a suicide note," he reminded Tucker. "They're usually found with the deceased. What else were you searching for?"

"Muddy boots," Tucker answered with a smile.

Kraus raised his eyebrows, forcing his hat up slightly. "Muddy boots," he repeated. "Oh, this should be rich. I can't wait to hear. Go on."

Marcie took a deep breath. "It occurred to us, as it must have to you, that the place where we found the shell this morning was on a more or less direct route from the Beer Bucket to here. Dusty said Dad was pretty upset when he told him about Lennie's selling cattle. A few minutes later, Dad rushed out of the bar. Given the sequence of events, we…I thought maybe Dad was on his way here to see Lennie, or maybe they'd agreed to meet, went up to the bowl and had a showdown. Dad was either killed up there or he died after being shot at the arroyo, and Lennie had to walk back.''

Kraus scratched his fingertips across his jaw. ''Seems to me your brother said he couldn't remember what got your daddy all fired up at the Bucket. Sounds like he's been holding out on me, too. I may have to have a little private conversation with him about cooperating with the authorities and the penalties for withholding evidence.'' He gave Marcie a cold, hard stare. ''If I didn't know better, I might begin to think you folks don't trust me. As for your little story, it raises more questions than it answers. Like why go up to the bowl in the first place? And if they did, why wouldn't Gruen drive the buggy back? Knowing him the way I did, I can't imagine him walking ten miles back home in the dark…and then killing himself in remorse.''

''It was just a thought.''

''Yeah. Just a thought.'' Rudy fixed his glare on Tucker. ''Did you find those muddy boots you were looking for?''

''No.''

''Well then, let me ask you another question.'' He peered again at Marcie. ''Do you think your daddy was involved in the rustling?''

But the sheriff didn't wait for an answer. He leaned into the front seat of his car and opened the glove compartment. She involuntarily sucked air between her teeth when she saw the thing he pulled out.

''So you know what this is.'' His tone was sharp, his expression implacable, as he tapped his thumbnail on the plastic envelope containing her father's list of numbers.

Tucker jerked and straightened. "How did you get that?"

"Legally, McGee. I obtained a warrant to search your cottage."

"But why?" Marcie pleaded.

"Your mother told me McGee showed her a piece of paper he claimed he'd picked up when he found your daddy's body at the bowl, a piece of paper he professed to be confused about. Apparently, he showed it to you, too."

Marcie eyed Tucker. His face was stoic, virtually unreadable. He made no further movement, but from where she stood, she could plainly see the vein in his neck throbbing.

"You asked me the other day," Kraus observed to Marcie, though he kept flicking glances at Tucker, "if I thought you killed your daddy. I said no, and I still want to believe that. But, dammit, Marcie, you lied to me."

Her spine stiffened at his tone.

"I asked you where you were the evening your daddy was killed, and you told me the two of you were together. Turns out that wasn't quite true now, was it?"

Marcie stared at the sheriff but said nothing. Kraus glared back, waiting.

"I was the one who told you," Tucker said forcefully, "not Marcie."

"She didn't correct you. That makes her a party to the lie."

"How do you know it was a lie?" Marcie sputtered.

"Your brother told me."

"Dusty?"

She remembered his initially coming home with the truck and reporting their father going off in the dune buggy, but he'd left again shortly thereafter. She didn't know when he'd come back again. It must have been while she was in her room. The truck wasn't nearly as noisy as the off-road vehicle, and it was a sound she was used to, so she wouldn't have paid much attention to it. Besides, she'd been playing her favorite Elvis album. *Heartbreak Hotel* seemed to say it all.

"He says he was home all evening and confirms you were in your room. He's also sure McGee wasn't with you."

It occurred to her that her brother might be using her to validate his own alibi, just as Tucker had.

"I never said I was in her room with her," Tucker protested. "I said we were both at the ranch. As it happened, I was reading in my bedroom in the foreman's cottage after dark. I can see Ms. Browder's bedroom from mine."

"Oh, it's 'Ms. Browder' now. You're cute with words, McGee. I've also got a good memory. What you said was that you were together at the ranch. Now you're trying to tell me you were together separately." He pronounced the words slowly, letting them drip with sarcasm. "It seems mighty suspicious that a married woman would rather have it known she was spending time with a man not her husband than tell the truth about where she was—"

"I'm not a married woman," Marcie burst out. She tossed back her hair and scowled at him. "I'm divorced."

Kraus ignored her protest and addressed Tucker. "You also told me you hadn't found anything at the scene except Mason's body. Now it turns out you did.''

"I told you I'd looked for a gun and didn't come up with one."

"You knew what I was asking and you understood…'' Kraus gave a fatalistic shrug of indifference, then went on. ''But that's all right. It gave me something else to take to the judge when I asked for a search warrant. The fact that you are the registered owner of a 9 mm Beretta, the same caliber weapon that killed Mason Browder—''

"That *might* have killed—'' Tucker corrected him.

"The same kind of gun doesn't mean anything anyway,'' Marcie interrupted. ''You don't have to register guns in this state and there could be dozens, hundreds, thousands of them out there—''

"A slight exaggeration, but you're right. Still, it's a rare enough gun around here to get the judge's attention. And when I told her we had a witness to the fact that he'd withheld evidence taken from the scene of a crime, she was convinced.''

Kraus's glower was frigid enough to make Marcie wonder if wounded pride wasn't the underlying motivation behind his hostility.

"That piece of paper…'' Tucker began. ''At first, I didn't know what to make of it, and neither did Mrs. Browder. She was able to confirm it was her husband's writing, but the numbers meant nothing to her. When I showed it to Marcie, she couldn't make heads or tails of it—at the time. Later, though, she thought they might be dates and units of cattle stolen, so we checked the numbers with Fletcher Doggitt over at the Prudhomme place. They matched.''

"What did you conclude?"

"Lennie was probably out of money and needed cash," Marcie explained. "So he started rustling, mostly from Prudhomme but a little from us, too. When Dusty told Dad about Lennie selling cattle in San Angelo, cattle he obviously didn't own, Dad would have figured it out. He would also have gotten pretty upset at his friend for stealing from him."

Kraus examined the paper in his hands. "Nice try. But you seem to be forgetting one little detail. If I'm reading this right, the numbers go into the future."

Marcie hesitated, steadied her breathing, then acknowledged, "Dad may have been in on it and became worried Lennie might get caught and himself exposed."

The sheriff scratched his temple. "Steal his own cattle? Why?"

"Dad wasn't broke, but I'm sure he could always use a little extra drinking money. Maybe he made a deal. Lennie could rustle from both ranches, give Dad the Lazy B share and keep the larger proceeds from the Prudhomme ranch for himself."

"I've got a better theory," Kraus said. "I think your daddy was out to ruin his neighbor."

The obvious question was why, but Marcie was afraid to ask it, afraid what Kraus's answer might be. She'd been hoping the Mason-Carlinda-Vince triangle could be avoided.

"Why would he want to do that?" Tucker asked as he reached over and covered her trembling fingers with a gentle, comforting handclasp.

"Carli says there was an old rivalry between them, and Mason was getting more and more paranoid."

Had her mother explained the nature of the rivalry? Marcie wondered.

"Paranoia isn't uncommon with advanced alcoholism," Tucker pointed out.

Kraus nodded. "Whichever theory turns out to be true, the result is the same, and your reason for coming here is the same. To get Gruen to admit he was stealing cattle. Is that right?"

The question made her doubt for a minute her own sanity. What could possibly have possessed her to think Lennie would own up to having committed a felony, several felonies, maybe even murder? She was saved from having to respond by the approach of one of the uniformed deputies.

"Excuse me, Chief, but you said you wanted this."

He handed Kraus a scrap of paper. The sheriff read it. He looked at Marcie first, seemed to be considering something, then refocused on Tucker.

"Tell me, McGee, can you explain why both Mason Browder and Lennie Gruen were killed with your gun?"

An icy shiver careered down Marcie's spine. The hand holding hers suddenly stopped its gentle massage.

"It was stolen from my desk."

"The same one, I reckon, I got a warrant to force open, the one where I found this piece of paper."

Tucker's hand tightened around Marcie's.

"Yet you didn't bother to report it missing," Sheriff Kraus went on. "You lost a 9 mm gun, then found your boss's dead body shot with the same-caliber bullet, but you didn't bother to inform the authorities that your weapon was missing."

"I didn't notice it was gone until after Browder was killed."

"I see. And you still didn't think it was important

enough to tell me? I've done some checking on you, McGee. A few things don't add up. Like why a so-called professional investigator would withhold evidence in a murder case."

"At the time I didn't know what I had."

"Or why Vince and Carli would hire an ex-con to find cattle thieves?"

Marcie blinked, then stared at the lawman. "Ex-convict? What are you talking about? Tucker isn't an ex-con—"

Kraus scowled at him, lips slightly parted in an attitude of disgust. "So you haven't told her about your criminal record, huh?"

Marcie's heart began to pound. She tightened her grip on Tucker's hand and looked at him. "What's he talking about, Tux? You're not a criminal."

"No. I'm not," he declared between clenched teeth. "But..." He took a long breath and shot the sheriff a caustic glare.

"Quite a coincidence," Kraus continued, "that within a couple weeks of being hired to investigate rustling, the two men who were probably responsible for the thefts should be murdered."

Marcie turned abruptly to Kraus. There was a smirk on his face. "You don't think Tucker ki...killed my father?"

Sheriff Rudy Kraus intoned very formally, "Tucker McGee, I'm asking you to come with me to answer further questions relating to the murder of Mason Browder and the death of Lennie Gruen."

"Is he under arrest?" Marcie gasped.

The sheriff ignored her. "If you choose not to come voluntarily," he continued, "I'm prepared to place you under arrest." He motioned to a deputy who had positioned himself within a few yards of Tucker. The deputy stepped forward and removed handcuffs from the back of his belt.

Tucker stared at them and swallowed hard. "Those won't be necessary," he said, his voice gravelly. "I'll go voluntarily."

CHAPTER THIRTEEN

MARCIE WATCHED IN HORROR as a burly deputy grabbed Tucker by his arm and led him to another police car. Stunned confusion had her head spinning. Tucker insisted he wasn't a criminal, but he hadn't argued when the sheriff called him an ex-convict. It didn't make sense. It was unnerving enough that he accepted virtual arrest without a fight, that his hand had gone cold in hers when the sheriff "invited" him to be interrogated, but the way his body had tensed at the sight of the handcuffs shocked her. Tucker McGee didn't scare easily, yet for a fleeting moment she'd seen pure terror boiling in his eyes.

Feebly, she grasped for logic. Tucker's gun was registered. How could a felon get a license as a private investigator with the right to carry a gun? That didn't make sense, either.

She clamped her jaw and fisted her hands as impotent rage swelled inside her. She didn't know what to do, where to turn. The man she had given her faith and trust to had just been hauled away by the county sheriff, accused of murder.

She turned to face the lawman she'd known all her life. She needed answers and wondered if and how she was going to keep her voice from sounding strangled. But he had already moved over to his Cherokee and was climbing behind the wheel.

"Sheriff," she called out.

His arm shielded his face as he adjusted his hat. He lowered it only to roll up the window, cutting her out. Fury erupted inside her, while perspiration trickled down her back. She had an impulse to pound on the hood of the shiny vehicle, plant herself in its path, do anything to force him to answer her questions. But some remnant of reason convinced her it would be pointless and foolhardy.

Her body shaking, she watched Kraus trail after the patrol car. The uniformed deputy a few feet away observed her but made no move to restrain her when she charged over to Tucker's pickup. The urge to flee this place, where an ugly man lay sprawled in his own blood, was strong, but the desire to follow Tucker was even more overpowering.

Once she was out of sight of the enclave of official vehicles, she pulled to the side of the road. Her fingers still trembled as she snatched up the cell phone she'd earlier tossed on the bench seat, flipped it open and jabbed in the number of the Prudhomme ranch. She hoped she remembered it correctly from eight years earlier. Had it changed? Vince answered on the third ring.

"The sheriff's taken Tucker in for questioning," she nearly shouted into the receiver. "He said he was going to arrest him." She pressed her hand against her diaphragm and felt her heart pound with uncertainty and anger.

"Why? What's happened?"

Inhaling raggedly, she forced herself to calm down, to explain everything as unemotionally as possible.

"We went over to Lennie's house to talk to him," she said, encouraged by what she perceived as

Vince's outrage, "and found him dead, apparently a suicide."

"Lennie killed himself?" Vince made a humph sound. "So why did Rudy arrest Tucker?"

"The gun in his hand…it was Tucker's."

"Damn."

"Kraus thinks it's the same gun that killed… um—" the word *Dad* suddenly stuck in her throat "—that killed Mason."

If Vince recognized the hesitation and understood it, he gave no indication. "That's ridiculous. Even if it was his gun…" He paused. "Look, go to the sheriff's office and wait. I'll have my lawyer there as soon as possible. In the meantime, if you can, tell Tucker to keep his mouth shut. The less he says, the better."

She hadn't discussed Tucker's role at the Lazy B when she'd met with the man who was her biological father. There was so much they hadn't discussed. But now, when everything around her seemed to be crumbling, she felt comfortable talking to him.

She nodded her agreement, even though he couldn't see her.

"And Marcie," Vince said gently after a moment's silence, "try not to worry. We'll get this straightened out."

"There's something else. Kraus said Tucker has a criminal record."

The line went silent, but Marcie knew he hadn't hung up.

"He…Tucker didn't tell you?"

So it was true. *Why couldn't he have been honest with me?*

"No. What did he do?"

"It's a long story." Vince paused for several seconds. "I think it's best if he explains it to you himself."

"Did Mom know?"

After another short interval, Vince said, "Yes."

Her fingers didn't shake when she clicked off the cell phone, not because she was calm but because she was drained. So much duplicity. So many lies and half-truths. Her mother was continuing to hold back information, and Tucker had kept a secret from her, a vital secret. Was there no one left she could trust?

She squeezed her eyes closed in a silent prayer for understanding before putting the truck in gear and driving into town.

The sheriff's office and city jail were in a stark, two-story, native-stone building across the street from the nineteenth-century Gothic courthouse. There had been talk for years of tearing down both buildings and replacing them with more modern, more efficient structures, but nothing ever came of it. She wasn't thinking about the landmark architecture, however, when she pushed through the heavy wooden door, though she did note the low-budget modular furniture looked ridiculous crammed in front of the tall, narrow sash windows.

The air inside clawed, damp and oppressive. It smelled of fear and unwashed bodies and a hundred years of snuff, all overlaid with cheap air freshener. Marcie scanned the tin-ceilinged room. Tucker was seated, facing Kraus across a paper-strewn desk, in the glass-enclosed cubicle that had "Sheriff" stenciled in gold letters on the door.

She was about to push aside the swinging gate in the hip-high railing cordoning off the front third of the room from the work area, when a compact woman in uniform stepped in front of her.

"May I help you?"

"I need to see Mr. McGee."

"Who are you?"

"Marcie Browder. Mr. McGee is our ranch foreman. I have to talk to him."

"Not right now. He's busy with the sheriff."

"I've got to see him." But the cold stare she received in return made it clear that wasn't going to happen.

Marcie went to the designated waiting area, an ugly corner to her left. The tubular frame furniture clustered there should have been arrested for vagrancy, she mused, and almost gave way to a fit of hysterical laughter. Feeling limp with depression, she plopped onto the lumpy red vinyl couch. But a minute later she was on her feet again, pacing past the front door. It opened and a trim man in a dark business suit and conservatively striped tie, gold-clasped against a white shirt, stepped in. Lawyer.

He moved confidently toward the swinging gate. She stepped in his path.

"Are you the lawyer Vince sent for Tucker?"

He looked at her cautiously, his raised-brow expression asking who she was.

"I'm Marcie Browder."

"Ah, Ms. Browder. I'm Nelson Spooner. Mr. Prudhomme called me." He held out his hand, his formidable gaze softening. "Can you tell me very briefly what happened?"

They relocated to the corner and sat on the edges of grungy plastic chairs. She filled him in on the sequence of events in a few short sentences. He nodded as she spoke. When she finished, he reached out a hand and rested it on her fluttering fingers. "Relax," he said calmly. "I should be able to get this matter resolved quickly."

"Is he going to be arrested?"

Spooner pursed his lips. "I'll do my best to make sure he isn't. From what you've told me, I'd say—"

"I want to go with you."

He shook his head. "Not yet. Give me a few minutes with him and the sheriff first."

TUCKER KEPT RUBBING HIS wrists. The cuffs hadn't been put on—this time—but the memory of helplessness at having his hands locked behind his back had shaken him. He gritted his teeth and took slow, deep breaths to keep the phantoms of fear at bay. He wondered if the lawman sitting opposite him was aware of the torment he'd imposed.

At the moment the sheriff was playing the silent game, shuffling papers on his desk as if they were vitally important. Tucker wasn't fooled. Kraus would wait until he started fidgeting before asking questions. Already he could imagine the vicious, sneering tone. It would be hard not to react to the distorted accusations the old man was likely to level at him, hard to suppress the instinctive urge to fight his attacker. But Tucker also knew in this kind of situation silence was his best defense. When they recited "Anything you say can be used against you," they meant it. He knew that firsthand.

There was a tap on the door behind him. Kraus muttered an expletive and called out, "Yeah."

Tucker turned as the door opened. "McGee's lawyer is here, Sheriff,'' the deputy announced, and returned to her station in the outer office.

A well-dressed man walked in.

''Spooner, what the hell are you doing here?''

''Nice to see you, too, Rudy.'' He didn't offer his hand. ''Now, if you'll leave us alone for a few minutes, I'd like to confer with my client.''

Tucker watched the two men square off and strained to keep his face blank. He had no idea who the pinstripe was or who sent him.

Finally, Kraus emitted another profanity, before stomping to the door. ''You've got five minutes.''

''I'll take as long as I need to properly represent my client.'' He'd put his hand on the doorknob, inviting the sheriff to leave, when they heard the commotion up front.

''I want to see the sheriff,'' a man's voice demanded.

''That's Uncle Fletch,'' Tucker murmured, even before he'd turned to see the man through the greasy glass partition.

''He's not available at the moment,'' the woman replied implacably. ''Is there something I can help you with?''

''You can get me the sheriff, dammit.''

His imperious tone had her on her feet, her back stiff. ''I told you—''

''I'm not deaf. I heard what you said. And I told you I want to see Kraus. Now!''

''That's not possible. If you'll wait—''

''No, I will not wait.'' He raised his voice to a belligerent tone. ''I demand to see the sheriff immediately.''

Kraus stepped into the main room. "What's going on?"

"I'm sorry, Sheriff, but this man—"

"I need to see you right away," Doggitt insisted.

"Fletcher, what the hell's so all-fired important you have to see me now? I'm busy."

"You've got the wrong man, Rudy," the old cowboy announced. "I'm the one who killed Browder and Gruen."

Tucker's fists automatically tightened. "Damn!" He glared at his attorney. "What the hell does he think he's doing? For God's sake, man, stop him."

"I'm your lawyer," Spooner pointed out.

Tucker stabbed with his eyes. "Not if you don't help Uncle Fletch, you're not."

The attorney hesitated hardly a moment, then went into the main room. "Sheriff, if you'll allow me a minute with Mr. Doggitt."

"This is none of your business, Counselor."

"It is now," Tucker said from behind the suit. "Uncle Fletch, get in here."

"Now, just a minute, McGee," Kraus flared.

"Are you prepared to formally charge either of these men with a crime?" Spooner inquired.

"McGee withheld evidence and—"

"We'll talk about that a little later. In the meantime, I hope I don't have to remind you that a violation of a person's civil rights, specifically his right to counsel, is a serious charge. It's not likely to play well at election time, either."

Kraus's already high color turned to a deep crimson. "Are you threatening me?"

"Simply advising you of the possible repercussions—"

"Don't you guys ever say a simple yes or no?" Kraus threw up his hands. "Aw, go on, dammit. Confer."

Marcie used the opportunity to take Fletcher by the arm and lead him through the swinging gate. The deputy stepped forward and started to say something, but her boss motioned her off. Marcie and Fletcher entered the office, and Spooner closed the door quickly behind them.

That the sheriff had capitulated surprised Tucker. The usual procedure was to keep suspects and other people apart for questioning. Did it mean the sheriff's case wasn't very strong and he was looking for a graceful way out? Or could it be he felt his case was so compelling he had no fear that their meeting would weaken it?

Marcie rushed to Tucker and threw her arms around him. The fact that she was shaking unsettled him even more than the feminine contours of her body crushed against him. He attempted to soothe her with gentle words as he ran his hand along her cheek. She turned her head and pressed her lips to his palm. The sensation, soft, sweet, desperate, was like a spark igniting dry tinder. Holding his breath, he eased her away and gazed into her eyes. He didn't want to hurt this woman, but the nagging doubts and questions he saw reflected in the set features of her beautiful face told him he had.

He guided her to the cracked leather couch. Fletcher took the matching overstuffed chair, while Spooner leaned against the front of the desk facing them.

Tucker glared at his uncle. "Okay, Uncle Fletch,

start talking. What the hell is this crap about you kill-ing—''

''I killed Browder and Gruen,'' Fletcher repeated.

''Bull!''

''Explain how you did it,'' Spooner pressed him calmly. ''First, Browder.''

Fletcher looked down at his folded hands, his jaw working back and forth. Everybody waited.

''I was driving back from town Monday afternoon. Must have been about six, because it was already getting dark. I saw the dune buggy on the other side of the road. Wasn't even pulled off onto the shoulder. Not completely, anyway. Figured it was Dustin, that he had engine trouble or something. I slowed down and was about to yell at him through the window that he better get his stupid contraption off the road before someone came along and rear-ended him, when I realized it wasn't Dustin but Mason. He had his head resting on his arms across the steering wheel. Figured he was drunk. I've made it a policy to stay clear of Browder, drunk or sober, but I couldn't ignore that damned machine in the road. It'd be dark pretty soon.''

Fletcher kept his hands in his lap, concentrating on his twirling thumbs as if they were the most fascinating things he'd ever seen.

''Go on,'' Spooner prompted.

''He was passed out. Actually snoring. Couldn't leave him there. Poked at him, roused him. He looked at me bleary-eyed and started cussing. Well, they weren't any words I hadn't heard before. Told him to get in my truck, that I'd move the silly damn vehicle off the road and drive him home. He reached for the ignition, but I snatched the keys from him before he could get them. Naturally, he exploded. Started ranting and raving about thieves and rustlers. I didn't pay much attention until he accused me of stealing his cattle. Got my dander up, and I shouted back. Shouldn't have. Stupid to argue with a drunk. That's when he took a swing at me. Easy to duck, but when I straightened up, he had a gun pointed at me. From under the seat, I guess. Told him to put it down before he hurt somebody. He kept waving it around like it was a toy. Just a matter of time before the damn thing went off. Didn't reckon going for it increased my chances of getting shot much, so that's what I did. But he wouldn't give it up. We struggled, probably not more than a few seconds, and it went off. We both froze at the sound. It took me a minute before I realized he was dead.''

Tucker loosened his grip on Marcie's hand. He hadn't realized how much he'd tightened it until she squirmed. He smiled apologetically at her, then laced into his uncle. ''How did you get him and the buggy up to the bowl?''

Doggitt worked his jaw. ''Went back to the ranch, got the flatbed and carted the thing and Mason up there.''

Dubiously, Marcie asked. ''Why?''

''Remote but accessible.''

''Why didn't you leave the gun, too?''

''Should have. At the time I knew only that he was dead and I'd killed him. Didn't think of trying to pass it off as suicide.''

''What about Lennie?'' Tucker asked.

''Got a call from him a couple of days later, said he saw me, saw what happened. Threatened to go to the police. He wanted money, of course. Knew it would never stop. Blackmail. Never ends. Went to his house to talk to him. He wouldn't back off. Shot him, too, except this time I remembered to leave the gun.''

"Why didn't you report your encounter with Mason to the authorities?" Spooner asked.

Doggitt bowed his head. "Guess I didn't think anybody'd believe me."

"So why are you coming forward now?"

"Can't let them think Tucker did it."

Tucker shook his head. "Uncle Fletch," he said, his voice almost breaking. "I appreciate what you're trying to do. But first of all, I didn't do it—"

"Didn't do you any good last time," Fletcher lashed back.

Tucker ignored him. "And second, your story won't work. It's got more holes than a piece of chicken wire."

Fletcher bunched his lips and kept his eyes averted. "Like what?"

Tucker turned to Marcie. "You tell him."

She considered the man Tucker respected as a role model and wondered why he would confess to murders he hadn't committed.

"Mason wasn't killed along the side of the road," she told him, "but in the mesquite several hundred yards away. We found the spot and so did the sheriff."

"You couldn't have driven up to the bowl with a flatbed, either," Tucker pointed out, "because the ground there was too soft. You would have left deep tracks."

"There's something else," Marcie interjected, "something essentially wrong with your scenario."

"What?" Fletcher muttered, looking like a very angry but chastened schoolboy.

"Whoever killed him brought the gun. Dad didn't."

Spooner's brows went up. "How do you know that?"

"Because Dad hated handguns. He wouldn't have one in the house." Everyone was looking at her now. "As a kid, a friend of his accidentally killed himself with his father's pistol. Dad never touched a handgun after that."

"Well, I'll be damned," Fletcher mused. "When he was in the state legislature, he sponsored a bill to control handguns. Never could understand why. He had a rifle and shotgun in the back window of his pickup like everybody else. But he wanted to ban handguns. Didn't make sense."

Kraus rapped on the door and came in. "You've had your time. Now it's mine." He peered at Spooner, who didn't raise any objection, so he turned to Doggitt. "Now, you old fool, I want to know why you pulled this stunt a few minutes ago. Why did you say you shot Browder and Gruen?"

"I remind you, Sheriff," Spooner said, "that Mr. Doggitt was not read his Miranda rights. Any statement he made cannot be used against him."

Kraus waved the legalism aside. "Why'd you say it, dammit?"

"You don't believe me?"

Kraus shook his head impatiently. "I've known you for nearly thirty years, you old coot. You don't go around shooting people in cold blood."

Fletcher fumbled again with his fingers. "You arrested Tucker. I couldn't let that stand."

"So you think he did it?"

Fletcher raised his head. "Of course not."

"But you thought I'd railroad him—just for the fun of it."

"It happened before. I won't let it happen again."

Tucker watched the lawman fighting with himself. There was anger, certainly. But it was hard to tell who it was directed at: Tucker, his uncle or maybe the system.

"What happened to McGee shouldn't have, but I'd like to remind you that it wasn't me who did it to him." He turned to Tucker. "You lock my jaws, McGee. I won't deny it. Instead of leveling with me, you held back information, treated me like the goddamn enemy."

"I'm sorry," Tucker began, "but I didn't know who I could trust. I had to—"

"Sheriff," Spooner intervened, "if you've gotten over your pique of injured pride, I think it would be appropriate for you to release Mr. McGee."

"Why should I?" Kraus snapped.

"Because, very simply, you have no prima facie case."

"His gun was used to kill both of them."

"A gun anyone could easily have gotten hold of."

"I have only his word it was taken."

"And no evidence to contradict that statement."

"He withheld evidence," Kraus persisted.

"If you're referring to the paper you took from Mr. McGee's desk, it isn't evidence of a crime. Nor is there anything to suggest it is, directly or indirectly, related to Mr. Browder's murder. I have a question for you. Have you any proof that Mr. Gruen did not commit suicide?"

"The autopsy is going to take some time."

"Do you seriously doubt he died of anything but the shot to his head?"

"Probably not," Kraus conceded. "But if there are no powder burns on the victim's hand, it means he wasn't the one who pulled the trigger."

"So right now, you have one murder and one suicide," Spooner reminded him. "Is it possible Mr. Gruen killed Mr. Browder and then, perhaps in remorse or despair, killed himself?"

"It's possible but—"

"Then you have no reason to hold my client."

Tucker had to hand it to Spooner. In a few short sentences, he'd cleared two people of murder charges and apparently solved the crimes. Or had he?

Kraus chewed on the side of his mouth. "Ah, get out of here. All of you. Now. Before I change my mind."

Once outside, Spooner shook everybody's hand, gave each of them his card, then wasted no time going to his illegally parked Cadillac and driving away. Tucker waited until they were in the parking lot before addressing his uncle. "I understand why you did what you did, Uncle Fletch, and I appreciate it, but it was a damn fool thing to do."

"I saw what prison did to you once. I wasn't going to allow it to happen again. You're still young, got a whole life ahead of you. Get on with it, boy." He turned quickly on his heel and stomped to his pickup.

"Quite a guy," Marcie murmured as she watched the old man climb heavily into the cab of his truck.

Tucker wrapped his arm around Marcie's waist. "I'm a lucky man, all right," he whispered, and kissed her earlobe. "Look," he said, straightening, "I have to go with Uncle Fletch. He and I need to have a man-to-man talk. Can you go home by yourself?"

Fletcher started his engine.

She smiled at him. "I think I can find the way."

Tucker gave her another kiss, this one on the lips. "I'll explain everything later." He turned and ran over to his uncle's truck as it was backing out of the parking space. Marcie watched the two men exchange words through the window. Finally, Tucker opened the door and mounted the running board. Jaw clamped tighter than ever, the old man shifted over on the bench seat as Tucker slipped behind the wheel. He gave her a thumbs-up as he pulled past her.

Marcie felt dirty, disgruntled and more than a little confused as she drove home. She didn't know why Tucker had been sent to prison, though she knew now from what the sheriff had said that it had been unjustly. And she was disappointed Tucker hadn't told her about it. She remembered his startled expression when she'd compared his cottage to a barracks or prison. That would have been the perfect time for him to tell her his experience. Instead, he'd dismissed the comment with a joke. Given the pains he'd endured, she could understand his reticence. The very thought of him behind bars, forced to live with cutthroats and thieves, had her heart sinking.

She turned onto the highway that would take her home. Home. She wasn't sure where that was anymore. Of one thing Marcie was certain, however. She was falling in love with Tucker McGee. No matter what their mistakes of the past, no matter what the trouble of the present, she felt a glimmer of hope that her future happiness was inextricably woven with his.

She was crossing Ten Mile Bridge, halfway home,

when a bang startled her. Simultaneously, the wheel jerked from her hand, and the truck veered sharply to the right. The acrid stench of burning rubber drifted in through the open window. She grasped for the wheel, but not soon enough. She watched, as if in slow motion, as the guardrail loomed in front of her. Then came the nerve-shattering screech of metal violating metal. With her heart in her mouth, her blood pumping painfully in her chest, she felt the front end of the truck jump above the corrugated fence, and she saw the dry riverbed rise up to meet her.

CHAPTER FOURTEEN

IT WAS DIFFICULT FOR TUCKER to read his uncle the riot act when the man was trying to help him, but Fletcher's charade had been both foolish and dangerous. Suppose Kraus had believed him. Or suppose the lawman had been so eager to pin the murder on someone he'd willingly have allowed Fletcher to take the rap—maybe even slip him details that would convince the D.A. they had the right man. It wouldn't be the first time someone had been set up.

Awareness of what his uncle was willing to sacrifice to ensure Tucker never went back to prison was humbling, too. The prospect of a ten-year sentence had been hell on Tucker. What a life sentence would have meant to his aging relative didn't bear thinking about. But he couldn't ignore it, either.

"Do you have any idea what your little stunt back there would have done to Mom if you had succeeded?"

Helen McGee had lost a husband and a granddaughter, as well as Beth, who'd become a second daughter to her. Then she'd had to stand by helplessly while her son was sent off to prison.

"*Hrumph,*" Fletcher growled.

"You might have thought of her. You're her big brother, her hero. If you had—"

"I got you out, didn't I?" the old man bellowed, and Tucker knew he'd embarrassed him.

Backing off, he laughed. "Yeah, you got me off, you old fool. Thanks."

"Shut up."

Tucker smiled to himself and felt that the special bond between them was as strong as ever. "Spooner's probably right," he said a minute later. "We already have a reasonable explanation of what happened."

Fletcher stroked the back of his neck. "You mean about Mason and Lennie rustling cattle to ruin Vince? Yeah, it's the kind of cowardly, underhanded thing Browder would do."

"If Dusty told his father about Lennie selling cattle in San Angelo on his own—"

"Pretty stupid to double-cross your best friend," Fletcher scoffed. "Mason was his meal ticket."

Tucker decided he'd have to find out if Dustin mentioned specific numbers to his father, and if they jibed with the ones on the paper.

"So Mason, all liquored up, decided to go over and confront his old buddy, got bogged down in the mud and ended up going on foot to get Lennie to help him," Fletcher summarized. "Is that how you see it?" He didn't seem to disagree with the scenario.

Tucker remembered the caliche on the bottom of Mason's boots when he found him up at the bowl. "It fits. Then they got into an argument and Lennie shot him."

"With your gun? How'd he get it? Mason wouldn't have brought it. He hated handguns, remember?"

"That was a long time ago. Liquor can change a man's attitudes."

Fletcher lowered his head and tugged on his ear-lobe. "I'll grant you that."

"Besides, Dusty was probably the one who took the gun from my room. He most likely left it in the buggy. It's illegal to carry them into bars."

"Okay, so Mason...or Lennie finds the gun. They get into a fight... But why take the body up to the bowl?"

Tucker scratched his chin. That was still the most troubling part. "How's this? Lennie didn't want Mason found where he'd killed him, because it was in a direct line to his place and would put him under immediate suspicion. Better to move him to a remote spot. He wouldn't have been familiar enough with the Lazy B to know where to take him and not be seen, but he knew the bowl. So he took him up there."

Fletcher wobbled his head uncertainly. "Then a couple of days later, when he realizes his free liquor is gone, he commits suicide. Hmm. Maybe."

"I wouldn't expect Lennie to leave a note," Tucker went on. "Why should he? And to whom? As for not finding any muddy boots at his place, he probably cleaned them as soon as he got back from the bowl—or got rid of them."

"Hell of a long walk for a man in his shape," Fletcher pointed out. "Stop off at Calhoun's," he added as they approached the crossroads to the ranch. "We need sweet feed."

Tucker turned left instead of right at the next intersection. Half an hour and twenty sacks later, they were back on the farm-to-market road to the ranch. He was thinking about Marcie's reactions today. She'd rushed into his arms at the jailhouse, but even the tremor beneath her embrace and the murmured

concern for his welfare hadn't diminished the shock
and disappointment he'd seen in her eyes.

The narrow paved road ran straight as it approached Ten Mile Bridge. Fletcher's old Chevy lumbered up the incline before descending toward the
shallow gorge of the Little Coyote River. Tucker
would have liked to stop on the ridge, get out and
soak in the endless prairie. But this time when he
crested the peak, his attention immediately locked on
the pickup pitched nosedown over the edge of the
bridge. It took a moment before he realized it was the
ranch truck he'd been driving.

His stomach muscles clenched, and cold dread
rocketed through him. "My God. It's Marcie!"

Fletcher, too, had spotted the wreck. He leaned forward, peered through the windshield, his hands
against the dusty dashboard. "Nice and easy. Don't
get too close. It looks like one strong breath might
send it over."

As they rolled to a cautious stop, Tucker could see
the back of Marcie's head through the Ford's rear
window. She was motionless. Tucker's heart
pounded. Was she injured? *Dear Lord,* he prayed,
please don't let her be dead.

He jumped from the cab and called out. "Marcie,
are you all right?"

"Tux? Is it really you?" Her voice quivered
through the open window. The sound of relief in her
words tugged at the male pride of protectiveness.
"I'm…I'm afraid to move. It keeps rocking."

Sheer terror ricocheted through him. He was on the
driver's side of the truck, looking at her. The cab was
tilted downward. She had her hands clamped to the
steering wheel, bracing herself in the seat. She

seemed hesitant to even turn her head to look at him. How long had she been frozen in this tortured position, staring at the yawning boulder-strewn riverbed?

"Stay absolutely still. First thing we've got to do is get the truck stabilized."

"I'll bring the chain," Fletcher shouted from behind him, and ran to the rear of his pickup.

"Sweetheart," Tucker said, "we're going to get you out of this. I promise."

Marcie's pulse thickened. *Sweetheart.* The word sounded so perfect coming from him, his assurance so full of confidence. She felt a surge of hope. Suddenly, the cramping in her legs as she held them stiffly against the fire wall didn't ache quite as much. Maybe with his help she would survive this horror.

Tucker surveyed the vehicle from the side and rear, squatting to examine the underbelly. Not only were the front wheels beyond the rail of the bridge, so was the transmission. In fact, most of the weight seemed to be on the wrong side of the pivot point. From what he could see, the one thing keeping it from careening into free fall—a fatal fall—was the sharp edge of guardrail wedged between the transmission and the universal joint. How long would it hold? Even as he studied the situation, the south wind had the vehicle rocking like a seesaw.

"Damn," Fletcher exploded behind him. Marcie groaned in despair.

Tucker's head shot up. "Hang on, honey."

"Please hurry." Her words were strained and terror filled.

He didn't want to leave her but had no choice. He sprinted to his uncle's Chevy. "What's the matter?"

The old man frantically moved a fifty-pound feed

sack. "The damn chain," he barked in frustration.
"It's trapped under these things."

Tucker's gaze shot back to the crumpled rail. "If
her tailgate were down..." he thought out loud.
Adrenaline pumping, he hoisted two sacks on his
shoulder. "Bring more," he ordered.

Brows knitted, Fletcher looked at him as though he
were crazy, then realized what Tucker had in mind.
"Might work if we do it real gentlelike."

What are they talking about? Marcie could hear
bits and pieces of their conversation, but she could
see nothing. The downward angle of the truck had her
rearview mirror catching only the clear blue sky. She
didn't dare turn around in her seat for fear of rocking
her already shaky world.

Fletcher grabbed one of the brown paper sacks and
followed his nephew. Tucker deposited his two on the
ground and relieved Fletcher of his. The end of the
truck was above him. No way could he deposit the
sack in the bed. Tossing it was not an option. If it
rocked the truck or slid forward, it could jolt the vehicle over the edge. For that matter, changing the balance at all might tear the teetering pickup off its pre-
carious fulcrum.

He hoisted the fifty pounds of feed over his head
and with infinite care placed it in the ledge formed
between the tailgate and bumper. Nothing happened.
No sound. No movement. He picked up a second sack
and did the same, placing it to the right. Again, it
didn't seem to do any good—or harm. The third one
went to the left. Meanwhile, Fletcher had brought another sack.

"It hasn't shifted." The old man examined the situation, then brightened. "I think you've helped hold it some."

"Bring more," Tucker ordered.

The problem now was where to place them. If he could get up higher, he could hang them on the top of the tailgate.

"No, don't bring any more," he countermanded himself. "Back up the truck."

They both ran to the Chevy. Fletcher climbed behind the wheel while Tucker jumped up into the bed.

Marcie heard an engine start. *Tucker, don't leave me. Please don't leave me.* She could barely make out the sound of gears meshing above the painful thudding of her heart in her ears. But the wreck seemed to go nowhere. *What are you doing, Tucker? I want to see you.*

He guided the Chevy to within a few inches of the Ford. Having gained the advantage of height, he began carefully loading feed sacks onto the tailgate of the tilted vehicle.

Fletcher, too, climbed into the bed and started shifting sacks. "Got it," he panted triumphantly as he dragged out the heavy chain and deposited it by Tucker's boots. He hauled himself back into the cab and gunned the Chevy forward.

Tucker gripped the side of the truck and jumped down onto the pavement. He pulled the chain out of the bed, then slammed the tailgate shut. By this time, Fletcher was back at his side. Tucker wrapped the chain around the hitch of the Ford while the old man did the same to the Chevy.

"Think we can pull it back?" Fletcher asked.

"We haven't got the weight or the power. The best we can hope for is to hold it stable."

Frustrated because he couldn't be in two places at once, he stood by while his uncle again slid behind the wheel.

How much tension should they put on the chain? If the Ford slipped, would it take the Chevy with it? The last thought sent ice through Tucker's veins. His uncle shouldn't be doing this. He was in danger of being killed.

Fletcher inched his truck forward. Tucker guided him with hand signals and shouted words until the chain was taut.

The pickup shivered, and Marcie stopped breathing. Her white-knuckled grip on the steering wheel tightened. She didn't want to look at the rocky riverbed far below, but it was all that filled her windshield. Still, she couldn't close her eyes. Suddenly, the trembling stopped. Not hers but the truck's, and the seat somehow felt more firm, less wobbly. She expelled the air in her lungs and took a deep, fortifying breath. She also knew the ordeal wasn't over yet.

The old man turned off the engine, left the transmission in gear and set the hand brake. "What about Marcie?" He stood beside Tucker, his shirt soaked with perspiration. "Should we try to pull her out or wait until we can get a heavier vehicle here?"

Tucker needed desperately to touch her, to hold her in his arms. He'd lost one woman he loved. He couldn't lose this one. Better to die with her... He shoved the morbid notion aside. He would be taking an unnecessary chance if he encouraged her to move. "We wait. Where's your cell phone?"

Fletcher scrunched up his face and shook his fists. "I didn't bring it."

An involuntary curse exploded from Tucker's mouth. But there was no time to waste on anger. He ran to the edge of the pavement and called out to Marcie. "Where's the cell phone?"

"On the floor...on the passenger side. I can't reach it."

Should they wait until another vehicle came by to get help? There was little enough traffic on this road during daylight hours, even less at night. In another hour the sun would be setting. The wind was already picking up.

For a split second all energy seemed to drain out of Tucker. He refused to give up. "We've got you stabilized, but you're too far over the edge to crawl out. Move very slowly and see if you can reach the phone."

He watched her bite her lip. She was terrified...and probably near exhaustion.

"Okay," she said with a resolution that startled him. Her courage was so powerful he wanted to crush her to his chest. Her strength would get them out of this.

She held her breath. With one hand clamped to the steering wheel, she released her seat belt and guided the strap back into its holder. She shut her eyes for a second, then looked over at him. He tried to smile encouragement, but the expression froze on his face as she cautiously leaned to the side.

Her scalp tingled. Her vision went dark, illuminated by tiny white pinpricks of dancing light. Nausea threatened, but she forced it back. She slowly blinked, trying to clear her vision. At last she was able to make out the position of the cell phone. "It would be in the far corner," she mumbled. With her left hand hanging on to the steering wheel, she reached for the small black plastic object.

The Ford creaked. Tucker went rigid, paralyzed with fear. *This is a bad idea.* She was completely out of sight. There was another shudder of the tipped vehicle. He called out. "Forget it, Marcie. Sit up. We can't take the chance."

He got no response. *Oh, God,* he thought. *Maybe she got dizzy and passed out. Maybe she's injured and didn't tell me. Maybe…*

Her head reappeared at the window. Or was it a mirage? Were his eyes seeing what his heart wanted them to see?

"Got it." Pride and hope colored her voice.

He watched as she punched in 911. Her smile turned him to putty.

Exactly twelve minutes later the sheriff and two patrol cars arrived at the scene. No bluster on the lawman's part this time. No snide comments. He listened to Tucker, his concentration focused on the situation.

"Gary, Neil," Kraus called out to his deputies, "I want both ends of the bridge blocked off." He reached inside his own car and grabbed the radio. "Dispatch, this is SO-1. I'm on location. Send engine three. Have Medic-3 follow."

Less than ten minutes later, the fire department showed up.

Kraus conferred with the team chief, while Tucker remained at the side of the Ford.

"A few more minutes, sweetheart," he assured her. "It's almost over."

The heavy tanker truck inched around the front of Fletcher's pickup. The bridge shook under its rumbling weight, rocketing Tucker's blood pressure into overdrive. Two firemen strung out the cable from the engine's front winch. One of them crawled under the precariously tilted Ford and fastened it around the rear axle. The motor lugged down as the cable was drawn up tight.

Another man got in the Chevy's cab and started the engine. But instead of pulling forward, as Tucker expected, the driver backed up.

The Ford shuddered as the chain tension eased.

''Stop. What are you doing?'' Tucker yelled, sure the crippled truck was going to plunge to the rocky chasm below.

Fletcher put a firm hand on Tucker's upraised arm. ''Let them do their job,'' he urged. Tucker stared at him as if he were a traitor, then realized the old man was right. He lowered his arm but couldn't control the pounding in his chest. The fireman removed the chain and the pickup pulled out of the way.

Tucker watched Marcie through her open window, her arms outstretched on the steering wheel. He would give his life to trade places with her, to know she was standing on firm ground, untouched, out of danger.

He loved Marcie Browder. He'd been drawn to her the moment he saw her, but now he knew the depth of his need. Without her, there would be nothing but emptiness. Sweat streamed down his face and threatened his vision. Angrily, he wiped it away with shaking fingers. His heart hammered as the fire truck tugged against the force of gravity.

The mangled lip of steel guardrail fought to keep its hold and refused to give up its captive. Impasse. The world stopped.

Tucker ran to the fire chief. "Do you have a wrecking bar?"

"Yes, but—"

"Give it to me."

"What do you have in mind?"

"I'll get underneath and pry—"

"Too dangerous," the man said dismissively. "When it springs loose, you'll be crushed."

"Not if I stay close to the rail itself," Tucker argued. "Besides, you got any better ideas?"

"We can get a crane."

"When?" Tucker snapped. "In a couple of hours? Do you honestly think this bridge is going to take the weight of a crane and the fire truck?" Tucker saw the man waver. "Look, I know the danger, but it's a chance I'm willing to take—I've got to take."

The man nodded grudgingly, then turned positive. "Okay, but I want a lifeline on you. If the truck starts to slip, roll off the edge of the bridge, out of its way."

Marcie heard muffled conversation behind her. Feeling more secure with the cable attached to her truck, she reached out the window and adjusted the side-view mirror. Tucker was getting into some sort of harness. *What are you going to do? Please, don't take any chances.* She watched a fireman check the harness, attach a nylon rope. *Let someone else do it.* She knew he wouldn't. Dread and pride volleyed inside her. He was going to risk his life for her. *If anything happens to you,* she silently argued with him, *I'll never forgive myself.*

Tucker saw her staring at him in the mirror and gave her a smile and a thumbs-up before he crawled under the cantilevered Ford. It took several tries to get the long, heavy steel bar wedged between the end of the transmission and the metal rail.

"Pull," he called out to the chief.

The engine of the fire truck revved up. The winch tightened its hold on the pickup with a growl.

Hot sweat blinded Tucker's vision. His arm muscles burned as he fought to maintain his purchase on the improvised shim. Then came the tearing, screeching agony of metal scraping metal.

Suddenly, a bang like a gunshot rocked the bridge, and the air around him compressed. Tucker gradually opened his eyes to find the grimy transmission less than an inch from his nose. The rear wheels of the Ford were safely on the ground a few feet away.

"Get him out of there," a man's voice ordered.

Strong hands grabbed his ankles and Tucker felt himself being dragged from the dark cavity. Reluctantly, he released his hold on the steel bar and was amazed when it didn't move.

Once more in the sunlight, he took a huge breath and rose to his feet. His knees shook. He wiped the sweat from his face and stared through the window of the pickup. His gaze met Marcie's, but there was no time for words—or need for them.

Grating, grinding sounds followed as the Ford was pulled back from the brink.

Tucker was the first at the driver's door. He yanked it opened. Marcie fell into his arms.

He caught her, gathered her up, held her to his chest. The paramedics rolled a gurney toward them, but she refused to get on it.

"I'm sorry." Tears rolled down her cheeks. "I shouldn't be bawling like this."

Gently, he kissed each salty cheek.

"I was so scared."

He smothered her neck with his kisses. "I don't know what I would have done if I'd lost you."

He held her in a long tight embrace, felt the fear and terror slowly drain from her taut body. And as she softened, he hardened.

A wrecker finally showed up. Activity buzzed around them, but none of it was important. The only thing that mattered was that they were together. The pounding of his heart, her pulse throbbing beneath his lips, was a rhapsody of touch and taste and promise.

At the urging of one of the paramedics, he persuaded her to drink some water, then a container of orange juice.

They sat on the gurney. He wrapped one arm around her shoulder, the other hand holding hers. Kraus came over, glanced at them, said nothing, then turned to watch the front end of the Ford being lifted and secured to the wrecker's tow apparatus.

"What happened?" he finally asked.

"I had a blowout and lost control," Marcie told him. "I should have been paying better attention."

"Sheriff," Tucker addressed him quietly. "It's late. If you have any questions, how about letting them wait until the morning?"

Kraus looked at him, made a clucking sound and said, "Yeah. I guess you're right. Fletcher looks beat, too."

Marcie bounced up. "Fletcher. I haven't thanked him. If he hadn't been with you—"

Tucker almost groaned audibly when she pulled out of his grasp and stumbled over to the old man. He was sitting on the running board of his truck, head down, elbows on knees, hands clasped in front of him.

He looked up at her approach, started to rise, but she waved him back, sat beside him, said something, then leaned over and kissed him on the cheek.

Smiling at his uncle's embarrassment, Tucker got up and wandered over to where the sheriff was surveying the smashed-up front end of the Ford and the blown tire on the passenger side. Kraus twisted up his mouth in thoughtful concentration, jabbed at the ribboned rubber, then inserted his hand into the yawning cavity. He groped around for a minute, his brows narrowed, before withdrawing his hand, fingertips pointed together.

"What did you find?"

The lawman stared at him, as if weighing a decision.

"I reckon her blowout had some help." He turned his palm up, displaying the item he'd extracted. A dull gray object, slightly distorted. But there was no doubt what it was. A small-caliber bullet. "Looks like somebody took a shot at her."

CHAPTER FIFTEEN

FOR ONCE THE SHERIFF AND Tucker agreed on something—not to tell Marcie about the apparent attempt on her life, at least not until the sheriff could examine the vehicle and crash site more closely. Tomorrow morning would be time enough.

Marcie, Tucker and Fletcher left a few minutes later. The old man drove this time, while the two younger people sat side by side on the bench seat. Using the floor transmission gearshift as an excuse to give Fletcher plenty of room, Marcie snuggled up against Tucker. He hung his arm around her shoulder and pulled her against his side. The sensation of her body nestled against him was having a predictable effect and made it difficult to concentrate on anything else.

Yet Tucker couldn't completely forget the lead slug he'd seen in the palm of Kraus's outstretched hand. Somebody was trying to kill Marcie. But why? The case would appear to be closed. Lennie had killed Mason, probably in a dispute over the rustled cattle. It could have been an accident, two drunks fighting like teenagers. But it might also have been enough for Lennie to suffer remorse, and perhaps come to the realization that without Mason to support him, his future prospects were indeed bleak.

Why, then, would someone want to kill Marcie?

What did she know, or what did someone think she knew, that made her a threat?

Too late Tucker realized he should have asked the sheriff if Lennie's fingerprints had been found anywhere on the dune buggy.

In spite of Marcie's closeness, Tucker felt a raw ache knot his stomach. He'd almost lost her. He'd given up hope of finding a woman to love again, someone who could fit not only into his arms but into his heart.

When they went over a cattle guard, her body vibrated against him, sending heat waves dancing through him. He brought his lips to her ear, ran his tongue along its curl and whispered, "I love you."

Not heat but fire suddenly consumed her. She closed her eyes, willing the truck and Fletcher away, wanting only to be with the man holding her, to explore sensations she'd abandoned hope of ever feeling. It wasn't simply the urgency of sex. There was something more, a deeper need that went beyond primal passions.

Fletcher dropped Marcie and Tucker off at the Browder ranch, refusing an invitation to come in for something cold to drink. He wished them both a good-night and continued on his way home to the Prudhomme place.

"I better let Mom know I'm back," Marcie said as they stood hand in hand in the driveway, watching the old Chevy kick up dust. It reminded her of the last time she'd seen Mason drive away after their confrontation.

Unexpectedly, her throat knotting, she wished he were back—with all his flaws and failings. What would their lives have been like if her mother had been honest from the start, if she'd told Vince she was pregnant by him...or if she'd held her counsel and never told Mason she'd deceived him?

The hand holding hers tightened, then whirled her around to face him. She saw so many contradictions in his eyes, the fierce gentleness, the passion. She understood the passion. She felt it, too. Wanting him. Thrilled by his closeness, his touch. But she'd been holding herself back to give him space, to give herself space, as well. He'd been blessed with love, then had it wrenched away. She'd been promised love, but never tasted it—until now.

"Oh, thank God, you're all right." Carlinda rushed though the kitchen doorway, slamming the screen door against the side of the house. With outstretched arms she lurched at Marcie and pulled her into a tight embrace. "Rudy called. He said you had an accident."

Marcie, stunned by the depth of her mother's emotion, hugged her back. "The truck had a blowout," she said, trying to underplay the seriousness of the crisis. She eased away and coaxed her mother to return to the kitchen.

"He said you were almost killed," Carlinda told her when they were inside. Her face was blotchy, her eyes swollen.

Marcie's mood plummeted toward depression. She went to the cooler, poured herself a full glass of water and drank nearly all of it before lowering the tumbler. She didn't want to relive the ordeal she'd just survived. "I was crossing Ten Mile Bridge, when a front tire blew. I almost went over the edge." She finished off the water. "But I didn't. Tucker and his uncle weren't too far behind me. They saved my life."

Carlinda clutched her arms to her stomach and sank onto one of the kitchen chairs. "Rudy also said you found Lennie."

Marcie's mouth turned coppery at the memory of the bloodstained corpse. "Yeah, we found him."

"Oh, honey, I'm so sorry."

Marcie sat at the table, facing her. "I guess the mystery's solved. It looks like Lennie was behind the cattle rustling. Dad must have confronted him, they fought and Lennie shot him, then tried to hide the body up at the bowl. Then he killed himself."

Carlinda sighed. "It doesn't sound like Lennie—murder and suicide, I mean. But the way he drank, I suppose it's possible." She turned to Tucker. "Vince called, said Rudy was giving you a hard time. I'm sorry. He also said Fletcher was going in to meet with the lawyer and straighten it out."

"He did," Tucker assured her.

"If it's my fault...because I told him about—"

"Don't give it a thought." He could be generous now. Marcie was safe. "We worked it out."

As her mother ran a hand nervously though her newly permed hair, Marcie noticed she was wearing lipstick.

"Are you going somewhere, Mom?"

Carlinda's gaze had wandered. "Oh... The memorial service for your...is going to be on Monday. The governor's supposed to be there. I was going to spend some time at the funeral parlor, then I thought I'd stay in town with Shelby."

"Good. You need to get away from here for a while. Where's Dusty?"

"After riding with Lula all afternoon, he changed

clothes and went in to Smithson's for a couple of hours.''

''Another riding lesson, huh?'' Marcie was suddenly glad her brother had someone in his life, too. ''Now, get out of here, Mom,'' she insisted, feeling guilty herself for not being able to offer more comfort. ''I'll get cleaned up and join you at—''

''Not tonight. You've had enough for one day. Tomorrow will be soon enough.''

''You don't mind?'' Her mother shook her head. Marcie kissed her cheek. ''Say hello to Shelby for me.''

''Go on,'' Tucker seconded. ''Marcie will be fine. I promise.''

The older woman got up from the table, then hesitated. She looked from Marcie to Tucker, finally resting her hand on his arm. ''Thank you for being here, Tucker. Thank you for protecting my little girl, for saving her life.'' She placed her hand on his shoulder, pulled him down toward her and kissed his cheek.

Carlinda's unexpected sentimentality was like an old woolen shawl being wrapped around Marcie— warm, familiar, cuddly. If she still harbored doubts about her mother's wisdom in concealing the truth for so many years, there was no doubt now what had motivated her to absorb her husband's abuse. In those few words, ''my little girl,'' she had conveyed a world of love that no mistake, real or imagined, could ever diminish.

Tucker gave the rancher's widow a thin smile and an embarrassed shrug, but he didn't really see her. Before him flashed the pictures in his bedroom. The portraits of the woman and child he'd loved but had been unable to save. He gazed at Marcie. He loved this woman, too, and he'd been able to save her. He reached for her hand, and she gave it to him. The tingling warmth of her touch was more than physical. It went to his soul. Redemption. And hope.

The three of them walked out to the carport. Carlinda chose to drive the old sedan, not Mason's truck, and once again Marcie and Tucker stood in the driveway, still holding hands, and watched a cloud of dust curl down the long dirt road to the highway.

"Come over to my place?" he murmured in her ear.

Tonight, she thought. How much there was to explore with this man. Tonight. She turned to face him and lifted her hand to touch his sandpaper cheek. The setting sun's fire reflected in his eyes. Yes, there was passion there. Deep passion and longing and love. She wanted him more than anyone or anything she'd ever wanted in her life.

She let her hands slide down his hard chest, felt his heart hammering under her palm, and stepped back.

"I need a shower," she said, then added, "and so do you."

He inclined his head toward his shoulder and sniffed. "You're right about that. I smell like last week's gym socks." He eyed her, imagining his hands touching her skin, exploring the contours of her body. "We could lather each other's backs."

She laughed at his lustful gleam of impatience. He had a wonderful back, and she'd love to dance her hands across it. Of course there was more to him than backbone. "I need to wash my hair."

He brushed his fingers against the lank tendrils of brown silk, his voice a low, seductive murmur. "I'd be glad to help."

The suggestion sent a wave of heat shimmering through her body. She covered his hand with hers. "Thanks, but not this time."

He ran a velvet caress down her arms. "Fifteen minutes?"

"It may take a little longer." She started to turn, but he clasped her wrist and held it even after she faced him. "I'll be waiting." He released her, but she didn't back away. Instead, she stepped forward, hooked her hands on his shoulders, pulled herself up on tiptoe and brought her lips to his. The soft contact lasted a mere second, but as her fingers brushed the pointy peaks of his aroused nipples, her pulse skipped. Spinning around, she dashed to the house. The screen door banged behind her. She pivoted. He stood in the middle of the yard, watching her. Her breathing stopped. Her heart pumped harder. The sudden heat in her belly descended and intensified. Slowly, their eyes still locked, she closed the wooden door.

Forty-five minutes later, she crossed the dusty yard and stood at the base of the steps to the foreman's cottage, feeling suddenly shy, nervous. He was leaning against a post of the narrow porch, thumbs hooked in the beltless loops of comfortably worn jeans that snuggled his narrow hips. A skein of black hair peeked above the top button of a faded, short-sleeved denim shirt.

The smile on his face hinted of mischief. "A little more time, huh?" He held out a hand, inviting her to join him.

"I decided I needed a soaking bath rather than a shower to get all the sweat and grime off me."

She mounted the bottom step, accepted his hand,

and felt a warm flutter as he pulled her up toward him.

"We need to talk," he said.

She almost giggled. Social intercourse wasn't exactly what she'd been expecting. But the serious expression on his face, the reticence in his eyes, inhibited her. Off balance, she negotiated the last two steps on rubbery legs, preceded him inside and accepted the easy chair he offered. He settled on the opposite end of the couch, his posture far from casual. Ankles locked, he curled his hands on his thighs and seemed to fight the urge to clench them into fists.

"What Kraus said today about my being an excon...I need to explain."

She wanted to tell him it wasn't necessary, but it was. She remembered the shock of the sheriff's statement, the feeling of having been deceived yet again and her renewed sense of despair in ever finding someone she could trust completely and unconditionally.

"I told you my wife and daughter were killed in a fire while I was deployed overseas," he said in a conversational tone that didn't quite hide the underlying agony of the loss. "What I didn't tell you was that after they died, I received a letter from my wife, the last one she ever wrote. In it she said she'd had some problems with the furnace and had tried reporting it to Patterson, the landlord, but that he kept evading her calls. When she was finally able to get through to him, he said he had other problems to attend to and would get to it when he could. Beth wrote me that evening. She'd gone ahead and called a heating service on her own, but they wouldn't be able to get there until the next day.'' Tucker's hands were knuckle-white fists.

"But there *was* no next day,'' Marcie heard herself say in a soft voice.

He raised his chin and stared up at the ceiling, his face a mask of pain. "A few weeks after the funeral, I tracked Patterson down in a bar. I hadn't been drinking, but I probably acted as if I had. I confronted him, slammed him against a wall and accused him of murdering my family. I threatened to kill him.'' He lowered his head, looked at her. "I lost control, Marcie. It took a couple of pretty good-sized guys to pull me off. I honestly don't know what would have happened if they hadn't. Two days later, Patterson was found dead behind his house, stabbed with a knife the police claimed was mine.''

Tucker stared down at his compact fists and opened them. He didn't look at Marcie but straight ahead.

"The trial lasted two weeks. The jury took pity on me because I'd lost my wife and daughter. They convicted me of manslaughter, even though the prosecutor had pushed for first-degree murder. The judge sentenced me to ten-to-twenty years. I appealed, of course, but to no avail. Six months later, another tenant who'd lost his family in the same fire confessed to stabbing Patterson. It was his knife, but it happened to be from the same kind of set Beth and I had. They'd never found any fingerprints on the weapon.''

Somewhere off in the distance, a coyote howled like a lost soul, and Marcie shivered.

"Why did he confess?''

"He'd been diagnosed with terminal cancer and figured he might as well set the record straight before he died. It still took nearly three months for me to be released.''

"So you were pardoned?" Relief flooded her. "Then you're not a felon. The sheriff said—"

"The sheriff called me an 'ex-con.' Technically, he's correct since I spent almost a year as an inmate of the state penitentiary." Tucker snorted. "Kraus was playing word games, the very thing he was accusing me of doing."

It was all beginning to make sense now. Tucker's strict code of justice, yet his hesitation to cooperate with the sheriff. And Kraus's distrust of him.

"That's why you were able to be licensed as a private investigator and allowed to carry a gun."

He nodded.

"Why didn't you tell me about this before? Why did you wait until you were forced to explain?"

"At first I saw no reason to tell you. You hadn't hired me. My background was none of your business." He stopped, clamped his jaw when he saw the enigmatic expression on her face. "Then I began to feel things for you, Marcie. Emotions I thought I'd never experience again. A joy at being with you..." He inhaled deeply. "I decided I had to tell you. If anything is to come of what I feel for you, you have to know the truth about me." He shook his head. "But I kept putting honesty off, just as I'd put off resigning from the Corps for Beth. It's not something I'm proud of." He shoved his jaw forward. "The truth is I really did want to kill Patterson. If those men hadn't held me back—"

"You still wouldn't have," she flared, surprising herself at the force of her conviction.

"I had murder on my mind."

"But not in your heart," she insisted. "How could you? Your heart was broken." She looked intently at him, at the dark doubts hardening his features, masking the love and devotion she knew were within him. "I suspect deep down you knew those men would stop you."

She offered him a gentle smile as he shook his head in denial. If only she possessed the wisdom to free him of the uncertainty and self-recrimination clouding his eyes.

She understood, if only imperfectly, the agony he must have suffered at the loss of his family. She'd endured pain and remorse at the death of the man she'd called her father. But Mason Browder had lost all affection for her. How much more devastating must it be to have someone you truly love and cherish taken away? As for the death of a child…she couldn't begin to imagine the anguish.

She understood, too, his sense of culpability. Hadn't she tormented herself for years wondering what she had done wrong, why she'd been found undeserving of love and kindness? Why she'd been rejected, seemingly without a backward glance?

That his guilt and hers were unreasonable and unfounded didn't diminish the depth of its impact. For him, prison could only have reinforced it. Only a very special man could survive such ordeals and come out whole.

"I've learned something important these past few days," she went on. "I've learned that what we have in our hearts counts for nothing if it doesn't influence how we act. My father, Mason, may have loved me. I think he probably did in his own way, but not enough to overcome his vanity and anger. Not enough to forgive my mother for what she did to him. I know my mother loves me, too. But their love for each other was inadequate in the face of their shame and humiliation.''

Marcie rose from the chair and sat beside Tucker on the couch. The vulnerability and hope she glimpsed in his downcast eyes had her insides trembling with the impulse to touch and soothe. ''Victims aren't responsible for the crimes committed against them, no matter what their imperfections might be. You loved your wife and daughter enough to give up the profession you treasured. A miscarriage of justice that compounded your loss wasn't your fault any more than the fire that took them away from you was.''

She placed her hand on his thigh and only realized the intimacy of the gesture when he flinched like a man burned...or burning. She lifted her other hand to his face. He'd shaved away the coarse afternoon stubble from his cheeks. She could smell the musky scent of aftershave and the erotic smell of the man beneath it. Nervously, he wet his lips and stared at her, his clear eyes searching hers.

She leaned forward, bringing her mouth closer to his. Exhilaration swept through her when he moved toward her. Searing heat warmed her breasts when they touched his hard chest and his arms encircled her.

With a ferocity that no more frightened than surprised her, he seized her in a desperate embrace. He pressed his lips to hers, his tongue probing their edges. There was no holding back. She opened her mouth in eager liquid welcome. His kiss wasn't a gentle flirtation but a savage plunging, a conquest to which she willingly surrendered.

His hands swept recklessly along her back, grazed the sides of her ribs. His racing exploration was rough, frantic—until he captured her breasts. Then his touch slowed and gentled with a tenderness that had the volcano that simmered inside her erupting with such burning heat she nearly wept. Passions long pent-up, sensations too long numbed by alternating intervals of abstinence and abuse, exploded with a fearless pleasure she'd never experienced before. She skimmed her hands along the taut contours of his chest and yanked at his shirt. The sound of each snap button popping was like a suspense-filled countdown. At last, she settled against the warmth of his skin and listened to the pounding of his heart.

"I love you, Marcie." He rested his cheek against the top of her head. "I don't know what I would have done if I'd lost you today," he murmured. She lifted her head, her eyes glassy. His mouth found hers. His hand slipped inside her blouse to cup her breast. His coarse thumb grazed the hard tip of her nipple. "Stay with me tonight," he begged, his words slurred by passion.

THEY SLEPT PAST SUNRISE, snuggling against each other as the first molten traces of light squeezed past the edges of the yellowed window shade in Tucker's bedroom. The mattress on the old iron bed was saggy and lumpy, but neither of them seemed to notice or care. What pulled him out of his warm, dreamy slumber was the sound of a vehicle crunching the gravel in the yard. He turned cautiously and stretched out his arm to part the curtain enough to identify the visitor.

Easing away from the sweet, soft flesh nestled against him, he managed to get out of the bed without waking Marcie. After groping a moment in the semidarkness to find his jeans, he pulled them on, picked up last evening's shirt and stuck his arms through the sleeves. He was still stuffing the tail into the waistband when he walked through the living room to the front door. Boots. He needed boots. He found them where he'd left them near the couch and stuck his sockless feet into them. He'd come back later and dress properly.

"'Morning, Sheriff," he said pleasantly as he stepped out onto the porch.

Kraus grunted a greeting. "Got any coffee?"

Tucker didn't dare invite the lawman inside in case Marcie padded out of the bedroom unaware they had company. But the thought of coffee had his mouth watering.

"Nice and cool this morning," he said with a stretch. "Stuffy inside. Why don't you make yourself comfortable out here on the porch while I turn on the coffeemaker."

The old man cast him a curious glance, then shrugged. "Don't be long. We have to talk."

"WAS THAT THE SHERIFF?" Marcie asked as she threw her bare legs over the side of the bed and combed slender fingers through the long tresses of her light-brown hair.

Tucker sucked in his breath at the way her upraised arms lifted her naked breasts. He had an uncontrollable urge to kneel at her feet, span her waist with his

hands and taste. But he knew it wouldn't stop there.
"A grass fire's burning over on the Huddsen place."
And one inside me that will blaze forever.

She looked up at him, and he saw the same urgency
in her eyes just before she glanced at the old mechanical clock on the side of the bed. "Bad?" The
biggest danger of grass fires was in the hot and dry
weather of late summer and fall, but spring fires were
a menace, too.

He couldn't help but stare. Her flawless skin was
as smooth as alabaster but with the color and flavor
of summer peaches, and warm as only a woman's can
be. "Apparently, they didn't get any rain out of the
last storm." Huddsen's place was south of the Lazy
B, less than ten miles away.

She leaned over and picked up the shirt they'd
carelessly tossed on the floor at the side of the bed
the night before. Tucker's breathing came to a full
stop now, the pressure in him encompassing far more
than his lungs. His blood pounded as she shrugged
into the cotton garment without bothering with the bra
at her feet.

"I'll go with you," she said as she fastened all but
the top button.

There was no question that Tucker would go to
Huddsen's ranch. Neighbors helped neighbors in a
crisis. It was also a matter of mutual protection.

"No," he said more sharply than he'd intended.
"I'll go and take a couple of the hands with me. Your
place right now is with your family. Kraus says Huddsen doesn't think it'll take very long to get it under
control." *But I'll never be able to control my need
for you.*

Kraus had also told Tucker he'd found the spot

where the rifleman had taken a potshot at Marcie. His men had recovered a casing on the rocky bluff at the far side of Ten Mile Bridge. A .22 wasn't a very impressive weapon, but one that could still be deadly in the hands of an expert. Had the rifleman been trying to kill Marcie and missed, or had the front tire been the true target? If she'd plunged off the bridge into the ravine, chances are neither the bullet nor the bullet hole would ever have been discovered.

Last night, he'd considered telling Marcie what the sheriff had found at the scene of the accident, but after explaining about his prison record, they'd proceeded to other things. He grinned at the memory of their lovemaking. It had been intense and gentle, spirited and beyond anything he'd ever experienced.

Should he tell her now? They were already running late, and she had planned to join her mother at her "father's" wake. He didn't want to burden her with more worries. Besides, where could she be safer, he mused wryly, than at a funeral home?

"Go on into town, sweetheart. I'll join you at Smithson's as soon as I can get away."

STANDING OVER MASON BROWDER'S casket, Marcie was both stunned and relieved when she realized she felt no bitterness toward the man who had rejected her. Anger still snarled at the edges of her thoughts about him and what he'd done to her life and her mother's. But foremost in her reaction now was pity, not for them but for him. He'd robbed himself of honor, achievement and love. No, there was no bitterness, just a sad, searing ache for what might have been.

The people who came to Smithson's to pay their

respects amazed her. They welcomed her back to the community as if she'd simply been on vacation. It had certainly been a journey. They spoke with Carlinda about the deceased, but whether it was by instinct or some quiet conspiracy, they always talked about his youth, about what a great football player he had been, so talented and popular. No one mentioned the last ugly years or the time he'd spent at the statehouse, as if those stages of his life didn't count. The Mason Browder they would remember was the handsome football star of twenty-five years before. Marcie found it a consolation to know that was how he would have liked to be remembered.

In the pauses between waves of visitors, and even while she was talking to old friends, Marcie kept daydreaming about Tucker. If anyone had ever told her that within two weeks she'd fall completely and wonderfully in love with a tall, dark Texan, a man she'd just met, she would have laughed. Yet that was exactly what had happened. Except it was hard to think of Tucker as a stranger. Ten days, and it felt as if they'd known each other all their lives. It didn't seem possible. But it was true.

Was she fooling herself? There were so many details about him she still didn't know. Did he squeeze the toothpaste tube from the middle? Always leave the seat up? She didn't even know how he liked his steaks cooked or what he ate for breakfast.

But the light in his eyes, the way he touched her, the way he whispered her name, made everything else fade into the background. He loved her. He needed and wanted her, and she loved him. She smiled at the recollection of this morning, the expression on his face as he watched her dress. She didn't have to see his briefs still wadded at the foot of the bed to know there was nothing under his jeans but man. Did he know how much she'd wanted him, too? How much she'd wished the world would go away and leave the two of them to reexplore and rediscover each other? A lifetime's adventure, she told herself, and smiled.

CARLINDA HAD APPLIED FOR and received special permission to bury her husband in the private family cemetery on the Lazy B ranch. The governor and his wife attended and were seated with Carlinda, Marcie and Dustin in the first row of cloth-covered folding chairs in front of the shiny mahogany casket suspended over the grave. Onlookers formed two loose groups on either side. Tucker stood with the people on the left, closest to Marcie.

He'd never made it to town the day before. An erratic wind had spitefully scattered the fire at Huddsen's, so that as soon as one sector was under control, another blaze erupted somewhere else. It was after four in the morning when he'd finally rolled into the courtyard. A small light was on in Marcie's room. Wanting her, he'd tiptoed to her window, to find her curled childlike in sleep. His heart ached for her. Rubbing his eyes with tired hands, he'd retreated to the cottage, washed off the smell of smoke and sweat and gone to his solitary bed for two restless hours of sleep.

Observing the pallor now on Marcie's face, the unconscious wringing of the hankie in her hands, he sensed she hadn't yet moved past the guilt stage of grief. He knew time would soften the pain of Mason Browder's death, but it would never go away, not completely. She wasn't to blame for what had happened to the man she'd called her daddy or for the relationship his drinking had destroyed. But Tucker also recognized that even though her mind had accepted those facts, Marcie would always feel a nagging unease that somehow she might have been able to make it different. It wasn't rational. It wasn't right. It was reality. He wasn't responsible for the deaths of his wife and daughter, either, but he, too, would always be haunted by their memories.

He listened to the carefully phrased words of the clergyman, praising the dead man's virtues, ignoring his vices. Then the governor got up and diplomatically recalled the former state senator's political skills, lauded his public dedication and mourned the state's loss. The minister recited a final benediction and it was over. Tucker glanced at his watch. It had all taken less than forty-five minutes.

The crowd disbanded with an air of relief. Most had come out of curiosity, a few with compassion for the family, even fewer in sorrow. Under clear blue skies, they followed the limousine carrying Carlinda and her children to the Browder ranch house.

Shelby had shunned the service, volunteering instead to stay behind and supervise setting up the reception that would follow. She'd arranged long trestle tables in two rows, one for hot dishes, the other for cold foods and desserts. Ever the organizer, she'd also borrowed folding tables and chairs from the Veterans of Foreign Wars hall and scattered them around in cozy little groups. White linen tablecloths, pinned at the sides to keep them from blowing away, snapped and fluttered in the relentless spring wind.

Wearing a dark-gray business suit, Marcie stayed with her mother and brother to greet people. Tucker joined the men cutting up slabs of skirt steak, crushing garlic and slicing onions and green peppers for the fajitas to be cooked in black iron woks over propane burners. Beer was poured into plastic cups from a keg mounted on the tailgate of a pickup truck nearby. Limiting himself to one brew didn't inhibit his participation in the tall-tale-telling contest that spontaneously blossomed at every wedding, funeral or family picnic.

The governor and his wife stayed long enough to shake everybody's hand, then left, taking their security and aides with them. Voters smiled and waved goodbye, then got down to serious "visitin'."

"Where's Marcie?" Tucker asked Shelby an hour and a half later, after the last fajita had been wrapped in a flour tortilla and served with spicy *pico de gallo*. Marcie had let down her hair and changed her clothes after the governor's departure. He craned his neck over the milling crowd for a glimpse of her blue cotton shirt and shiny brown ponytail.

"Took off a few minutes ago with her brother," Shelby responded between generous forkfuls of cream-cheese-frosted carrot cake. "I've got to give Dustin credit. Always figured he was a chip off the old Masonry." She snickered at her own pun. "But since the old man's untimely death, the boy seems to have matured, acting more like a responsible adult than a kid for a change."

Tucker wasn't sure why Shelby's revised assessment of the young Mr. Browder disturbed him. "What do you mean?"

"Heard him telling Marcie he was leaving the ranch and Coyote Springs, wants to go to New York, maybe Hollywood, and be an actor."

Tucker lifted an eyebrow.

"Said he knew Marcie loved the ranch more than he ever would."

"He told her that? Today?"

"Yep." Shelby licked icing from the corner of her mouth. "Just before he asked her to go with him up to the bowl. Said he wanted to leave a small bouquet there in memory of the old man." Shelby shoved another hunk of cake into her mouth. "A bit of sentimentality I wouldn't have expected from the spoiled brat," she said after swallowing. "But then, I reckon it's the kind of dramatics you could expect from an actor."

"They went up to the bowl?"

"Yep. On horseback. She took Sparkle. He took Skipper."

"Skipper? Why didn't he take his regular horse, Duke?"

"Something about him still being lame."

Tucker felt as if he'd slammed into a wall. How could he have been so stupid?

"Did anyone go with them? Lula?"

"Nope. They went alone. Marcie wanted to invite you, but he said he wanted it to be just the two of them. I guess he wouldn't let Lula tag along, either, because she went storming off just before they left."

"How long ago was this?"

Shelby scratched her head. "I dunno. Half hour, maybe."

Tucker rushed to the barn and saddled Cisca. If they had a thirty-minute lead, they'd almost be there by now. He'd have to hurry to catch up. Even then, he might not be in time. His insides churned as he threw his leg over the saddle. He kicked the pinto into a lope and said a silent prayer that he would catch up to them.

Before it was too late.

CHAPTER SIXTEEN

TUCKER ADJUSTED THE FIT of his hat and tipped his head into the wind as he rode due south. The sky overhead was clear, but clouds were building to the west. Rain, always welcome, wasn't wanted now. A heavy downpour, no matter how short-lived, would slow him up and could be dangerous. Even an old trooper like Cisca might lose her footing on the slick clay and caliche mud.

Carefully following the hoofprints that led up the gentle slope to the Green Valley bowl, Tucker kept playing a scenario in his head, hoping to find a flaw that would make his worries about Marcie unfounded.

It was ironic that Fletcher, in concocting his tall tale to explain how he'd supposedly killed Mason Browder and Lennie Gruen, might inadvertently have hit upon what actually happened. But the more Tucker reviewed the situation, the more his uncle's scenario seemed the only possible explanation—Mason's body was at the bowl simply to get it out of the way.

Dustin had left the Beer Bucket to gas up the truck right after his father had charged off in the dune buggy. Concerned about his sports vehicle, if not the driver, he would logically have gone searching for the old man. Maybe he saw Mason swing through the gate, or he discovered the gate was open. In any event, he followed. What they fought about at the mesquite grove was still open to conjecture. It might have started with Dustin finding his dune buggy mired in the mud and progressed from there to the old man taunting his son about being a sissy actor. Or it might have had something to do with the rustling. Whatever the specifics, Dustin had ended up shooting and killing his father.

The murder may not have been premeditated. Regardless, Dustin would have been wise to report it immediately as an accident, a family squabble gone bad. The case might not have come to trial. And even if it had, a good lawyer could probably have gotten him off with probation or a light sentence.

But Dustin panicked—which was another good argument that the killing had not been premeditated. Half drunk himself, he did what most people do when they're scared: he tried to hide the crime. Since the mud hole was out of sight and the body wasn't likely to be found right away, he returned to the bar and established his alibi for the time Mason was probably killed. Later that night, he saddled Duke, went back to where he'd left his father, loaded the body into the buggy and took him up to the bowl, leading Duke with him. Somewhere on the return trip the horse went lame, not an unpredictable occurrence in the dark.

Tucker settled deeper into the saddle. A late flock of mallards was flying north in perfect formation. Bees hummed industriously over flowering cactus blossoms. And bright spring colors vied with one another for attention. Only the turmoil within him contradicted the beauty of the world around him.

Okay, he'd worked out how the crime was committed and by whom. The questions remaining were why Dustin had killed his father in the first place and why he wanted to kill his sister now.

Had Dustin uncovered his father's cattle rustling and tried to stop him? Tucker mentally shook his head. More likely, Junior wanted in on the action. Had Marcie said something this morning that alerted him she was close to figuring it out? She must have been unaware that what she said was a threat; otherwise she would never have willingly gone with him. What could it have been?

Cisca stumbled as she clopped across a shallow, spring-fed creek. Tucker gave the mare her head, letting the horse recover balance, then urged her again into a steady lope.

But why take Mason's body up to the bowl? Why not leave it where it was with the gun in his hand? Suicide might have been a reasonable conclusion— especially after Mason was discovered to have cirrhosis of the liver and cancer. But, of course, Dustin didn't know his father was terminally ill.

The breeze was subsiding, making the crystal-clear air warmer. Tucker scanned the terrain ahead, alert for snakes out sunning themselves.

Maybe, Tucker speculated, Dustin was hoping his father's body wouldn't be discovered right away and the evidence of what had actually happened would be destroyed or at least made ambiguous by the delay. Or maybe—Tucker reined Cisca around a fat cadmium clump of spring sow thistle—Dustin wanted the location itself to be a mystery. He was an actor, after all; a showman. Perhaps confounding the audience was part of his performance?

Sweat began to trickle down Tucker's back as he

approached the bowl. Had he made it in time? Or was he too late?

Cisca shied at a covey of quail scooting between tufts of violet locoweed, but Tucker kept a tight rein and urged her up the incline. They were almost to the rim when he heard a crack and echo. A rifle shot! His heart stopped.

ALL MARCIE COULD SEE WAS the blood. All she could feel was surprise. She slid from the saddle, felt the horse shy away, and slumped to the ground. She gaped in amazement at her brother, saw his jaw tighten, his eyes darken at her in a dead stare. Her pulse pounded in her ears. *"No-o-o,"* she wailed.

CISCA, WIDE-EYED, STARTED to rear. Tucker fought her down, then prodded her in the flanks to advance once more up the gravelly slope. Reaching behind him, he unbuckled his saddlebag and withdrew his old .38 caliber Colt revolver. The mare pumped her way up the hillside. Tucker's pulse chugged viciously, his muscles rigid with tension.

He reached the edge of the bowl and looked down.

Nothing.

No sign of Marcie or her brother.

No horses.

Another shot split the air. This one closer.

It had come from his right, from the small area within the huddle of rocks where he and Marcie had hitched their horses and waited for the sheriff's helicopter to arrive. The memory flashed across his mind even as he nudged his horse toward the spot. But not too close to it. He dismounted and crept toward the rocks.

''Marcie,'' he called out.

''Stay back, Tucker,'' Marcie's voice blared.

She sounded scared. Scared but determined. At least she was alive. His pulse raced. Was she injured?

Another shot rang out. This time the whine of the bullet's ricochet was barely inches behind him. He dove to the ground and rolled hard against a waist-high outcropping, not sure if it offered protection or made him a better target.

Damn. He'd left the cell phone in his saddlebag. It might have been more useful than the revolver he still carried in his hand. He couldn't even be sure where the shooter was.

If the buffeted sounds weren't fooling him, Marcie was among the boulders directly behind him. Was Dustin there with her? Marcie had obviously foiled his first attempt to kill her. Was he holding her now at gunpoint? Dread coiled in his stomach.

''Marcie,'' he called out again.

Ping. The bullet glanced off the rock to his left. It had come from in front of him, not behind. Dustin was facing him; Marcie was alone. A hollow-stomach wave of relief washed over Tucker.

Dustin's last shot had missed him by a wide margin, which meant he must be firing based on sound and couldn't see his target. That was some consolation. But not much. Dustin was an expert marksman. Sooner or later, he'd find his quarry.

Tucker scurried to his right, crouched against the base of the rock and waited for another shot. None came. He dashed farther. Still no shot. Dustin hadn't yet spotted him.

Scouring the area above him, Tucker saw only the jagged rim of the bowl and the cerulean-blue sky above. An open stretch lay between him and the next prominence. If his calculations were accurate, Marcie was behind that barrier. He had to get to her.

He raised himself into a three-point runner's stance and sprinted the twenty yards to cover.

Tsing-bang. A rifle barked.

One bullet splatted against the jagged limestone just above Tucker's head. Strangely, he felt as if he were in slow motion as he dove behind the boulder. He landed hard, came up short and stared.

Marcie, on her knees, faced him. There was agony in her glance, then she returned her concentration to the prostrate form in front of her. Dustin.

"He's bleeding, Tux," she said, her voice choked. "I can't seem to stop it."

Tucker could see her hands shaking as she stuffed a red-stained handkerchief into the gaping wound in Dustin's chest.

"I've got to stop the bleeding," she muttered.

"What the hell—" He duck-walked to her and bent to examine her brother. Dustin was unconscious and had already lost a lot of blood.

"Here, let me." He nudged her aside, tore the soggy shirt away from the gaping hole and examined it. An inch lower and the bullet would have penetrated a lung.

Tucker pulled his own handkerchief out of his hip pocket. Not exactly sanitary, but he had no choice. He removed the crimson cotton Marcie had been using and carefully positioned his own on the wound, pressing down hard with his hand. Old training came back without conscious thought.

"We have to get help," he said with military detachment. "Have you got your cell phone?"

"No. Where's yours?"

"In my saddlebag," he answered.

"I'll get it."

"No." But he was too late. She'd already scooped up the revolver he'd dropped on the ground and crept around the other end of the rock. He wanted to order her back, but he dared not call out. Besides, this wasn't the Marine Corps. And Marcie Browder didn't take orders.

Tucker looked down. Dustin's breathing was steady but shallow. Shock, of course. Tucker examined the cloth beneath his hand. It wasn't completely saturated yet. The flow had slowed. He kept on the pressure. He could control the external bleeding, but what damage the bullet might have done inside its victim he had no way of knowing. The feeling of helplessness twisted his gut.

MARCIE SLIPPED OUT FROM behind the boulder and crawled to her right into the low growth of young ironweed. She had to consider her options before the shooter spied her. A small table rock sat straight ahead of her. No good. Not high enough to give cover. Besides, a thick patch of prickly pear cactus grew just beyond it. She'd be hemmed in.

Marcie surveyed the countryside. The rifleman should be behind the dome-shaped prominence to her left. It might be possible to run up to it, using it as a shield against the shooter behind it. Then what? Ring-around-the-rosy? Her handgun would be an advantage against a rifle in a face-to-face encounter, but maybe she had a better alternative.

Marcie examined the terrain to her right. It led away from the shooter. If she could sneak through the little passage between the rocks there, she would be able to circle around.

Had the assassin caught sight of her yet? Marcie looked up at the clear blue sky. Where was a storm when you needed it? Thunder and lightning would have been perfect cover. Instead the afternoon sun smiled down on her, scalding her back.

Marcie bolted through the breach and flattened herself against the granite monolith. She waited for a gunshot. None came, and she allowed herself to start breathing again. Cautiously, she moved through the thick undergrowth of mesquite, last year's dry broomweed and fresh clumps of ragweed. Was the rifleman allergic? A fit of sneezing...

She circled around, confident she was invisible—if the gunman was where she thought.... She checked the gun in her hand. All six chambers were loaded. Six shots. Would they be enough? Would she get a chance to use any of them? She approached the backside of the boulders.

Marcie had fired rifles often enough, but rarely pistols. When she'd realized her husband's propensity for violence, she'd taken a course in self-defense that had included handguns. But even though the paper targets had been shaped like men, they'd still been inanimate objects. Now she was faced with the prospect of aiming a gun at a living human being. Not an image but warm flesh. She thought of her brother's punctured chest and looked down at her hands. They were caked with his blood. But they were steady.

A killer, Marcie reminded herself. That was what this sharpshooter was. The person who had murdered her father, robbing her forever of the chance for reconciliation with him. A murderer who had tried to kill her brother. Marcie didn't want to think of Dustin dying, but she knew he might. Tucker would do everything in his power to save his life, but even he, no matter how much she loved him, couldn't perform miracles.

The murderer had also tried to kill Tucker.

Marcie didn't want to shoot anyone, didn't want to take a life. Could she? Her teeth bit down hard. Yes, if that was the only alternative. She would do whatever was necessary to protect the people she loved.

A dust devil sprang up out of nowhere, filling her eyes with dirty grit, blinding her. She struggled against panic. Shielding her face with her hands too late, she blinked furiously and managed to clear her vision. But her vision was still blurred by stinging tears.

"Drop it."

Her veins filled with ice. She squinted. The sniper stood less than twenty feet in front of her, rifle tucked expertly in the crotch of her shoulder.

TUCKER WAS FRUSTRATED. He had to stay with Dustin, yet he wanted, needed, to go after Marcie. He'd promised himself he would protect her, guard her from danger, and here he was hiding behind a rock while she faced a killer.

He bent over Dustin's still form. Blood continued to seep out of his chest, but it was a trickle now. Could he leave the wounded man?

No. Relaxing his pressure would increase the flow of blood.

A bandage? Even if he had one or could improvise one, he didn't dare lift the victim to wrap it around him. He had to keep the pressure on.

Then he had an idea. It was dangerous, but it might work. If it didn't…Dustin would bleed to death.

"I SAID, DROP IT." LULA HELD her rifle steady.

Marcie hesitated. Could she raise the pistol and fire off a shot before Lula pulled the trigger?

"I'll give you one more chance to drop the gun," Lula snarled. "It won't take more than a tiny twitch of my finger to kill you."

Lula's squinting glare was so cold Marcie did all she could do to keep from shivering. She held out the pistol by the trigger guard and tossed it lightly into the nearby thicket. It hissed through the dry brush and hung on a slender branch.

Lula smirked with satisfaction. "I never supposed you were stupid. It would have been a lot easier if you were." She backed against a round boulder. "Now, move away, over there." She motioned left, to a silvery green salt cedar wedged between two stone outcroppings. "Nice and easy."

Marcie maintained eye contact and sidestepped in the direction Lula indicated. "Why?" she asked. "Why did you kill them?"

Lula's grin was careless, but Marcie saw the vulnerability in it and the pain of someone who'd been deeply hurt.

"I told him to leave me alone," Lula said, her words bitter. "But then, you probably know he liked 'em young."

"Who?" But Marcie knew.

Lula snorted. "Your daddy, of course. Though it went for his smelly pal, too."

Marcie winced, her stomach turning sour. "Dad came on to you?"

"Came on to me?" Lula made an ugly sound. "He damn near—"

"Oh, God." Marcie felt suddenly dirty. She had a flashing urge to sink to the ground and fold herself into a fetal position. Raw determination quickly flung the temptation away.

"I fought him off once," Lula said, "and told him if he ever touched me again, I'd kill him. He thought it was all a big joke. I saw the gun McGee had with his stuff when he moved in. Breaking into that cheap metal desk in his room was no trick."

Lula seemed eager to talk, and Marcie wondered if by hounding her with questions she could distract her enough to grab the rifle. "But how did it happen?" Marcie asked. "I don't understand what happened."

"Simple." Lula lowered the rifle to waist level, but her grip didn't relax. Even a poorly aimed shot could stop her captive and probably kill her. "The day you and your pa had that fight, Dusty had invited me out to the ranch to teach me riding. Hell, I can handle a horse at least as well as he can, but it made him feel like a big man to think he was giving me lessons." She shrugged. The lazy lifting and dropping of her shoulders was filled with derision. "So I let him. After you threatened to kill the old man and he went driving off, Dusty said he needed to go after him. I told him I'd be fine. You and your mom had already gone in the house. So I decided to go riding by myself."

"And you found Dad stuck in the mud?"

Lula shook her head in disgust. "I offered to get the buggy free for him. Figured he was drunk enough to be harmless. Then the son of a bitch started pawing me. I warned him to stop, but he grabbed my wrist.

I struggled, even slapped his face, but all he did was laugh. So I shot him.''

Marcie felt an icy shiver ripple through her bones. ''That means it was self-defense. Why didn't you just come forward—''

''Self-defense?'' Lula cackled. ''Yeah, right. And who do you suppose would have believed me? I was the one who brought the gun, not him.''

From Lula's perspective, she was right. She was the outsider, he former state senator Mason Browder. The irony, Marcie realized, was that people probably would have believed her. The girl just didn't realize it.

''Besides, I know what people think of me,'' Lula went on. ''I haven't been a virgin in a long time. Ma's boyfriend took care of that.''

Marcie winced at the implication. But this wasn't the time to explore those wounds. ''So you brought his body up here to the bowl,'' she stated, trying not to sound accusatory. It seemed to work. Lula's reply was almost conversational.

''I tied Duke to the dune buggy, came up here, left the body and the cart and rode the horse back to the ranch house. It was after dark by then. Dusty was just getting home from the Bucket. Not nearly as sloshed as his daddy, but drunk enough that he didn't notice Duke was beginning to favor his right foreleg. I wanted to hose it down and put liniment on it but was afraid Dusty would start asking a bunch of questions, so I didn't. The jerk actually thought I'd been waiting for him all that time.''

''Why the bowl?'' Marcie asked. ''Why here?''

''Dusty brought me riding here a week earlier, before the rain. He told me nobody ever came to this area, and that the place used to belong to Lennie. Figured it was as good a spot as any to dump the body. Maybe when they did find it, they'd think Lennie killed him.''

Marcie thought she saw movement in the bushes on the right of the column behind Lula. It was a strain not to look closer. With an unsteady pulse she wondered if it was Tucker. It had to be. Had he abandoned Dustin? Did that mean her brother was dead?

Then a piece of the puzzle that had been bothering Marcie from the start suddenly fell into place. ''You were up here when Tucker and I found the body, weren't you? It was you I saw among the rocks.''

Lula nodded. ''I'd screwed up—should've left the gun in his hand like he'd committed suicide. It would have worked, too, especially when they discovered he was sick, and dying was going to be painful as hell for him. Then you two showed up and spoiled everything.''

Shrillness was creeping into Lula's voice, and her mouth tightened. So did her grip on the rifle. *Keep her talking,* Marcie told herself. *Buy as much time as you can.*

''And Lennie?'' she asked, trying to conceal any intimation of distress from her words.

''That old sot,'' Lula spit. ''He was even more disgusting than your pa. He saw me riding in the woods near the road, put two and two together—''

''Was he going to turn you in?'' Marcie prompted.

''That's not how he got his jollies,'' Lula sneered. ''No, he tried playing the consoling uncle, but he didn't fool me. I've had uncles like him before, too.''

Marcie tried not to imagine what Lennie might

have proposed. "So he was blackmailing you," she said sympathetically.

"He invited me over to his house to discuss it. Since I still had the gun, I took it with me. Putting it to his head and pulling the trigger wasn't hard, wasn't hard at all. I'd wanted to do it to a few other guys—" her lips curled in a malicious grin "—but he was the lucky one."

"But why did you try to kill Dusty?"

"That's enough talking," Lula snapped. She kept the rifle pointed directly at Marcie's midsection as she sidled over to where the pistol dangled in the shrubbery. Holding the rifle confidently with one hand, she reached with the other for the revolver. It tumbled the rest of the way through the bush.

"Don't move," Lula warned when Marcie raised one foot.

The rattle, hiss and scream came so closely together, Marcie froze. She saw the burst from the rifle's barrel, heard the shot, felt the echoing thud ripple through her, and fell to the ground.

CHAPTER SEVENTEEN

TUCKER HAD BEEN CIRCLING the stone pillar, slipping toward the sound of the women's voices. He could see Marcie, and though she kept her attention riveted on the woman with the gun, he knew she'd spotted him. What he didn't know was Lula's exact position—snug up against the column or a few feet in front of it? If she caught sight of him before he had a chance to make a move against her, she might shoot Marcie. But doing nothing was unthinkable.

Then came her bloodcurdling scream and the explosive blast of the rifle. Tucker sprang forward. Lula was dancing around. A three-foot-long rattlesnake, whose territory she'd invaded, had its fangs embedded in the heel of her hand. She let out a high-pitched howl of uncontrolled panic and terror, the .22 target rifle still cradled under her right arm.

Tucker lifted his foot and, in one swift motion, kicked the weapon skyward. But the rifle was no longer Lula's concern.

"Marcie, you all right?" he called out.

Marcie had instinctively dropped to the ground when Lula shrieked. The carelessly discharged round had gone wild, and except for the heavy pounding of her heart, Marcie was unscathed.

"Fine," she huffed as she booted the fallen rifle out of the way.

Tucker grabbed Lula by the waist from behind and hauled her, kicking and screaming, off her feet. She continued to shriek and dance around, begging someone, anyone, to get the snake off her. Desperate and terror-stricken, she was nevertheless too revolted by the writhing creature to grab hold and pull it off herself.

"Stop fighting," Tucker commanded in a voice that almost succeeded. The young woman continued to thrash. Tucker tightened his hold, practically suffocating her.

Marcie had a healthy respect for rattlers, but she also knew they were more deadly in legend than fact. That was rational thought. Lula was beyond reason. In spastic jerks, she flipped her hand violently, unwittingly digging the snake's fangs in deeper and provoking it into a maximum discharge of venom. Staying cool was vitally important in minimizing the effects of snakebites—which was exactly what Lula wasn't doing.

With one hand Marcie clamped Lula's left wrist. With the other she grabbed the rattler behind its head, squeezed its jaws open and unhinged the serpent's fangs from Lula's bleeding hand. Swinging her arm in a great arc, she whipped the poisonous snake far beyond the neighboring rocks.

"It's gone," Tucker whispered in Lula's ear, his encircling grip unrelenting. "Now stop bucking. You're making it worse. You have to calm down."

Lula was obviously torn between the impulse to fight and conviction that she was doomed. She stiffened, held the rigid pose for a moment, her eyes wide and terrified, then she slumped. Tucker lowered her to the ground.

Marcie didn't wait around. She bolted behind the massive boulder to where she'd left Dustin, convinced she'd find a lifeless corpse.

Her brother lay on the ground, arms by his sides, eyes closed. A rock the size of a softball was balanced on his chest. The handkerchief Tucker had used to replace hers was under it, crimson stained. She knelt at Dustin's side, unsure he was alive, and touched two fingers to his neck. Miraculously, she found a pulse in his carotid artery. It was slow but strong, and his breathing, while shallow, seemed unimpaired. She closed her eyes in a grateful prayer of thanksgiving.

By now, Lula had lost all her fight and lethargy had set in. Whether it was from the poison in her bloodstream or awareness that further resistance was futile wasn't altogether clear. Tucker carried her to where Marcie was with her brother.

"How is he?" he called out.

"You saved his life, Tux. You saved mine."

"I love you."

The air between them vibrated with his words, their resonance isolating the two of them from their surroundings. The sensation of intimacy lasted but a split second, yet it seemed to fill all time. His gaze consumed her even after he shifted his attention away.

He ordered Lula to lie flat on the ground, then pulled the thin belt from her narrow waist.

Eyes wide with fear, she whimpered, "What are you going to do to me?"

"Try to save your arm and your life," he answered. "Now, stay still."

Using the belt, he bound her right forearm as tightly as he could to slow the flow of blood without cutting off circulation. Marcie examined Lula's face.

It had gone from red to white and was now slightly green. She wouldn't be running away.

While Tucker checked Dustin and adjusted the pressure on the bloody wound, Marcie went searching for the horses. She found them not far off, munching new grass and succulent wild vegetation, seemingly oblivious of the human drama that had just transpired. After removing Tucker's cell phone from his saddlebag, she punched in 911. It would be another fifteen minutes before the medevac helicopter landed at the spot where she had found her father's body.

Once she'd corralled the horses, she returned to their makeshift camp. Dustin was still unconscious and Lula subdued. Realizing this might be her last opportunity to talk privately with the woman who had murdered two men, Marcie sat beside her.

"Why did you try to kill Dusty?" She studied Lula's left hand. The bleeding had stopped, but the skin was already inflamed and shiny, and the fingers were beginning to swell. Red streaks were inching their way above her wrist into her forearm. Rattlesnake bites were extremely painful, but they were a significant threat to life and limb only if left untreated. Antivenin was on the way. Lula was in no immediate danger of dying.

"I wasn't aiming for him," Lula said in a strained voice, her eyes pinched half closed against the pain burning her hand. "I was aiming for you."

Marcie's breath caught in her throat.

"I tried to get you yesterday. Almost did, too," Lula said without even looking in Marcie's direction. "I didn't bargain on you being so damned quick behind the wheel. Any other driver with a front-end blowout would have gone off the side of the bridge."

Marcie felt the blood drain from her face. "Ten Mile Bridge? But…that was an accident." She looked over at Tucker; he was busy getting the handkerchief out of Dustin's back pocket to use as a dressing.

Lula snickered. "Yeah, with a nudge from me. I'm a damned good shot with a target rifle. Used to give shows in a carnival. If your stupid horse hadn't stumbled when he did, I would have gotten you instead of Dusty a little while ago."

Marcie's mind wasn't on today's shooting, though. "You shot out my tire?"

Lula squeezed her eyes shut and bit her lips. "Where's that damned chopper?"

"Why would you want to kill me?" Marcie asked, her voice faltering. "I've never done anything to you."

"God, it hurts." Lula tried to prop her head up with her right hand; the position was more uncomfortable, however. Defeated, she rested her head back on the hard, uneven soil.

"Why?" Marcie repeated more firmly this time.

"Simple," Lula replied, her eyes still closed. "Dusty told me he was going to leave, and he wasn't taking me with him. He's just like every other man I've known. Happy enough to use me, never willing to give, never willing to share." Her brows came down and her eyes opened into narrow slits. "Thanks, sweetie," she mimicked in singsong mockery. "I sure did have a good time. We must do it again someday. See you around."

"But why kill me?" Marcie demanded, thoroughly confused.

Raising her chin and throwing her head back, Lula looked for a fleeting moment like an innocent teenager sunning herself. "All I wanted was a home and family like other people. I thought I had a chance with Dusty." She pouted. "I should never have told him what a good actor he was or taught him how to mime." She gestured with her injured hand, as if to make a point, and winced in pain. Gasping, she swallowed a deep breath. "I figured he was just interested in amateur stuff, the civic theater, that sort of sh—" Her voice turned acrimonious. "I didn't expect him to take it seriously. But all of a sudden he's got it into his stupid head that he's God's gift to Broadway, or the next Hollywood superstar." Lula opened her eyes and glared bitterly at Marcie. "When I first met him, he said he wanted to stay here, run the ranch and have a flock of kids."

Family and kids weren't values Marcie would have attributed to her brother—until she'd seen him entertain the waifs at the orphanage. More contradictions. Will the real Dusty Browder please stand up?

"Then your pa hired that new foreman instead of letting Dusty run the place, and you came home." Lula fumed. "Dusty said he had no reason to stay anymore. Then...with his daddy dead, I was sure he'd have to stay. Maybe, I decided, killing the dirty old man hadn't been such a bad idea after all."

Marcie looked over to where Tucker was monitoring her brother. He cast a brief pitying glance at the murderess and returned his attention to Dustin.

"When he told me yesterday that he was going to turn the ranch over to you," Lula continued, unaware Marcie's mind had wandered, "I figured the only thing that would keep him here was if you left. But you seemed to be digging in your heels. Even Dusty said you were well organized. He didn't like taking orders from you, but he said you'd probably run the place better than he could. He didn't have any reason to stay, so I had no alternative but to kill you. That way Dusty would have to stay to help your mama run the place.''

The chill that clawed at Marcie's heart was relieved by the throbbing sound of helicopters approaching. While Tucker continued to monitor Dustin's condition, she got to her feet and went out to greet their rescuers.

MARCIE FLEW IN THE MEDEVAC helicopter with Dustin and Lula. After he called one of the ranch hands to come get the horses, Tucker followed in the Ranger chopper with the sheriff and filled him in on what had happened and why.

Dustin was in the operating room by the time Carlinda arrived at the hospital. The stoicism she'd shown at the news of her husband's death was back in place but was far less convincing. By the time the surgeon came out to report on her son, Carlinda seemed so brittle Marcie was afraid to touch her.

''Your son's lucky,'' the doctor explained. ''The bullet missed his lung by a fraction of an inch and lodged in his shoulder. Fortunately, it was small caliber, so it didn't do too much damage. He'll have to undergo physical therapy to regain strength and full mobility of the joint, but otherwise he's going to be okay.''

Only then did Carlinda put her arms around Marcie, break down and cry.

Persuaded that her son wouldn't be awake for several hours, she agreed to return the following morning to see him. She'd driven to town in Mason's pickup, and now the three of them shared its bench seat for the ride home. Tucker drove. Marcie sat next to him, her mother by the window. Carlinda asked about the events that had brought them to this latest crisis. Tucker explained about Mason and Lennie rustling cattle, while Marcie repeated Lula's account of what had happened between her and Mason. She'd considered sanitizing her report, downplaying Mason's attempted assault as a misunderstanding by a paranoid young woman, but there had been enough rationalizations and lies. Marcie was convinced the only hope for closure regarding the life and death of Mason Browder was in complete truth.

By the time they were halfway home, the three of them sat in morose silence, Carlinda snuffling softly into a shredded tissue.

The automatic security light had come on hours ago, and flooded the yard with its unnatural halogen glare as Tucker pulled up the driveway. He parked in the pickup's usual spot. Carlinda was already out of the cab by the time he circled around the rear of the vehicle to assist her. She kissed Tucker on the cheek, mumbled a hoarse thank-you and rushed to the back door of the house.

Tucker extended a hand to Marcie.

"Did you know about the bullet in the truck tire?" she asked him.

He nodded. "The sheriff found it."

"Why didn't you tell me?"

"I didn't want to worry you."

"You didn't think I was strong enough to handle the truth?"

The question, quietly asked, was like a slap across the face. "I didn't think telling you someone had tried to kill you would do any good,'' he explained. ''I'm sorry, Marcie. I should have told you. I made a mistake. I know it's not a good excuse, but it wasn't that I didn't trust you. I love you.''

Her heart skipped a beat—as it did every time he said those magical words. She knew he meant it. He opened his arms to her now, and she had no choice but to let herself be folded into their reassuring shelter.

She pressed her cheek to his chest, listened to the beating of his heart. ''Without trust…''

''Shhh.'' His hand stroked her hair. ''It wasn't a matter of trust, Marcie. I hope you know that. Besides—'' his voice played with her now ''—when was I supposed to tell you? Before or after we made love?''

Levering herself back, she looked up into his seagreen eyes. How safe she'd felt in the dusky light of his bedroom, spooned against him.

''Please don't keep things from me,'' she pleaded, ''even to protect me, Tux. I can't bear the thought of secrets between us. I've been surrounded by lies and deception all my life. Mom wasn't honest with Mason about me. She wasn't even honest with *me* about me—all in the name of protecting me, sparing me.''

He ached to be able to relieve the grief and sadness in her heart. ''Marcie…''

She snuggled more tightly against his body. ''You went up to the bowl to find me today because you thought Dustin was going to kill me. You saved my life, and I love you, Tux. But do you see that if you'd been right, you put me in greater danger by not telling me the whole truth?''

He flinched and she realized she'd hurt him. He

felt he'd failed to safeguard his family, and now she was berating him for failing to protect her, as well. If there was anything she wished she could take back, it was the last statement. She didn't look into his eyes this time. She didn't have to. No, she admitted, she was afraid to. Her legs felt rubbery as she gently separated herself from him.

"I want to be with you tonight more than anything in the world," she admitted. "But I can't, not yet." She looked toward the house. "I'll come to you later, but right now she needs me." She gazed into the mysterious green pools of his eyes. They were so changeable. At one moment soft and dreamy, at others stern and fiery. She'd seen sadness and joy in them. She knew some of the sadness would never go away, just as the anguish burning in her could never be completely wiped out. But they'd also found a unique freshness and renewal in each other's company, in each other's arms, that made those secret moments of sorrow and regret endurable. The memory of what they'd shared and the promise that they could again partake of that selfless generosity gave life new meaning.

He brought his hand up to her face, brushed the back of his finger along her cheek. "I love you, Marcie," he whispered, "for being who you are, a caring and devoted daughter and the woman in whom I can entrust my soul." He kissed her forehead, a sweet gentle touch that sent hot ripples of desire shimmering through her. "I'll be waiting."

He turned and walked slowly toward the small wooden cottage a few yards behind her. Marcie bit her lip at the sound of his footsteps receding across the gravel yard. She ached to follow him, yet even as she heard his tread on the porch steps and the squeak of the screen door opening and closing, she didn't feel alone. The warmth his lips had conveyed was still inside her.

She went to the back door of the ranch house and entered. Her mother was at the kitchen counter by the coffeemaker.

"I know I shouldn't be drinking coffee at this hour. I'll never get to sleep, but I don't think I have much chance of sleeping anyway. You want some?"

"Sure," Marcie agreed. "Caffeine doesn't seem to bother me." *Besides, I don't plan on doing much sleeping tonight, either.*

She watched her mother measure out ground coffee into the paper filter, then sprinkle salt over it. "What are you doing, Mom?"

"Am I making too much? Didn't you say you wanted some?"

"I mean, why are you adding salt?"

"Oh, I always do. Gram used to add salt and an eggshell to her coffee. I don't bother with the eggshell anymore."

Marcie started laughing. Her mother stared at her, her curiosity gradually turning from confusion to offense. Marcie finally managed to regain control. "Mom," she said, then chuckled again. "A touch of salt works with boiled coffee, but not with drip." She laughed again. "No wonder you make the worst—"

She beheld the forlorn expression on Carlinda's tired face, and the mirth of a few seconds earlier faded to guilt. She walked over to her mother and wrapped her arms around her. "Oh, Mom, I love you...even if you do make lousy coffee."

Before she could fully comprehend what was happening, her mother was crying. Marcie was about to apologize for her comment when she realized her mother's outburst of emotion had nothing to do with coffee. The tears had been a long time in coming. She rocked her mother tenderly in her arms. "Let it out, Ma. Let it out."

At last the convulsive weeping stopped and Carlinda, head still bowed, disengaged herself and shuffled over to the other end of the counter. She grabbed a handful of tissues from the dispenser and blew her nose.

"You must hate me," she said raggedly. "It's all been my fault."

Marcie moved up beside her, placed her arm around her mother's quivering shoulder and guided her to a chair at the oak table in the middle of the dining area. She sat next to her and took one of her hands in hers.

"I don't hate you, Mom. I love you, and I know you love me."

Carlinda's head shook gently in contradiction. Marcie raised her chin.

"You had to make some very hard decisions," she said. "I wish you had told me earlier about Mason and Vince. It might have made it easier for me to understand why Dad…why he acted toward me the way he did."

Carlinda wiped her nose with a wad of tissue. "I should have told you. It was wrong of me not to."

"I've learned something from Tucker, Mom. I've learned that we're not responsible for other people's actions, and that no matter what we may have done in the past, what we do now, this moment, is a new responsibility, a new opportunity for truth."

The older woman gauged her with watery, blood-shot eyes. "What do you mean?"

Marcie stroked her hand. "Dad was hurt by your not being honest with him. Okay, maybe he had a right to be, but he should have been man enough to get over it. He had choices, too. He could have accepted what he couldn't change. He could have left you if he was unable to forgive you. He had it in his power to be a better person." She paused and swallowed the last, most bitter pill. "And no amount of wounded pride justified his rejecting me."

She rose from the table, retrieved the box of tissues, placed it at her mother's elbow and resumed her seat.

"He could have been honest with me, also," Marcie continued, "but he chose not to. Those were his choices, Mom, not yours. Don't you think it's strange that he could be so dishonorable about so many things—his affairs, his wasting money, his stealing—yet he kept his promise to you not to tell me about my paternity." She looked directly at her mother. "I don't think he did that out of honor, Mom. Maybe part of the reason was humiliation—he didn't want to acknowledge that he'd been deceived. But I think the real reason he kept your secret was to hold you hostage, to hurt you, to be cruel. You didn't deserve that, Mom, and neither did I."

Carlinda nodded, sniffled, patted her eyes with a dry tissue and got up and went over to the counter. "Tad Radic, your father's...Mason's lawyer, was looking for you today, but you'd already left with Dusty. He gave me this for you." She picked up a small box wrapped in plain brown paper and handed it to her daughter.

"What is it?"

"I don't know. Tad said Mason gave it to him about ten years ago and asked him to deliver it to you in the event of his death."

Marcie couldn't explain why her hands suddenly trembled as she slipped her fingernail under the corner of the wrapping and pried it loose. The white pasteboard box it revealed was ordinary, unremarkable. She removed the lid. Inside was a cloth-covered jeweler's box, one too big for a ring.

Carlinda, still standing, moved closer, and Marcie's heart began to pound. Folding her lips between her teeth, she slowly opened the container. Inside was an antique pocket watch, intricate scrolling etched in its gold surface. Marcie looked up at her mother.

Carlinda's hands had flown to cover her mouth, and fresh tears were streaming down her cheeks. "It's his mother's and grandmother's lapel watch," she moaned. "I'd forgotten all about it."

TUCKER SAT ON THE PORCH steps, whittling a piece of wood. He'd never been a whittler, but then, he'd never felt the way he did now, stimulated, edgy, worried. He'd almost lost her today. He didn't want to think about the possibility, but he had to face facts. His misjudgment, his failure to alert the woman he loved of danger, had nearly cost her her life.

The evening was growing chill, but not nearly as cold, he realized, as his world would be without her. What if she didn't forgive him. No, he wouldn't even consider the possibility. She must understand that he loved her, that everything he'd done, everything he'd ever do, was to protect her, that he couldn't live without her.

The sound of the kitchen screen door slamming had

him on his feet so fast he almost stumbled off the step. His blood heated as he watched her walk across the gravel yard toward him. The harsh overhead floodlights bleached the color from her face and for a moment he became frightened. Had she been crying?

He nearly sprinted the distance between them. "Is something wrong?" he asked as he slowed a few feet away.

"Everything's fine," she said with a smile.

"Is your mother—"

A chuckle bubbled inside her. "Mom's all right, too."

He came within a few inches of her, his hands still by his side. "Am I forgiven? I promise to never—"

She threw her arms around his neck and pulled herself against his hard body. "Shut up." Before he had a chance to register her words, she rose on tiptoe and smothered his lips with hers.

His arms instantly encircled her. She felt warm and soft, and she smelled of night air and woman. His mouth adjusted itself to hers. The kiss was hot, urgent. Her delicate moan heightened his hunger.

"Marcie—"

She shook her head. "I said, shut up."

She tugged him by the hand to his cottage and bounded up the steps, dragging him behind her. She waited until they were in his bedroom before turning to face him.

"I love you, Tucker McGee."

He scooped her up into his arms and placed her on the sagging iron bed. It creaked, then creaked again as he lay beside her. They both beamed. But the grin gradually faded to a smile, melting at last into a plea as they peered into each other's eyes.

He ran his tongue along her earlobe, down her neck, across her chest, tracking the sweet contours of her body. Her nipples peaked under his breath.

She brushed the tips of her fingers along his jaw, paused and traced the outlines of his parted lips.

Clumsily, his hands shaking, he managed to loosen the buttons of her blouse, slipped his hand under the fabric and cupped her breast. "I love you, Marcie."

He brought his mouth down to one hardened nipple, then raised his head. "I'll always love you." He tasted the other one, then laid his head between them and listened to her heartbeat.

She ran her hand through his hair.

He shifted, threw his leg over hers and straddled her, then hovered above her. "Marry me. Let me love, honor and cherish you the rest of my life."

She laced her fingers behind his neck. "Till the end of time."

Looking For More Romance?

Visit Romance.net

Check in daily for these and other exciting features:

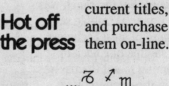

Hot off the press

View all current titles, and purchase them on-line.

What do the stars have in store for you?

Horoscope

Hot deals

Exclusive offers available only at Romance.net

Plus, don't miss our interactive quizzes, contests and bonus gifts.

PWEB

HEART OF THE WEST

Every Man Has His Price!

Lost Springs Ranch was famous for turning young mavericks into good men. So word that the ranch was in financial trouble sent a herd of loyal bachelors stampeding back to Wyoming to put themselves on the auction block!

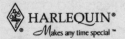

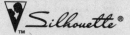